THE BILLBOARD
BURNER

BOBBIE SUE BUSBY

THE BILLBOARD BURNER

iUniverse books may be ordered through booksellers or by contacting:

iUniverse
1663 Liberty Drive
Bloomington, IN 47403
www.iuniverse.com
1-800-Authors (1-800-288-4677)

Because of the dynamic nature of the Internet, any web addresses or links contained in this book may have changed since publication and may no longer be valid. The views expressed in this work are solely those of the author and do not necessarily reflect the views of the publisher, and the publisher hereby disclaims any responsibility for them.

Any people depicted in stock imagery provided by Thinkstock are models, and such images are being used for illustrative purposes only. Certain stock imagery © Thinkstock.

ISBN: 978-1-5320-2574-7 (sc)
ISBN: 978-1-5320-2576-1 (hc)
ISBN: 978-1-5320-2575-4 (e)

Library of Congress Control Number: 2017914044

Print information available on the last page.

iUniverse rev. date: 09/09/2017

Mark ...

He stared blankly through the blue curl of smoke, until it stung his eyes and slowly rolled over in the grass, sparkling with early morning dew. He hated smoking, and god, how he needed a shower! While lying on his stomach, Mark watched the grass slowly try to erect itself where he had laid all night. Of all the thoughts coursing through his mind, the only coherent one he could articulate at this pristine, pre-sunrise time of day was, *Has the whole world gone completely mad, or is it just me?"* Mark could admit to being mad occasionally— or at least, his friends often accused him of dancing on the line between sanity and craziness. He mused and smiled as another cavalcade of thoughts invaded his reverie. If they could only see him now!

There was Jim, Greg, and Dan. One shouldn't think they didn't all have their neuroses. Jim was a health food nut; imagine being in a restaurant, and every waitress was required to give a list of ingredients, additives, and preparation instructions for everything on the menu. Jim had a 'delicate' gastrointestinal system; those were embarrassing experiences. About now, though, he would give anything to be having breakfast in a greasy spoon somewhere, listening to the nauseous preservatives in substitute bacon. Mark grudgingly thought about how abnormally normal Dan was, except that he loved to fly. Dan was innocuously calm; nothing ruffled his feathers. As long as he was transporting someone, somewhere, into some other time zone at three to seven thousand feet, he was happy. To Mark, this was incredibly abnormal because he appreciated solid ground. Greg was the yuppie and a perfectionist golf pro. He had the attire, the clubs, the Izod label, and the passion—all over a little white ball!

Each one of these guys was an overachiever, which contributed to their abnormalities too. The bond for their friendships was their common ability in athletics. Mention any adventure, activity, trip, or campout, and all four of them were physically and mentally glued together. That had been the case ever since high school, a few failed relationships, and now their avowed bachelorhood.

Reminiscing inspired Mark to begin stretches for his daily jog—not that it took a lot of inspiration. He estimated the cornfield to be at least eight miles in perimeter, and he bolted lightly into the fresh morning haze.

But back to the world being mad ... Life had definitely, unequivocally degenerated into madness! Humidity seemed to be hampering his progress this morning, but there was no rest for his mind. *Why does a mind perversely persist in torturing you with avalanches of thoughts? It takes you into dark corners you'd rather not face. It revisits the sentimental and, sadly, jogs something out of the recesses that you'd so long ago forgotten. Whoever came up with that banality "Life goes on"? That is only true if your mind lets you go on.* Which Mark's did not. He continued his trek through weeds and undergrowth on a cow path, and soon he felt the loosening of limbs and muscles, as well as the flexible freedom of a well-exercised body. That feeling was intoxicating and was why he jogged every day of his life.

Actually, he felt lean, strong, and sinewy. He even felt young for his forty-two years. It was impossible not to enjoy the beauty of this ethereal morning and place. The outdoorsy air was medicine to his lungs and brain—the pulchritudinal atmosphere surrounding him on this one special day out of thousands of days in his life, and of the millions of days in the whole scheme of eternity, was mercilessly fleeting. The time was nearly 5:00 a.m. He should not have wasted time standing in awe as the doe and her new twins crossed the path in front of him; this was *their* backyard, and he was the intruder. He had been compelled to quiet his pounding heart while they dallied across. Next was a fine family of quails, with ten little chicks and Madam Quail leading and gently clucking. Birds' wake-up calls then made their territories known as they announced the perfection of this dawning day. To this activity of sounds and busyness was always a deep love and appreciation for nature in Mark. Several times Mark slowed the pace, quietly revered, and almost religiously acknowledged the only normal thing of that day: nature in all of its beauty and magnitude.

Too bad that the matter to which he was attending that morning might involve destroying any part of this beauty.

Ruby ...

Ruby Jewel sighed as the already-large project on her drafting table grew to an even more immense size. Her tawny, curly hair fell forward around her finely sculpted cheekbones as she surveyed the task set before her. For the twentieth time, she asked herself why she had agreed to such a mountainous job. The clients were Type A, hard to please, finicky, and always in a hurry. *An impossible hurry*! They wanted this finished in less than six days. That seemed to be precisely the moment her creativity quagmires.

She absentmindedly alerted Chloe that it was time to get up for school. No response. She sighed. *Why is it so hard to get a daughter going in the morning?* Ruby rolled her eyes as she briefly remembered not wanting to get up herself at that age, especially when the reason was school.

Back to the drawing board ... The clients wanted graphics inside of the lettering, which always required a tedious, slow, excruciating computer process. Plus, they wanted twelve originals for advertising, and they wanted it yesterday. After poring over stagnated ideas, reworking them, and going cross-eyed from the late hour she'd worked, 2:00 a.m., she began to formulate the start of brilliance. The task was to not only complete it professionally and creatively, she also had to *stay awake*. Ruby predicted that her boss would call no later than 6:30 a.m. The pay was good, but sometimes she wondered if the caffeine running through her system to achieve it was worth the kidney damage.

Ruby hollered up the stairs at Chloe once more. She thought she heard a groan of resistance, but at least her daughter, eleven years old going on sixteen, was waking up. Ruby began the first stroke of genius with a splash—*Yeah, right!* she mocked herself—carelessly throwing her hair behind her shoulders—and glanced out the studio's picture window into the dim morning light. She became aware she was being watched from across the street.

Mark took in a deep, satisfying breath—not just because of the massaging touch of the cool, pink sandstone building he was leaning against after his two-hour-long run, but also because of the vision of this lovely, concentrating woman working hard in the wee hours of the morning in her studio, losing the battle with her unruly hair. His expression was approving, and his mind said, *Wow!* When she finally noticed him watching her, he lingered long enough to make sure she noticed that he was appraising her. Then he turned on his heel and stepped into the humdrum café where one could easily get the notion that mornings in this cafe had been similar for the past one hundred years.

Before the inviting aroma of coffee reached his lungs, the feeling of *There's a stranger in town* permeated the place. Mark purposely found a stool with his back to that prim little studio from across the street, and then began the noxious task of intermingling with the semifrowning locals. It never worked to swagger into a joint and try to fit in. Mark sat patiently until the perky waitress came over with a mug and coffee pot. Then he smiled and shyly said, "Good morning."

She responded with, "My, you're up early for a city dude!"

Careful, his mind cautioned. He said, "Really, I'm up late— been driving all night. Going to visit my cousin in Montana." Mark always figured if stranger types were always on the road, there would never be any motel paper trails or security camera sightings of comings and goings.

The buxom waitress chirped, "Well, then, I guess you really need coffee, don't you? You've still got a long way to get to Montana." She said that as though the entire café of ranchers, businessmen, and regular louts did not let it go unnoticed at him leering at the lady in the studio across the street, and as if he obviously did not know the great distance away that Montana was. He shrugged. He couldn't prevent his eyes from returning time and again to the studio—and, he noticed with an internal sneer, neither could the rest of the menfolk in the cafe.

As Ruby noticed the man watching her, she immediately looked down and uttered, "Perv!" Always Ruby erred on the side of caution not only for her own sake, but now for Chloe, who was growing up so fast into a dangerously beautiful young lady. Ruby worked often in the early hours without blinds or the need for them, and nobody seemed to bother watching her; at least, she'd never noticed anyone watching her before. She was a little disconcerted, and she quickly glanced up again and thought, *Nice ... lean ... muscular ... boyish perv!* Even as she negated that last thought with a smile, she wondered who he was. With only split seconds to size him up, she knew she had never seen him around before. Secretly, Ruby almost wished she had spent an extra forty-five seconds on her hair before attacking the studio this morning, but, then she chided herself for even entertaining the idea of noticing a man. The last thing she needed in her life was another ship anchor.

But she dared another glance. Then, as though waiting for her to look twice, he turned on his heel and entered the Red Rock Café with what she thought was a bit of a swagger.

"Snob!" she said out loud.

Chloe, standing sleepily beside her, suddenly said, "What? Who's a snob? Where?" Chloe truly looked like she'd just rolled out of bed and had to pick herself up off the floor.

Ruby said, "Doesn't matter, sweetie. Ready for breakfast?" As the two of them headed for the back of the studio to the kitchenette, Ruby glanced backward without letting Chloe see it, and she noticed that the guy sat with his back to her side of the street. Ah, it *was* true! A snob after all, and a perv! *Still, he's one nice-looking perv, compared to the jokers around here who know better than to ask me out.* She proudly wore the invisible banner of man-basher to discourage any unwanted advances. This time around, if anything was going to happen—of which there was not a snowball's chance in hell—it would be on *her* terms.

She'd slipped into a comfortable buddyship with most of the men in Tepid Springs with zero expectations. Unbeknownst to Ruby, however, was the fact that they were all vying with each other to prove their chivalrous intentions toward her. Most of them—the smart ones—treated her like a younger sister from a safe distance; the rest of them soon learned exactly what "cat scratch" was all about, psychologically and physically.

To get the strange encounter off her mind, Ruby began the granola and yogurt routine, which she and Chloe both enjoyed every morning. Often Ruby tripped over to the café to pick up a white mocha double shot just to hear the small-town gossip and have a semisocial outlet, but she decided against it on this morning. The locals did enjoy her coming over to chat, tease, and exchange non-information, and they considered her a vital part of their daily routines. In fact, some of Ruby's graphic art and advertising design helped put Tepid Springs on the map. Tepid Springs liked young entrepreneurs, and Ruby liked the small-town ambiance in which to raise her precious only child.

Breakfast together never took more than ten minutes, and then Chloe was back upstairs, beginning the long process of getting everything perfect for the inevitable sixth grade posturing.

Piercing sirens—unusual here—coming from far up the street were temporarily ignored by both mother and daughter.

After the waitress returned and took his order, Mark feigned a trip to the men's room. Actually, he did need to wash his hands just in case there was any residual wax or gunpowder remaining, but he was also contriving a way to resituate himself so he could gaze across the street after he was sure she'd had enough time to notice him sitting with his back to her studio. Call it ego or whatever; he did not spend much time dallying with women who needed to be chased and wooed—entirely no patience for mind games. He responded more to women who made up their minds. Without much faith in relationships, he did not believe in love at first sight, but that woman—even from a distance—was mesmerizing.

As Mark was checking in the mirror to see if there was grass, leaves, hay, et cetera visible anywhere on his person. His heart almost collapsed into his shoes when he heard the nearing police sirens. Always the same reaction: a sinking, head-bowing, sick-in-the-pit-of-the-stomach feeling. Braving a *What the hell* kind of expression, he reentered the main room of the restaurant to a flurry of people moving and crowding around the crackling scanner and the front windows. As the first sheriff's unit raced past the café, Mark guessed that this sort of excitement didn't happen too often in this podunker. He ventured a glance while everyone else was preoccupied. The gal across the street was also rubber-necking against the studio window. In all of this confusion, it was easy to reposition himself in the optimal view of *her* while he waited for his ranch-sized cowboy platter of grub.

As Ruby crashed the dishes into the sink, she became indignant over the notion that a total stranger could prevent her from joining her crowd, her turf, her café, simply because he thought he commanded so much space! How dared he! She threw her hair up into a casual plop of curls at the back of her head, smeared on some lip gloss, and banged the door behind her as she trotted across to *her* local hangout.

Chapter

2

THE DIN OF the Red Rock Cafe continued as the locals speculated on what could possibly warrant such official excitement this early in the morning and on this languidly, peaceful promise of another day. Some listened intently to the scanner to get the first of the news; others took the opportunity to accuse and to announce suspicions and imaginings of their own in order to get the proper amount of delicious gossip started.

Everyone knew already it was a fire.

"It's that bastard boy of Dickendacker's, I'll bet. He's just got hisself out of JDC for arson last month."

"Before rushing to judgment, maybe lightning hit a power pole. Don't forget about those blokes that got hit by lightning on Sheridan Lake out of a clear, blue sky."

"They were on a lake, Shad! Water—duh!"

"Ah, now, come on. Think about it: they say the apple don't fall none too far from the tree, and his old man's had a few buildings 'accidentally' burn down on his ranch." More chatter of this variety continued.

Just as Mark sat down, his plate of sausage, eggs, toast, and juice was delivered, with pancakes on the side. He was famished, and the food looked deliciously unhealthy, but he knew he had better interject some feigned concern about the crisis now in full swing. He loudly exclaimed, "Geez, is it always this crazy around here?"

Mark was dismayed as the words got the wrong type of

attention. One of the popular and reputed rowdies suddenly turned and just as loudly retorted, "Are you calling us crazy, man?" Then others began to notice him a bit more, looking him up and down.

"Didn't you just fly into town from that direction about a half hour ago, buddy? Maybe the sheriff needs to have a little chat with *you.*"

"What's your name, stranger, and where ya from?"

In answer, Mark jammed half of a scrambled egg on toast into his mouth and muffled back, "Do you want my business card?"

"Yeah, I wanna know what business you're in, and what business you've got in our town." He said *our town* in an attempt to garner a mob, but most of them were still gathered around the scanner or dispersing back to their coffees.

Mark took another oversized bite of breakfast to avoid answering.

Ruby zipped across the street and was getting ready to step up on the curb when the fire trucks screamed past directly behind her. *Good heavens! What is going on?* She had never seen them out of their building, except in the holiday parades. Now she was glad she'd decided to claim her usual white mocha (and turf). She lightly stepped into the frenetic activity of today's café.

Both the rowdies and Mark's semiaggressive comments were temporarily drowned in the screaming fire truck's sirens as they charged by at the exact same time Ruby opened the door.

Mark tried to think fast without appearing to do so. No, he did not want a visit with the sheriff; but he was confident that he had covered his trail. No law from this out-of-the-way conurbation could possibly have anything to pin on him. The trick was to get out of town at just the right moment without looking suspicious. He mindlessly continued jamming food in while planning the exact moment to exit. When the front door of the Red Rock opened, the screaming sirens were still audible from further down the street. Mark, now facing the door suddenly looked up into the most beautiful green-blue eyes he had ever seen.

Without taking his surprised stare away from her eyes, he was still conscious of piles of auburn tendrils, a flustered but perfectly sculpted face, slim body in tight-fitting jeans, and one of those rare, eye-locking, can't-take-my-eyes-off, time-warp, never-to-be-forgotten, forever-savored-and-fantasized moments that only a man and a woman experience. It was the kind of first-time encounter when one simply *knew* one wanted more of that candy.

He swallowed, gave a nonchalant half-smile while hoping he did not have butter dripping off his lips, and said, "Hi." His cell phone began ringing in his pocket. It was on the final ring when he fumbled it out of his pocket, opened it not intending to answer, and closed it to finalize the call.

He did not, could not, remove his eyes from Ruby as she breezed past him and up to the counter behind him. Then he observed the back of her from the reflection in the café's front window (still perfect) and listened to her silky voice murmur out a white mocha double shot order to go. *To go!* Not to miss this rare and quickly passing opportunity, he decisively chose that moment to pay his tab and sidled up behind and beside her. He exhaled on her bare, delightful neck.

Ruby was taken aback at stepping into the café right into the path of heart-arresting trouble. First, the fire trucks had rattled her. Second, she did not know that the guy had changed seats and now faced the door. Her wild, half-startled eyes landed straight into his. She was always greeted by café regulars in the same fashion as Norm did on *Cheers.* Today, she'd intended to slip in more anonymously. Instead, she found herself in the awkward position of being center stage, flustered and aware of the chaotic atmosphere of the café, the sputtering police scanner, the noise of some crisis taking place—and him—all in the same instant. She found herself maddeningly locked in an admittedly pleasant but disconcerting eyeball showdown. *Damn! Damn! Dog damn!*

With only a shred of superficial dignity remaining, Ruby glided her way directly to the counter to hurriedly order her coffee to go, aware all the time of his eyes following her every nervously flinching muscles. She distracted herself from thinking about what a gawky teenager she felt like by asking Marsha, the waitress, what the heck was going on.

"There's a fire out on Highway 385 by the Smithwick turnoff," then looking directly at Mark's person, continued... "our local expert speculators have deemed it arson."

Ruby knew to whom Marsha's gaze went.

"What? Arson *again?*" was all Ruby could muster, a gazillion thoughts crowding into her mind. *Goll dang, am I flirting with an arsonist?* And, facetiously... *isn't this something great to write home about?* As her alarm escalated, she was soon aware of the stranger standing very close behind her, and she nearly fainted from the warm, sensual feeling of his breath on her neck. It was pleasant. *I've got to get out of here,* screamed a voice in her head as her feet remained riveted to the floor.

Buxomy Marsha handed her the white mocha and said, "That'll be $3.95, dearie." Ruby fumbled in her obviously empty pockets.

Damn, damn, double damn. She cursed herself silently for forgetting her purse in her haste and lamely looked at Marsha to state the obvious, "This is awkward. I'll bring my money over when I come back for lunch later today."

As Marsha was mouthing "Okay," Mark slapped a twenty on the counter and said, "This should cover the lady's white mocha."

Marsha was still mouthing "Okay" in stunned lip sync like this sort of thing didn't happen every day in her café—and of course, it didn't.

Ruby immediately said, "Thanks, but I'm fine." She assumed that had dismissed the stranger. She began backing away, nodding to Marsha a *You know* gesture that she'd return later. She had to get out of this awkward—

"—Oh, but I insist," he replied as he shoved it closer to Marsha and told her to keep the change. Ruby was bristling with overstimulation when a huge, strong hand lightly touched her back. "I'm a former boy scout." He wickedly grinned with irresistible boyish tease. "I was taught to do a good deed every day!"

Mark finished the transaction by handing over another excessive twenty for his unfinished breakfast, nodding for the waitress to keep the change, and holding out his hand to show Ruby the direction of the door—as if this were her very first time in the café.

After this scene, the only choice was to exit this ungainly circus safely back across the street. Ruby grabbed her mocha, spilling foam out of the top, and was guided by this overconfident, masculine person to the door. Mark intended to follow her out to the street where they could engage with less commotion.

"I need to ask you some questions, sir," bellowed the deputy sheriff, who had entered through the back door of the café just moments ago. "Don't be a-leavin'."

Mark opened the door for Ruby, lowered his voice, and said, "I'll see *you* later, ...emphasizing the *you*." Then having ushered her completely out the door and waiting for it to close, Mark reluctantly turned back to face the deputy.

Chapter

3

RUBY NODDED AND continued across the street in a complete daze. She risked one more look over her shoulder, saw that he was waiting for her to look back at him, and then observed him stiffening his back to deal with the deputy behind him. Now at her studio, she bent over the advertising project to get her mind off the disorder of the past six and a half minutes. Ruby called to Chloe to see if she was ready to leave for school. Of course not. Well, no sense in wasting time waiting. She at least tried to look productive by attacking her drafting table. Ruby allowed herself the luxury of peering across the street, now busy with the traffic of locals having to get to work. Chloe was going to be late for band practice, but she'd never missed before, so Ruby indulged her.

Ruby could see the deputy engaging the stranger in serious conversation, and she knew that ol' boy could get down to the nitty-gritty. Soon they left together out the back of the café. *Did the deputy take him to the smarmy little police station to question him? Could he have had anything at all to do with this fiasco, as several locals intimated? Who was he, and from where had he come? And why do I even give a crap?*

Ruby could not shake him out of her mind. She savored and relived the eye-locking moment, and she could still feel the masculine hand on her back. She disgusted herself by nearly going into a swoon over his sensual breath on her neck. Jerked back to the present, Ruby lunged upstairs to drag Chloe to school. The girl had already missed band practice at 7:30, and Ruby was not about to allow her to be late for the 8:00 bell. If she could truthfully admit it, she was mostly irritated that she hadn't caught the stranger's name.

"Mom, you never hollered at me before for being late," Chloe almost bragged as she met her mother at the top of the stairs.

"Well, you've never been late before!" Ruby replied through her gritted teeth.

They went together out the back of the studio and hopped in the purple pickup. Ruby loved her truck. It was only a six-banger with decent gas mileage that she'd bought brand-new ten years ago. It was her very first new vehicle and her first truck. Her father's comment was something to the effect that women did not need to drive pickups. She could have traded it off a dozen times, but her own mother loved when they came to visit back home in Omaha, and she often stated that she couldn't see Ruby driving up in anything but her purple truck. She figured she'd pass it down to Chloe when she learned to drive—and she immediately shuddered at the thought. *Worry, worry, worry!*

The distance was only a roundabout mile to middle school, where Ruby dropped off Chloe in a happy mood. Then she began the trek back to the studio and her piles of work. She was very tempted to go past the police station on her way to the studio. Would it be obvious? Would she be noticed by anyone? Worse, maybe she would run into him again! She recoiled from the earlier humiliating encounter and decided against a repeat. Then again, her mind took her back to his extremely dark, intense eyes—eyes that could easily seduce and undoubtedly had done so more times than she would want to know. *Stop this schoolgirl foolhardiness!* she told herself. *Haven't I got enough on my mind with these crazy clients and being a single parent?*

The police station was just a block from her usual

route back from middle school so it wasn't a stretch to see a strange pickup parked on the street at the front door to the station. It was not recognizable to Ruby; in fact, it was a pretty shabby one: older, rusty, dented, bumper sagging, with a cracked windshield. *Just drive home, girl!* Somehow, she accomplished it.

For the rest of the day, Ruby willed herself to concentrate and forget about the day's odd (or, was it exciting) happenings. She considered going back to the café at lunchtime but decided against it; Marsha would most likely comment about her white mocha getting paid for by the stranger. *Does anyone know his name?* She was getting tired of referring to him as *him* all morning.

Belatedly, she realized she could have used a trip to the café as a reason to sneak-peak the police station and see if he was still being questioned or was truly passing through, like every old Western she'd ever seen in her life. No longer being able to withstand the suspense, she contrived an errand to run to the post office and pass the station. The dilapidated old truck was gone with the wind. With that knowledge, only one decision needed to be made: get back on task, and complete the advertising project, and forget about the whole incident ... forget about *him.*

Her parents were visibly disappointed when she'd announced that she was going for a marketing and advertising degree in college, beginning with graphic arts. Dad vehemently asked, "Are you going to be a starving artist somewhere in the ghetto?" Mom had always based her hopes on Ruby going into special education like she had done. Ruby loved her parents to the end of the world, but she could not succumb to their goals for her life. There was one point, however, where she'd wished a hundred times over that she had listened to their wisdom: her marriage to Jashawn. Mom and Dad had reluctantly pointed out some traits that would probably disagree with their family's value system. They were correct, of course, but just try to tell that to a hot-blooded, got-the-world-by-the-tail twenty-one-year-old who was freshly graduated from college. After being introduced as Mr. and Mrs. for the first time, and Jashawn bodily picking her up in front of the entire congregation, twirling her around with white fairy tale organza flowing everywhere, and carrying her out of the church, things unfortunately changed. He changed like night and day, just as her parents had predicted. Ruby hid their marriage problems from her brother, parents, aunt, grandparents, and everyone until Chloe was born. Then she simply snapped, moved out, and rebooted her college education. She'd been in Tepid Springs, scratching out a living from project to project, ever since.

She rationalized her advertising career by saying it was good money—when she landed clients who spared no expense. But up until this spring, it had not been paying off like she'd hoped. Ruby knew where her parents stood regarding advertising: they hated it. They were products of the sixties and thought capitalism, the establishment, and affluence were evil.

It did no good to argue that her brother, Jake, was laying a cement metropolis all over creation and contributing to the asphalt jungle. But she and her younger brother were very close and tried not to allow parental issues to cloud their relationship. After all, it was what their parents taught them: siblings should be best friends. They certainly did fulfill that parental dream.

Ruby jerked herself into the present. She spoke to herself and didn't care if anyone was listening. "Back to the drawing board—literally."

Mark hoped it appeared to the deputies now interrogating him that he had nerves of steel. After the first of their guaranteed insipid questions, "What are you doing in Tepid Springs?" Mark knew it was going to be long and tedious, with much jumping to judgments—and insufferably boring.

He'd said, "Touring ... like a tourist tours." They did not appreciate a smart ass.

"Do you know anybody here?"

"Yeah, I'm distantly related to the mayor." He couldn't resist one minor guffaw. *Dang, mistake.* That only incited them. Mark decided to cool it and made an attempt to be more contrite. He asked if the highway was or was not public domain. Mark was beginning to wonder how a beauty like Ruby had landed in this small-town mentality. *How could such a lovely person* ... Mentally, he was tripping away from the reality of being in a police station until more questioning was peppered at him.

"What shoe size do you wear?"

"What? Are you kidding? My shoe size? It's eleven and three-fourths!" That information always confounded small-town cops.

"Eleven and three-fourths? What kind of size is that?" All the deputies could do was look at one another befuddled.

"They're specially made."

Mark thought he was going to have to snap his fingers to bring the detectives out of their trance.

"My shoes are specially made ... in Italy."

"Oh."

"Oh."

"Oh," said all three cops, separately.

Mark knew he was going to be detained all day if he didn't take control of the situation.

"Okay, guys. I've got to get back on the road. Either read me the Miranda rights, get me a lawyer, or charge me with something. But it's obvious to both of us that you haven't got diddly shit because I haven't done anything wrong." He almost said "nuttin' wrong" but decided not to stoop to their level. "It looks like I'm just in the wrong place at the wrong time, for some asinine local incident, and you need a fall guy."

"We'll do the questionin' and the releasin', buddy," they shot back at Mark. "And you might be findin' yerself back in this here town for another little visit with us—and perhaps a complimentary room for a time. So don't be goin' on any disappearin' international flights anywheres!"

Mark rolled his eyes at "anywheres" and planned a nice, long laugh about it later.

They did not take gunpowder samples off his hands. There would be none anyway because he had scrubbed up, but they wouldn't know until tests came back from the site of the burning that gunpowder was even involved. He was certain that they wouldn't know what chemical was involved. Jim, his chemist friend, saw to that, along with Mark's own impeccable research.

Mark was feeling fortunate to have gotten out of town with giving only his name, address, date of birth, phone number, and shoe size (which really was eleven and three-fourths, and it was that three-fourths that made all the difference in the world—as he'd previously experienced). *Wow, small-town cops! Always out to bag the biggest, baddest criminal in the universe!*

Even though he was free to leave town, a part of him was reluctant because of the perfect lady in the picture window of a cute little studio. How could such a few short, precious moments of a fleeting encounter grip his heart and mind so totally? He was not that much in need of a woman, with plenty of girlfriends at home and everywhere. He was now a declared bachelor and hadn't found a reason good enough to change that status, especially after listening to his closest friends lament the divorces, the money, the infidelity, custody, the kids, and the problems following court dates.

He and his crazy friends made pacts with each other to kill whichever guy decided to ruin their bachelorhood *and fun* to get married. One night several years back, he vaguely remembered the four of them having a few too many, and he signed some sort of a contract to that effect, although, the incriminating document had never surfaced since.

As soon as Mark drove his smooth-running truck to take the studio route out of town, he knew it was a mistake. She wasn't there! He checked the time: 11:30 a.m. Had he been with those jokers for three and a half hours? He quickly grabbed a scrap of paper, scrawled a quote from a favorite book he'd remembered reading recently, hopped out of the truck and stuck the note on the outside of her window with a bit of his own personal crime-scene wax, where she could not miss it. Then he headed northwest toward Montana.

Chapter

4

FOR THREE HUNDRED miles out of town, Mark fantasized different versions of the scenario of her finding his note stuck to her window. And there were many, many versions! It was such fun imagining them: her surprise, her shock, maybe disdain *(oh, no!)*, perhaps indignance, disgust *(please, no!)*, and more. No, the best scenario would be for her to smile. A vivacious, indulging, knowing, appreciative smile like she had known it all along. In his mind, she would think, *How romantic!* He knew her smile would be stunning and could probably melt stone into putty. He was glad that he had made an advance toward her, and so deliriously happy that he had noticed her—as if anyone could *not* notice her! He had noticed that many locals that morning had been noticing her all the way up and down, as if they were familiar with her, although she seemed completely oblivious. *Long legs, tight jeans; slim hips; square shoulders; thick auburn highlighted hair; and best of all, a perfectly sculpted, flawless, innocent face with unforgettable green-blue eyes ...* At least, he was pretty sure she was unaware of the men's greedy eyes on her.

The scenario he liked the least was that she never noticed his note at all; that somehow, the maniacal wind or some passerby prankster jerked it off, or an earthquake shook the window out, and it fell into the rubble ... He could imagine in that direction too.

Stop! It wasn't just the red light ahead; in his head, he couldn't bear the negative scenarios, and he flatly refused to entertain them. Then with a derisive laugh toward himself, the deputy, and the sheriff, he almost welcomed the chance for a threatened, second interrogation. *Could I get so lucky?* Then he belligerently laughed for another hundred miles after leaving yet another small town behind. On to visit his 'cousin'.

Because of his continual fantasizing, Mark had not been very focused on the many billboards that blew past his rolled-down windows. The weather was so fine: low humidity, clear blue sky, and flawless landscape of mountains, trees, hills, and wide-open spaces. It was unlike the busy, loud, almost angry noise of Kansas City, with insufferable humidity and more billboards than one could possibly read if one didn't want to veer into a ditch. Signage was simply a blur of information, more than a person could humanly remember or scribble down while driving along. It was oxymoronic to advertise telling people not to text on their phones while driving when they must read the small print to call an 800 number and report another driver texting while driving. *Now, that actually could not possibly cause an accident, could it?*

This was where Mark got off that mad merry-go-round called life as humans have made it: striving and driving and conniving for money, success, material possessions, information, technology, and the endless pursuit of what they thought was happiness! *Slow down, people, and just exist! Live! You don't have to possess, and gain, and fame, or go insane in order to live and enjoy life!* It reminded him of another quote from Bryson's *Walk in the Woods.* "Presumably, a confused person would be too addled to recognize he was confused, ergo, if you know you are not confused then you are not confused. Unless, it suddenly occurred to me—and here was an arresting notion—unless persuading yourself that you are not confused is merely a cruel, early symptom of confusion."

Oh, no! Back to the world going mad. He felt like he was going mad by watching the world go mad! The true test of insanity was thinking everyone else was crazy instead of oneself! *Such pleasant thoughts earlier, such delightful fantasies, and then this negative crazy-making!*

How could he interrupt such pleasant musings with thoughts of the whole world and everybody in it losing their grip? He quickly went back to the wonderful, wild encounter of *her*. Then along came the most obnoxious billboard he'd ever seen in his life. There were some pretty obnoxious ones, but this one was beyond belief. It was a garish, out-of-context scene for eastern Montana: a gauche interjection of stress and nerve-jangling politicking like a high school football team dashing through a paper hoop on homecoming game night into the peace of this beau-gorgeous, poster-perfect, Montana landscape scene. *What a downer.* He groaned audibly as he checked out the wooden posts holding up the double billboard. If that wasn't enough, there was the self-purporting phrase at the bottom of the sign: "Best food in town. Ask anyone!" Almost more than capitalism, Mark loathed competition. *Isn't there enough to go around? Isn't there enough for everybody to have a piece of the pie? What is it with human beings and greed?*

The truck almost made the U-turn in the middle of Highway 40 of its own accord, and Mark knew where he would be spending the night. His *modus operandi* was to light the slow-igniting fuse very early in the morning—where smoldering would not be detected for hours—and he hundreds of miles down the road and safely away from the scene.

At least Mark knew he'd have some downtime to return to his replaying of … He made up his mind to stop calling her *her*. She had a name and deserved to be called by her name, whatever it was. He reveled in the delicious thought of giving her a name of *his* choosing until he learned her real name. With that, he donned 'the work clothes': big, over-sized soles from some old boots, size thirteen; paper gown; gloves;

head bag; the drill; the charge; and the cigs. A pretty simple arson kit.

Ruby was practically gnashing her teeth that she'd allowed herself in this dire timeframe to wander so far off task. She noticed the clock and saw that it was nearing school being dismissed; she would need to pick up Chloe before the child invented an excuse to run downtown with her friends. As she dragged her eyes away from the clock, groaning over not getting enough completed on her project for such flighty reasons, her peripheral vision caught something stuck to the outside of her studio window. She barely blinked, and her eyes fluttered back to the object.

What the heck? Was this a practical joke? Who could have devilishly pasted something to her window without coming into the studio? Who would risk the note getting whisked off by the wind, unless it wasn't important and, truly, just a prank? Ruby moved closer toward the window and saw that there was writing on it. *That's just what I need—a few more distractions,* she thought. She moved around her drafting table to the door, still keeping her eye on the slip of paper in case the wind, perversely, snatched it at the last moment.

As she stood outside her studio window, taking the note and reading it, her brows furrowed. Marsha happened along behind her and asked, "Whatcha got, Ruby?"

Ruby, unaware of anyone near her, almost jumped out of her skin. "Uh, I don't know, uh, what this is. Not really ..." As Marsha persisted in being nosy, Ruby quickly decided for reasons unknown to her at the time that she did not need any rubber-necking and sure-to-follow speculative gossip, just in case. *Just in case? Just in case of what?*

Marsha began taunting, "Ruby's got a secret!"

"Oh, for heaven's sake, Marsha. Haven't you got anything

better to do?" Ruby grumbled. "I think this note must be from one of Chloe's friends."

"Whatever!" Marsha dejectedly intoned, starting toward the Red Rock for the evening shift preparations.

Ruby stepped inside into the dimly lit hallway of the studio, out of sight of Marsha or any other peering eyes that seemed to catch her off-guard. Ruby wondered, *Could it be? Could he have? Is it possible in the few minutes I took Chloe to school, he came by?* Ruby remembered he had said, "I'll see you later," but after seeing the unfamiliar truck gone, she gloomily gave up on that idea. She indulged herself with the usual thought that when it came to relationships, all men were pathological liars, undependable, stupid, and a waste of time.

The note started, "Whenever you're not looking for someone, there she is!"

What? screamed Ruby's mind, incredulous. *Whenever you're not looking for whom? A person, a partner, a woman ...? What else could it be? And the line 'there she is'. What is that supposed to mean?* All the while, her heart was pounding as she tried to deny what the message meant. *How could a man waltz into my hometown, give me a couple of up and down looks, lock eyes in an intimate way, pay for my coffee, get arrested, drive out, and leave a note riddled in questions, assumptions, guesses (wild ones), suppositions, doubts, wondering, astonishment, and general jaw-dropping whats?* It was maddening, and she had half a notion to toss it into the trash like so much poison—which was exactly what her brain told her to do. But her heart always trumped her brain, even though she would not admit it most of the time. Exasperated, she stuffed the note inside the middle tray of her drafting desk.

She was still reeling from the ostentatiousness of the note when she noticed it was time to pick up Chloe. Ruby opened the drawer to make sure she did not imagine the entire episode, and she mulled it over in her mind while she dashed for her truck.

Chloe was full of school chatter–more than usual because of the fire-setting gossip. Apparently, the "bastard" boy was not at school today and was being apprehended by police again. The entire school had poor little Rodney caught, charged, judged, and sentenced all in one day. That was quite a reflection on educators everywhere, teaching about democracy! Or perhaps it was just small-town mentality.

Ruby started, "But how on earth could you possibly decide so soon if he ...?"

"Was guilty?" Chloe rattled on, finishing her mother's sentence. "Because he just is! He's done it before!" Then Chloe went on to explain how Rodney had just gotten out of the juvenile detention center for burning down a rancher's old, abandoned outhouse. "He's an arsonist, Mom!"

"He burned down an abandoned outhouse? That sounds like something that *should* be burnt down!" Ruby was trying to get some clarification to settle her own mind about an entirely different nagging suspicion.

"Mom! That rancher has rights!"

"And so does Rodney, if you have opened a book on American history lately. That's as bad as everything that was going on in the Red Rock Café this morning."

"Oh, yeah? Tell me—I'm dying to hear it!" Chloe was almost begging.

"I think you've heard enough gossip for one day, little woman," Ruby often called her by cute pet names.

Chloe knew when it was time to shut up. She started talking about a party that was being planned for the weekend, and she wanted to attend.

They rode in silence to the grocery store to pick up a few fresh vegetables for dinner. As Ruby was squeezing the iceberg lettuce, Chloe wandered to the shampoo aisle and began reading how this or that shampoo was guaranteed to tame her curly light brown hair, which was sure to be as wild as her mother's.

Ruby hadn't realized her hand had not left the lettuce for a whole minute until Marsha surprised her from behind. "Goll, Ruby. What're ya gonna do, mash that lettuce to bits?" Marsha had to make a quick run for café supplies for the dinner rush.

Ruby's adrenalin rush nearly knocked her to the floor. "Marsha! Quit sneaking up behind me like that!" Ruby was drawing the attention of other shoppers.

"I didn't! I spoke to you a minute ago, and you never answered. I didn't think you heard me, so I came closer."

Ruby did not know why she was so on edge. Well, yes, she *did* know. *Him! The café! The coffee! The fire! The note! The day that never seems to end!* She wanted to go home to a bottle of something.

She grabbed the same head of lettuce that she was still massaging, beckoned for Chloe and her magic shampoo, and went to pay.

Marsha beat her to the check-out counter. "Is that all you're getting? A head of lettuce?" Marsha solicited, "Why don't you come over to the café for supper tonight? The special is buffalo and vegetables like only Badger can make."

When they got to the truck, Chloe agreed with Marsha that they should eat out because she had a lot of homework. Upon getting into the house and checking the fridge, Ruby was chagrinned that there was no salad dressing. *Oh, boy!* She threw the dishtowel on the sink and said, "Let's go."

The strong smell of wild meat permeated the restaurant as Ruby and Chloe settled in a booth, knowing already what they wanted to order.

Marsha rushed past and said, "The usual?" Ruby nodded, and she knew their dinner would be served within minutes. She looked around. Quite a few ranchers were there for the buffalo special, and many townspeople, too. Ruby noticed Dickendacker sitting alone near the back door, but soon he was joined by his "bastard" son, Rodney, to Chloe's surprise.

"I thought ..." she trailed off.

"Well, it doesn't look like the police held Rodney for very long, does it? Perhaps they didn't have enough evidence to hold him."

"But usually Kara is right with her inside information."

"Well, just because Kara's dad is the police chief, that doesn't mean she knows everything, Chloe. Please remember that, okay?"

"It's just that everybody's been texting all day, and, and ..." Then hunger took over in Chloe's mind, and she forked into her plate.

Not so with Ruby. She poked at her vegetables and hacked at her buffalo. Usually she was a healthy eater, staying away from sweets (except for her white mocha) and always eating a balanced three meals with nothing in between, just as she perfectly modeled for Chloe. Both of them were slim, strong, and healthy for it.

"What a day" Ruby said with a sigh. "And what am I doing over here again, after all of this craziness of today?"

She looked at where *he* had sat just this morning. In her mind, she replayed herself blasting into the café door this morning, with the whining sirens behind her and *him* directly in front of her. Both of them locked eyes. She enjoyed that brief nuance. She'd remembered the white mocha, the fumbling for money, the exchange of few words, and the awkward embarrassment of practically backing out of the door. The humiliation went on forever. *Why am I here again now?*

Chloe made mention of her toying with her food, remarking that *she* was not allowed to do that. Ruby marveled, *How can a child absolutely ignore you, and then the very instant you do not want her to notice you, she picks that exact moment to remind you of what you're always reminding her about?* She felt just as strongly about getting out of there as she'd felt that morning, which seemed to be about forty-eight hours ago instead of ten.

Marsha brought the ticket just as Ruby and Chloe stood up. "Ruby, you didn't touch your food! Is something wrong with it? You usually gobble up your whole plate. Or do we need a box to go?" Marsha finally got to the end of her diatribe after making a huge and successful effort of scolding, insulting, and calling attention to them, all in a single second.

"Yes, we need a box to go." By then, Ruby wanted to crawl in a hole and pull the hole in after her. With friends like Marsha, who needed enemas? Chloe observed Ruby rolling her eyes, and Chloe frowned because rolling her eyes was an attitudinal act she was never allowed to do.

They followed Marsha up to the register, paid, and were about to exit. Then Marsha couldn't resist. "Ruby, did you ever find out who left you that note on your window?"

Now the whole world, and consequently, the entire café knew—as did Chloe, who was immediately peering not too kindly at Ruby.

Ruby muttered an unintelligible no and darted across the street.

Chloe did not waste any time asking about the note on the window, and she tormented her mother all the way across the street. She didn't even notice the cruising carload of guys in an old Mustang convertible yelling at her.

Ruby stomped more than walked back. She headed straight upstairs to the bathroom and nearly slammed the door in Chloe's face. This was an evening for a long, luxurious, uninterrupted, bubble bath of solace and peace. She did not care whether Chloe did her homework; she was going to soak until bedtime, and she immediately began running the water.

Chapter

5

TWO HOURS INTO her Calgon-take-me-away bath, Chloe knocked on the door. "Mom, you have a phone call. Don't know who it is ..."

Ruby, fearing it was her antsy clients, asked her to tell whomever it was to call back tomorrow. When Ruby finally dragged herself out of the bathtub, Chloe had gone to bed and was asleep, her homework complete and lying on the dining room table waiting for Ruby to check it. If Ruby had not felt so absolutely wiped out, she would have felt guilty over Chloe going to bed without a goodnight hug and kiss.

She was grateful to have the luxury of finally dropping into her own pink, flowery bed. Ruby's tousled head hit the pillow just as the telephone rang. She did not care. Her eyes closed, and the phone stopped ringing. She slipped into an emotionally exhausted sleep.

Approximately three hours later, at the stroke of midnight, Ruby woke up. She had not drawn the curtains in her bedroom, so between the continuously flashing yellow stoplight and the Red Rock's blinking neon sign dancing on the walls, it was impossible to sleep.

Ruby wanted coffee ... no, a white mocha. Refreshed now after her short rest, she wanted to relive yesterday again and again. Except for the embarrassment—she could gladly let go of that. Ruby relived the look he had given her. She relived him watching her from across the street, leaning nonchalantly against the pink sandstone. She tiptoed quietly to the window and peeked out into the darkness, imagining him standing there. Now when everything was quiet and people were not bugging, embarrassing, or sneaking up on her, she felt like yesterday was actually normal. Okay. Good. Exciting. And Promising. *Well, maybe. Don't get carried away,* she warned herself.

Ruby made her way downstairs in the semidark, got out a small glass of wine, and went to read the note in her desk drawer with no lights on, because she already knew what it said. "Whenever you're not looking for someone, there she is." Ruby indulged herself in fantasy. Deep in her heart, she believed it was from him. She truly wanted to believe it. She willed herself to believe. Then she basked in the delicious events of the day and ignored the negatives as her fantasy took her wherever she commanded.

She thought that if the note was truly from him, he probably scrawled it out in a hurry. He did not make spelling or grammar errors—a real turn-on for Ruby, who considered herself a literati. Many people made the contraction error of *your* instead of *you're.* He did not. Elementary, to be sure... but Ruby had no patience for illiteracy. If it was he who'd written the note, it meant that he'd found someone, a woman ... maybe her! She allowed herself to let that prospect in her world of zero prospects feel good for a while, even if he was a complete stranger.

Now, that was a glaring assumption on his part, if *he* wrote the note—that he'd not been looking for a significant other but had still found one. Ruby was giddy and was certain the wine had gone straight to her head. She remembered that she had not eaten enough food at dinner to handle the spin. Also, in her heightened condition, she determined to march into the Red Rock Café tomorrow and ask Marsha his name, along with her usual white mocha.

Mark scouted for a place to hide his old workhorse. Mark loved his truck. It had served him faithfully for the past couple of years or so when he'd bought it from a convenient junkyard en route and ventured into his temporary calling. He knew that the business he was in required a vehicle that could disappear quickly and easily—perhaps permanently. At the same time, he sorely missed his leisurely, carefree KC driving in his classic Beemer.

Mark began the quick, easy process of applying fake tread to the tires of the truck, and he purposely drove it around the soon-to-be crime scene in order to leave the mandatory forensics. He scattered a few hairs around the site gathered from collecting samples in motels, gas stations, and interrogation rooms; hopefully there were some from the heads of some of the locals who undoubtedly rented rooms by the hour. He secretly hoped that the deputy's DNA from his thinning scalp was among the fake evidence he was planting.

Darkness was enveloping the pristine countryside. There were mountains as far as the eye could see. Orange, purple, and indigo combined themselves to create an outrageously beautiful sunset. Only dark greenish black remained of the grass and trees silhouetted in the fading horizon. A car zoomed past: one solitary driver who never glanced to the right, where Mark was crouching. A person could hear a car coming from ten miles away and have plenty of time to douse lights and conceal himself. The truck was safely behind a butte about two miles down the road—a perfect morning jog tomorrow bright and early, so he could give his mind free reign to think about topics of his choice tonight. *Her. Yeah, baby!*

Although that—giving his mind free reign and not concentrating—could be careless and dangerous. He forced himself back on task. The soles he wore strapped to his street shoes were ridiculously large and would need careful disposing of. Medical gloves were the easiest things to pitch; just find a hospital or clinic. After he gave thorough attention to every detail, he ground into the wooden post with the drill, placing the self-destructing charge in six of the eight beams at and below ground level. Mark was satisfied that he'd met all criteria for a successful burn. He lay down for a short nap now instead of leaving in the morning; he needed to drive to be at least several hundred miles away from the crime scene by daybreak. Each job had to be assessed and implemented individually to confound the crime signature, so often there were times when he spent the night at the scene. This was not one of them; it would serve no purpose. It would simply be best to make a phone call on his disposable cell phone far from this job. The challenge was to never create a predictable *modus operandi.*

Mark lit the slow-igniting, slow-burning fuse with a Marlboro cigarette and sprinted into the fading evening. He reached his truck by 8:55, precisely at sundown, and drove northwest into Montana, the never-ending land of big sky.

Mark was bothered by the mistake he'd made. He'd called her—not once, but twice! Whether or not trading cell phones with Jim would cover him well enough was only a matter of some smart-ass cop trying to think outside the box. Mark knew that didn't happen very often because they were so entrenched in their code manuals. Using the disposables helped greatly.

His mind repeatedly tormented him over those desperate, unnecessary risks he took, but it was easy, and so normal. Her phone number was plastered on the outside of her studio window! It was a great combination of numbers too, and he let the numbers roll over his lips. He guessed she was approximately thirty-eight years old, with a twenty-six-inch waist, thirty-six-inch hips, and an area code of 308—leaving out the zero—complementing her nice chest. Indeed, he liked those digits.

The wine had spun its magic on Ruby, and she rested her head on the drafting table for just a few minutes. She was lulled down the river in pleasant dreams of …

Bang! What was that noise? She jerked her head up so fast that she got a crick in her neck. *Oh, the paperboy hit the door with the lackluster news of Tepid Springs.* Ruby didn't know why she subscribed to the thing, except that her artwork, original graphics, success stories, and advertising were contained in its sparse pages.

The paper! It must be after 5:00 a.m.!

She massaged her neck where it had gotten stiff. She had fallen asleep on her drafting table—no wonder her neck hurt! *Crash!* Was Chloe bouncing around in the kitchen so early? The she heard another crash. Ruby dragged herself off the chair to cautiously encounter the chaos in the kitchen. Upon seeing Chloe so perky and bubbly, Ruby stifled a groan.

"Did we sleep well?" Chloe greeted, looking impish.

Ruby, feeling foolish, would not grace her insipid question with an answer. There was none, anyway. Instead, she shuffled into automatic pilot toward the coffee pot. Her first thought, which was gaining less bravado at this early peak of morn, was how she was going to storm the café and ask his name. Then she took another look at the bottle from which she partook around midnight and was astonished at the amount she had consumed. She quickly relegated the bottle to under the sink, to escape Chloe's scrutinizing gaze. Ruby was not yet awake enough to realize it was much too late for a cover-up.

When the coffee pot was happily gurgling, Ruby drifted into the hallway leading outside to pick up the newspaper. Never expecting anything too earth-shaking from the local

Tepid Springs Star, Ruby fell back against the wall as she gawked at the front-page headlines and slumped to the floor.

Tourist Noted as Person of Interest in Billboard Sign Burning

A tourist passing through town was promptly apprehended by the Tepid Springs Sheriff's Department on May 8 after admitting to having traveled north on Highway 385 during the questionable period of time in which the crime of aggravated vandalism and possible arson, or both, near the Scheumaunekk Ranch could have occurred. If the Sheriff's Department collects enough evidence to detain a Mark Smythe from Kansas City, the penalty could be five years in prison, a $75,000 fine, or both. More information on this breaking story will be updated as our fine Sheriff's Department sleuths the case.

Ruby was still holding the front page when Chloe stepped into the hallway, knelt, and asked, "Mom, are you okay? I'm getting worried about you."

Ruby looked into her daughter's precious face and said, "Honey, will you please give me a hand up?"

More in a trance than in the present, Ruby replied that she was not feeling well and was going back to bed. She asked Chloe if she could catch a ride to school with her friend Ashley. Ruby didn't wait for her answer as she keeled down, face-first, onto her bed.

Mark reached White Rapids with no time to spare. He'd

had to drive ten miles southeast on Highway 65 in order to leave the fake tire tracks going in the opposite direction he would eventually take. Then he'd stopped, taken the clay and cords out of the treads, made a U-turn and headed back to the north.

Now he was hungry and looking for a local restaurant as good as the food at the Red Rock Café in Tepid Springs.

An all-night casino came into view, and Mark thought it a likely place for a tourist persona to hang out. Hardly anyone was still up from the night's gambling, but it appeared to have a pot of sure-to-be stale coffee. He was not disappointed. He called his cell phone to check how many minutes he had left and while telling himself not to make the same mistake three times—calling her number, by now indelibly etched in his memory.

Ruby wondered how long it would take for her to smother to death while lying facedown in her bed in this position. She felt humiliated, in despair, let down, and crappy. Mostly, she was furious that she'd melted like this into a near-tears fit like one might experience in a break-up—like she'd experienced in the divorce. When it got down to actually filing the divorce papers, her bravado had turned to Jell-O, and her resolve had evaporated like the quarter inch of rain on the parched ground outside of town during their seven-year drought.

She was furious because she'd been so stupid. She finally admitted that was the worst part—that she'd behaved like an infantile-minded female. No, like a brainless teenager! It gagged her to imagine herself among other desperate women in this pitiful condition.

"I should have known!" she chided herself for the thousandth time. Finally, the drool was so disgusting on the sheets that she stood up and ripped into them, yanking them from the four corners of the bed and flinging them with a vengeance down the stairs.

The wall telephone jangled right beside Ruby's ear. "Oh, shoot! I forgot to call the school!" she chided herself as she picked up. "Hello?"

"Ruby? This is Norma up at school, and we have to have verbal permission for Chloe to have ridden with Ashley to school today."

"She is at school, isn't she?" asked Ruby, slightly alarmed in this surreal trance while trying to get the clock into focus. She wasn't thinking about the actual time so much as about how much time she had spent facedown in her little bitty pity party.

"Yes, she's here, and safe," the secretary added. "But all students need a note saying with whom they ride to and from school."

Ruby could not believe it. It was so after-the-fact. And also mid-morning.

"You should have sent a note with her, but Ms. Powlee will accept a verbal."

Ruby's jaw dropped. Rather than bicker over this minutiae, she ingratiatingly agreed and hung up. Then she picked up the receiver and banged it down again three more times for good measure. *Why are such stupid people allowed to live?*

She'd been prostrate on her bed for over an hour. *Well, I guess I have indulged myself quite enough,* she thought, and she rolled her eyes and swore over the stupidity of school protocol. Ruby had followed the rules all of her life, but either she was going insane, or it was getting to be the time in her life when she needed to stuff a few of those rules where the sun didn't shine. With that rabid attitude, she punched the sheets into the washer, started it, and decided to get this advertising job finished today. Yes! She did not give a rip how she got this job done—forget the creativity and doing her best. At this moment, she simply wanted to shove something up someone else's pipes for a change. Ruby fairly dove into the project from hell.

She pasted, cut, reworked, stole graphics off the Internet, modified them, enlarged, cropped, reshaded, outlined, spreadsheeted, inserted pictures, files, planned, created, originated, and more nonsense until she was certain the project was a quite nice, doomed failure. She worked without a scrap of food and had even forgotten her morning coffee, all future white mochas, and lunch at the café in order to find out his name (which she now knew and, oddly, didn't want to know anymore). She was nigh onto plans for dinner and picking up Chloe at school when the phone rang.

If that is the school again, I'm going to go up there and ... She brusquely said hello.

There was a slight pause. Then, "Hi."

She knew his smooth voice, even on the phone. She would know that voice in a police lineup ... if ever they needed voice recognition in police lineups.

Another long pause. "Hi? Uh, I am the guy who—"

She interrupted. "I know."

"...who...", he tried to finish, "you do?"

"Yes, I do."

"How do you?"

"I don't know, I just do." She wanted to scream, *I know because your mug was all over the damn papers this morning. That's how!*

She ventured, "Is your name Mark, by any chance?"

"Yes. How did you know?"

"I guess I'm psychic."

"Wow, psychic and beautiful!"

Oh, just get real, you idiot. You really think I'm gonna fall for the "beautiful" thing in the first three seconds? She was in the mood to hang up—but her hand would not let go of the phone.

"Well," he drawled in proper gentlemanly Kansas City vernacular, "you have an advantage because I don't know your name."

Oh, and is this where I voluntarily fill in the blanks for your blank brain and give you my blankety-blank name? I don't think so! She wanted to say to him, *And you never will!*

Instead, she quipped, "Then you have your work cut out for you, because I'm not in the phone book, and I use my maiden name." Her heart wanted to squish down to putty, but her rock-hard nerves would not allow it.

"But I have your *numbers*, I mean, number. I mean, phone number."

She was silently mocking his stuttering and stumbling over his statements. For a guy who exuded so much confidence and cavalier nonchalance, he was almost tongue-tied. That felt like a small victory for her. But it was soon a shallow victory because she detected some honesty ... and could it possibly be vulnerability, or... innocence?

Yeah, Mark, and I've got yours too! She now knew he had absolutely no idea what she was talking about. How can a guy randomly travel through small towns and life, burning down billboards, destroying property, and thinking he could have romance all across the continent? *Geez, the gall, the absurdity, the ego!*

"I tried to see you before I left town so we could formally meet, or at least find out each other's names," he rather lamely persisted.

But I already know yours, dolt, because it was plastered all over the blasted front page!

"I thought we could exchange phone numbers or e-mail, but you weren't there. I scribbled a note to you and left it on your window. Did you get it?"

"Yes."

"Yes? That's it? Did you read it? Do you have any idea where that quote comes from?"

"No. Tell me."

"Then you have your work cut out for you ..."

Ruby was livid! *How dare he!* It was one thing to be sarcastic, but she sure hated it when other people flipped the tables on her.

He finally said, "Well, I'm sorry, I've gotta run. Can I call you again?"

She hesitated. "Um ... okay." It was spoken from her heart. Her brain thought, *Why did I say okay?*

"Soon?"

"Uh, okay." *And then I actually did it twice?*

"I like it better when you say, 'Yes, I do!'"

"Very funny." She could have ignored the obvious reference to marriage vows (which people usually said but didn't mean, as the current divorce rate would attest), but she flatly decided against further wordplay.

He totally threw her off when he merely said, "Thanks. I hope we can get to know each other better soon. Bye."

"Bye." Then she gave a deep sigh.

Ruby looked at the phone like it was a new invention she'd never seen or used before, and she shook her head in disbelief. *He called! No... wait—Mark called!*

Chapter

6

CHLOE CRASHED IN, coming through the front hallway door yelling, "Hey, Mom, did you forget about me? Ashley's Mom brought me home, so the school is probably going to yell at you again tomorrow!"

Ruby tried to conceal the glee in her recent leap into the mucky-muck as she slipped around her desk to meet her daughter. *What am I doing? What am I thinking? Why did I say he could call me? Oh, well. Needn't worry. Don't men always say they will call you back and never do?*

Ruby grabbed her only child into her arms and held on tightly.

"Mom, are you better than you were this morning? Did you have a migraine?"

"Much! What shall we have for dinner?" Ruby nodded and thought, *Oh, I have a headache, all right!*

Chloe knew it was usually reserved for Thursday night only, but she ventured, "Pizza?"

"Anything, sweetie!"

"Why so happy? I thought you weren't feeling well this morning."

"I wasn't, but I finished that impossible project, and whether it is right or wrong, I'm handing it back to those persnickety people in a heap. We probably ought to go out to celebrate me finishing it!"

"Oh, could we?" implored Chloe.

"How about bringing in the pizza and watching a movie?"

"On a school night? Mom, do you have a fever or something?"

It was true. Ruby rarely veered from her household rules and regs; she ran a pretty tight ship as far as school, homework, consistency, and Chloe were concerned.

"Why don't you start your homework immediately? I will go call in the order and pick it up. If you're finished before I return, you get to choose the movie, okay?" To save face with the rules, she added, "It's Wednesday—that's close enough to Thursday night!" Tepid Springs hadn't had a five-day school week for more than two decades, so essentially Thursday was like Friday for most kids. Teacher in-services and sports activities were scheduled on Fridays, but Mondays through Thursdays, the students attended class for more hours than any five-day schools. Ruby relished her Fridays with Chloe. Those were days they chose to ride the Mikelson Bike Trail, go horseback riding, or hike to Harney Peak, Bear Butte, or around Sylvan Lake.

Stunned from the phone call, but eternally grateful that it had terminated just before Chloe got home from school, Ruby breathed another huge sigh filled with nothing but convoluted thoughts. *What in holy heck is happening to me? I feel like a giant pendulum going back and forth and getting thrashed every time I reach the right or left.* She grabbed a light sweater because the weather this May was still chilly. Then she jumped into her purple Ford for the errand.

After two minutes of waiting for the pizza, Ruby realized it had been a mistake to even come out of the house. Everybody was talking about the front-page news. She had to admit Mark did not sound like or appear to be an arsonist, but why would they have detained him if there wasn't some truth to the rumors?

Usually Chloe cared nothing about local or national news, but she had the news station on when Ruby returned, and they were flagging Mark's name, truck, and Kansas City home all over like he was being profiled on *America's Most Wanted*. He had a nice house with a small, economic car in the drive; Ruby couldn't see that it was an older BMW. Some of his friends and neighbors were being interviewed. They said he was going to visit his cousin in Montana, and they liked her very much because she had visited him in Kansas City. On and forever on they went in the frenzy for new news. Ruby mostly despised the news programs as sensationalism (and obnoxiously probing people) at their worst.

Later, they settled into the couch side-by-side with a bubbling-hot cheese and vegetable pizza. They watched a favorite, *Princess Bride*. Between Ruby and Chloe, they knew the entire script of the movie and had their own personal jokes about common lines. They echoed several of their favorite movie lines, "I'll cut your heart out with a spoon!" "It's possible ... pig." "Stop rhyming—I mean it." "Anybody want a peanut?" It usually sent them into peals of laughter. "And make the stitches small!" was from yet another old favorite movie.

Ruby found herself sinking over the news program, but she made a heroic effort to be happy for Chloe's sake. *He'd called her!* She'd frosted him out, so it would be a miracle if he ever called her again. Dejectedly, she let her feelings reign with a foreboding that the tittle-tattle about Mark was probably true, and she could never allow herself to become involved with someone on the edge of the law—for her sake, but especially for Chloe's sake.

The movie was over, and they tromped up to bed. Another sleepless night, with the confrontation of facing the clients tomorrow. How was she ever going to get any quality rest tonight? Ruby's head hit the pillow, and out of emotional exhaustion, she slept soundly. Surprisingly, she woke up in the very same position she'd gone to sleep. When the alarm rang at 5:00 a.m., Ruby already felt like she was late for work. The clients would be in her studio by 10:00 a.m.

Julie, Mark's cousin, ran screaming out from the banging screen door, jumped into his outstretched arms, and wrapped her longs legs around him. "You came! I can't believe you actually came out here to God's country to visit me!" Julie was the nuttiest tomboy of a cousin he'd ever had. She'd always wanted to live on a ranch in Montana, and she'd found a pretty nice guy crazy enough to do it with her. They raised horses, llamas, and cattle on nearly four hundred acres. The view was beautiful in every direction one could see. The fragrance of sage, pine, and recent rain permeated the morning.

Mark sighed from the exhausting miles and miles of zooming under the radar and now being tucked in the backwoods of a safe place, where he could relax. He was ready for sleep and some recharging.

Julie said, "How about a cowboy breakfast? Pancakes and eggs, bacon, hash browns, oatmeal, toast ... I'm fixing the kids' breakfast right now. Come on in and join us!"

Although he was hungry, Mark did not want an overloaded, shovel-sized breakfast to go to sleep on. But he followed Julie's bouncing steps into the big ranch house kitchen as she hollered for everyone to snap to attention because company had arrived. First, though, he must make a phone call to establish his whereabouts. He dialed an enticing memorized number, using Julie's home phone.

Ruby's telephone rang piercingly through the docile morning's first one-eyed look in the mirror. *Oh, good grief. I look tired!* She looked first at her face. *If it's those clients bugging me at this hour, I'm gonna give them a piece of my mind. Their appointment was at ten o'clock.* "Hello?"

Ruby could not believe her ears. The caller was Mark.

As the phone picked up, Mark heard slight agitation, but

her *sweet, sexy* voice said hello. He tried not to think about her perky chest. Unlike most men who enjoyed big, oversized double-D cups occupying the entire front of a woman's body, Mark did not. He liked women who were slim, athletic, natural, and maybe flat by some standards. Like Julie, who was an active, outdoors woman—a gal who was tough in an extremely feminine way. Plain and simple, some women achieved that tough-but-feminine combination. Some never could. He loathed the ones with voluptuous bodies and no brains, who arbitrarily allowed their innocence to be turned into sleaze. Furthermore, he did not like blondes at all. Give Mark someone with hair color of brown, black, or red any day. He didn't even mind silver. Women worried entirely too much about how to stay looking young when the only beauty a man like him admired was being confident, intelligent, natural, and playful, and truly knowing how to be comfortable with herself.

Mark allowed his persona to be that of a playboy, but in fact he was *not* a playboy in any sense of the word; he was a one-woman man. Perversely, it made a fantastic cover for his real business—that of self-declared, self-employed, environmental activist.

His mind quickly wandered back to the present.

"Uh, hi again." He let out a breath.

So soon? She remembered that he'd asked if he could call her again, but she did not think it would be the next morning. She checked the clock: it had not even been fourteen hours! She didn't really expect him to call back at all!

"Hi again to you." *Back at 'cha*, thought Ruby.

"I hope I didn't wake you up."

Oh, by calling at 5:05 a.m.? Ruby didn't get it, Ruby didn't get *him*. Nevertheless, she was smiling. *Kind of a nice wake-up call.*

Technically, Mark supposed he was using her to establish

his whereabouts, but in fact there was no one else in the entire world that he would have rather called. "It's earlier *here!*" he added.

"And where is here?"

"Where I'm sitting right now."

Ruby rolled her eyes and thought, *Round and round! Must these initial conversations always be so crazy and droning?*

"I'm on the porch, looking at the beauty of nature, waiting for breakfast."

Was eating all men ever thought about? Her father, brothers, cousins, and ex were exactly the same regarding food. She asked, "Are you really in a different time zone?"

"No, just kidding. But I'll wager the sun is peeping over Battle Mountain at your house." He said *house* because he did not know whether she lived in the back of her studio or an apartment elsewhere.

How did he learn about Battle Mountain after being in town such a short time? That was one of Tepid Springs' secret, which most tourists never learned about—just like they didn't know that the "waterfall" splashing into the springs was pumped up from the Fall river. It was comical to watch all of those unsuspecting tourists meticulously cataloging vacation pictures in front of it like a treasured souvenir postcard.

"And the sun is not rising in your neck of the woods?" Ruby purposely changed the verb to *rising*; it was more sophisticated and less redundant. Then she grit her teeth over using the old Roker cliché of "your neck of the woods."

Mark laughed like he could imagine her gritting her teeth over her petulant banter. "This is not my neck of the woods, darlin'."

Oh, right! If she dared say she knew he was from Kansas City, he would immediately know she got her information from the newspaper or national news. She was not ready yet to reveal that fact and preferred to maintain the façade of being psychic. Also, she did not want their repartee to discontinue.

Wait a minute! He called her darlin'! That is just too familiar, too soon! Look out for a guy who starts right in with the flattering. Now she stopped smiling and struggled to get a better grip on the first few minutes of yet another upside-down conversation.

"Why did you call me that?" she asked.

"Call you what?"

"You know ... *Darlin'.*" She was chagrinned because it sounded like she called him *darlin'* back.

He took full advantage of it. "Well, thank you for calling me *darlin'*, darlin'," he teased. "Uh, sorry if that offended you, but remember, I don't know your name!"

"Yeah." Ruby was still not about to offer her name.

"That means I can take the liberty of naming you myself until I learn your real name." Mark thought that ruse might work, but he was in for a tantalizing surprise when she did not.

"Oh-ho! So you either think I am dumb or so forgetful that I didn't remember that it is *your* problem to discover *my* name."

He indulged her with a chuckle because he enjoyed their exchange.

That brought her smile back too. *What a sexy laugh his was!*

"So how did you discover mine? A newspaper, perhaps?"

Busted! He knows! Now what could she possibly say to cover up the source from which she had learned his name, plus a whole lot more? Ruby thought the psychic idea gave her some power, but it was dashed in a nanosecond by his infuriating guess, or luck—or perhaps insight from previous experience? *Or often? So it's true, then?*

Meet it head-on! This is a train wreck waiting to happen anyway. She said, "I saw it on a *billboard.*"

She did not expect Mark's reaction.

He burst into a full-blown, spontaneous laugh. It practically jangled her end of the wire. He continued laughing, seemed to be stopping, and then would start all over. Ruby waited rather impatiently for him to finish enjoying her accusatory, tactless honesty. She thought that tasteless comment would succeed in putting him on the defensive after prematurely calling her darlin', and she wasn't sure if he was ever going to be able to speak again.

"Oh, man. Let me ... get my ... breath!"

Whatever!

This dead horse was slammed on the table between them, and it was up to him to say the next words—but all he could seem to do was continue *enjoying* it.

Suddenly, a woman's voice could be heard calling him to breakfast. Still laughing and trying to get his words out, he said, "Gosh, I haven't laughed so hard in a year. I really have to go, darlin'. Can I call you again?"

No, wait—this conversation is not finished! He had confessed to nothing, and she was not about to let him go until he answered some of her questions. And where was he, that she could hear some other woman's voice?

Chloe was mumbling something. Ruby heard Mark being called to breakfast somewhere. She was on a rigorous time frame with clients. Could anything else descend upon her in her first ten minutes of the day?

"No! I mean, yes. I mean, *wait a minute!*" Ruby let down her guard all in one stuttering sentence.

Mark loved it. Not even a WWF contender could have wiped that devilish grin off his face. Now who was floundering? While Mark had been at the casino around midnight, he'd looked up Tepid Springs on their Wi-Fi kiosk and read the article in the *Star*. He already knew where she'd gotten her information and his name. However, she did not know that he knew about the headlines, and he was not about to tell her. *What, and ruin the most delightful banter and challenge he'd experienced in years?* He digressed just long enough to imagine how she looked this morning: hair tousled, lacey jams, infuriated expression. *So adorably irresistible.*

"Wait for what?" he continued baiting her.

"Wait for ... me to ask you ... Wait for you to ..." She faded. *Wait for me to ask you if you did the deed or not, or wait for you to confess to the truth!* No way was she going to be able to spit out the subject of the obvious—the arson issue. She came within a hair's width of finding out the truth, and then it went *poof*—all the while he laughingly dodged her reticence and enjoyed it. *Does he not know the consequences of committing arson? Is he taunting the law? Is he a repeat offender? Why else would he be so nonchalant about a serious charge like arson?* Ruby's mind spun furiously.

"Well, I've got to run. Can I call you, darlin'?"

"Uh, yes. No. Uh ..."

"Yes or no?"

"That's a trick question!"

"Either I can call you again, or you don't want me to. What trick is there to that?"

He's slimed through another skirmish! The way he asked that question could be taken two ways. "Can I call you darlin'?" or "Can I call you, darlin'?" She told herself she was going to have to perk up a bit and deflect his verbal traps a little better. She was definitely out of practice.

The best ruse was to change the subject completely and get back into safe territory. "You are taking advantage of having awakened me out of a deep sleep."

"Is that a yes or a no?"

"Yes, but only after my coffee!"

He replied, "Or your white mocha."

She walked right into that one and chose to ignore it.

Mark added, "I saw your lights come on at 5:00 a.m.

yesterday morning, while I was waiting for the Red Rock Café to open. Never did I imagine the ..."

He was going to say *exquisite creature that would emerge from that sandstone building.* But no, too soon, too familiar, too vulnerable. If there was anything that was a turn-off, it was getting to the mushy part too soon. He knew enough about women to know that it was the long, slow, tantalizing dance of romance that was the fun of seduction, not so much the sexual act. He had observed that most men skipped over what he thought was the best part in order to jump in the sack. Not him. Ninety percent of the women he dated bailed out because they thought he took too long getting to that consummating point.

"Never did you imagine what?" she prompted.

"Never did I imagine that you would not be up and going already," he finished lamely, hoping that his substitute comment came off as authentic.

"Okay, Ru—uh, darlin'. Next time I will call you after you've had your coffee. Thanks for saying yes." He'd nearly called her Ruby. When reading the *Star* online, he had come across her advertisements in the paper, and there was her name! He was lucky because he'd almost logged off before he'd noticed her ad. "Later, Darlin'."

"Bye." She sighed—a deep, invigorating intake of breath— surprised that she could still breathe at all. *What am I doing?* Already she wondered if she was in too deep, too far gone. She tried to shake off the euphoric feeling but smiled in spite of herself. He had blatantly and successfully evaded her inference about the billboard issue.

She was still shaking her head while consulting the mirror. *Better hop into the shower and get this bizarre day rolling.*

Chapter

7

SOON CHLOE WAS off to school without crisis or incident. Ruby had picked up the paper on the way back into the studio after taking Chloe to school and straightening out the after-the-fact permission note with Ms. Powlee. Quickly she checked out the front page. Thank goodness, no more glaring headlines. Maybe the incident would blow over and she could entertain the notion of being interested in this very interesting man.

On the back page of the first section was a blurb that a certain Mark Smythe would be reinterviewed by local law enforcement, including input from the FBI.

She thought, *Holy shit! Now what?* Ruby had so much to do to prepare for her clients' visit, and here she sat, bemoaning this recent development. *Maybe the media just needed to keep the story alive, or needed someone to blame, to make it look like the cops were working their hardest to get this crime—no, misdemeanor—no, crime solved. Our good taxes at work. Who knew?*

Ruby got the coffee pot hopping and went into battle with the inevitable work. It wasn't very long, and her mind was smiling over the fact that he'd called her *not once, but twice in nearly twelve hours.*

Back to business. Back to him. No! Back to business!

Ruby set her mind to concentrating and began to flourish in ideas and graphics and computer gyrations. She was determined to have a professional, stellar, irresistible presentation to offer the clients. With just a few indulgent smiles and thoughts of Mark, she slapped the last page together a half hour early—but just barely before her boss haggled at the front door.

"Hi, Jordan," she quipped as she beckoned him in and trotted back to the studio. "I think the clients will swoon over this." Ruby did not like last-ditch efforts that came together like magic—too much stress—but that seemed to be how she often accomplished her work. For the half-hearted effort she'd felt earlier, she didn't think the project turned out too badly; she decided to be a little bit proud of this achievement. The color was balanced but subtle; the lettering shadowed effectively, and the background was classy, giving the foreground the desired superior position.

He greeted her with, "How's life in your little back-bedroom Springs community?" Then he laughed, trying to ease into the important reason for his appearance.

The comment was condescending, and they both knew it but she chose to ignore it. He had flown in from Denver and must not have had a very smooth flight.

She gestured with satisfaction over her work for Jordan to scrutinize, and he was totally unreadable. He picked up the first poster, turned it, took it to the window for better lighting, and leafed through the manual with no expression, or maybe a critical frown here and there. "Hmm," was all he said.

Then, "Uh-huh."

Finally, "What do you think, Ruby?"

She was disconcerted by his aloofness; after all, she'd known him almost her entire career in advertising, she and considered them pretty good friends. He'd served as a character reference for her when it was difficult for a single mom to get a job.

"I have worked half the night. Weeks and weeks of hours without a breakthrough. Finally, last night, uh, this morning ..." She stopped. Without hesitation, she challenged, "I think most of this project is some of my best work ever."

"So do I, but I'm not so sure about the clients, and that is who we must please," was all he came back with. After an uncomfortable pause, he said, "Uh, does the message need to be so ... uh, political? Remember, they are just selling advertising space.!"

"I know. What do you suggest I tweak?"

"Frankly, it's going to require more than tweaking, darlin'." He stepped away just in case there might be uncharacteristic fallout.

Ruby concealed the thunderstorm gathering in her mind, and she suppressed a desire to lash out at Jordan. He usually represented clients fairly accurately—*that* she respected—but it always involved him being adept at squeezing additional hours, weekends, work, and modifications out of her. But she was in no mood today to give that extra inch.

"Don't ever call me darlin' again."

Jordan stepped another three feet back and said, "I haven't had coffee yet. Let's go on over to your quaint little café across the street and discuss this rationally, okay?"

Ruby was offended at his reference to the 'quaint' little café, and to discussing 'rationally'. His comment reminded her that he'd first insulted the small-town 'bedroom community' like it was second class, and he continued insulting with bedroom 'springs,' as if all people had to do around here was hop into bed with each other. Third, he'd trashed the town's historic name of Springs in the process. No, this was not acceptable, and she was in half a mind to tell him to jam it. This interface also reminded her of her ex-husband's relentless condescension.

"The café is *modern,* not quaint, with running water and indoor toilets, Jordan. Stop insulting the world with your global-sized ego!"

She gave him a bit of time to process the fact that he'd just been taken to task, and that she was not giving an inch. She regretted not doing that in her marriage. Then she quietly mentioned he should inform the clients that her work would be for sale to their available and despicable competitor.

Jordan stormed out.

Ruby gazed after him and let a thought momentarily possess her that Jordan was selfish, belligerent, and so demanding that anything less than getting his own way all of the time every day was abhorrent to him. Maybe the clients were not the impossible ones after all! Perhaps *he* was self-serving under the guise of helping her. What exactly was that sixty/forty split of the profits? Was Jordan cheating her and then feigning demanding clients in order to charge them more and give her less? Perhaps his ulterior goal was to keep her beholden to him—not a position she relished.

Ruby shook her head to clear it. Maybe she was getting paranoid. She already knew she was a bit on edge right now. Ruby went to the bathroom to rinse her face and cool her head. All the while, her gut feeling tried to deny the negative feedback regarding Jordan. He was her bread and butter. Chloe's bread and butter, for goodness' sakes! Still ...

Ruby slipped into a fresh ruffled blouse and trotted across to the café where Jordan looked somber. She knew immediately she would apologize.

"Jordan," she began as she slipped into the opposite side of the booth, "I'm sorry for blurting out that I will sell to our competitors. I've worked really hard on this assignment, and perhaps I am too partial for my own good."

He seemed to accept the hint of a truce. "It's okay. I just want what's best for the clients, Ruby, and your work is stellar—it *is* the best. They are pleased so far. I just want them to be wowed, if you know what I mean."

"Yeah, I suppose so."

"Well, let's talk about the changes tomorrow. I'm going to the bar to relax in Rapid, and I will plan on being back in the morning, okay?" She nodded. Jordan then excused himself and slid into his rental car for the hour-long drive to Rapid.

Ruby ordered her usual white mocha and hurriedly departed. She wondered what had gotten into her and what exactly had just happened. Ruby thought a bar wouldn't hurt her mood either.

Chapter

8

IT DID NOT matter that Mark didn't wish to eat a heavy meal before crashing for ten or twelve hours. Julie was too excited at his presence to listen to reason. Besides, the mountain of steaming pancakes dripping with homemade maple syrup and hand-churned butter was too much to resist, and Mark pretended to hate it but plunged in with two forks. He ate until he hurt—and then he ate some more. Finally, after refusing refills, seconds, thirds, and rolling more than walking away from the table, Mark headed to the nearest bed. He slept solidly for a seemingly brief four hours and then felt himself being pried out of bed and bodily dragged to the stable to be rigorously introduced to Julie's prize horses.

"Julie, you are a mean girl!" he sleepily choked out. He vaguely noticed Julie's husband evaporating into the tractor shed; by then, he knew he was in for a good whelping by an animal with a brain the size of a walnut. Before his eyes were completely open, he was astride a hot-blooded, green-broke gelding named Sheik, who could hardly be contained in his stall. Julie rode a young, sleek, reddish-brown Arabian mare named Nefertiti, meaning "the beautiful one has arrived."

While still buttoning up his shirt, he was at the mercy of Sheik, turned loose to ride into the sunset—or was it sunrise? Mark was dazed and felt only half there, but the exhilarating ride that horse gave him was so totally incredible and exciting that all was forgiven. Julie cantered easily and gracefully behind Mark and Sheik the entire way, until Sheik gave permission to walk by slowing down. Mark thought he'd seen breathtaking canyons, pristine woods, statuesque wildlife, and soaring eagles blur past, but he couldn't be certain— at least not while Sheik was in charge. As they splashed across clear running streams and paused quietly in wooded meadows, Mark thought he must still be asleep or had arrived in heaven. The beauty of this place commanded reverence and whispered wonder. Without explaining or sharing with Julie, who would totally agree with and possibly insist upon joining his "mission," Mark experienced an ethereal feeling as he surveyed the magnificence of this place from atop this powerful animal that he was indeed doing what was right— almost as if he had no choice. By the time they returned to the barn, both Sheik and Mark had become calm and were recommitted to their calling.

Mark tried unsuccessfully to disappear back into bed while simultaneously fearing the evil way Julie would most likely awaken him next.

"You've got to see my flowers and herb garden, and my honeybees and goats, and the rest of the ranch!"

On the way down into the middle of the king-sized bed, not knowing his next move or caring, Mark mumbled, "Great. I'm allergic to bees! God, please give me a delightful dream ... and, *please*, God. You know what I mean ..."

Chapter

9

RUBY PICKED UP Chloe after volleyball practice, and they headed home to a long, uneventful evening; out of boredom, they succumbed to slumber early and fitfully. Ruby dreamed of advertising: creating gloriously illustrated, multiple intelligence-style messages, eye-catching—no, traffic-stopping billboards that throngs of daily commuting drivers would enjoy and learn from. She envisioned her work being so well-known for their particular style that she would never be beholden to another snake like Jordan. The more she thought about their business relationship during the past five years, the less she trusted him. In fact, speaking of snakes, she considered sporting a handgun for the first time in her life.

Chloe flopped into bed with her and was soon curled up and asleep. Ruby got back up to watch some mindless TV—commercials, advertising styles, riff-raff, and guaranteed superficiality. The ten o'clock news was reporting a small but well-contained fire in Montana; the oddity was that only a billboard burned, and nothing much surrounding it—no grass, trees, fence, fields, or real estate property. An investigation was opened for suspected arson and would be on-going until solved.

Ruby had been mulling about Jordan's issues. She sat up, moved to the edge of the couch, and perked her ears, but the story concluded.

Now what was that again? screamed her mind. *A fire?*

Another fire? Wasn't Mark headed in the general direction of Montana? Could he have done it again?

Those sudden, interruptive alarms crowded Jordan to the back of her mind. So many questions, so little information, so many conflicting feelings, so much stress. Why wouldn't her mind let her stop thinking?

Ruby fumbled in the medicine cabinet for Tylenol PM, grabbed a glass of wine, and flounced on the couch, where she fell into fitful sleep. She perversely dreamed about Mark's smile, his athletic physique, his strong hand lightly touching her back. She shivered. She wanted to stay right there in Mark mode for the rest of her life.

It seemed like five minutes later that Chloe was straining at her to get up. "Mom, it's time to take me to school. I've got band practice."

Ruby ventured one eye open. "Isn't it Friday?" she mumbled.

"Yes, Mom, but I still have band practice. We're getting ready to march in the Fourth of July parade."

"Isn't it still May?" Ruby made another attempt to stay pasted to the couch.

"Mom, I'm going to be late!" Chloe said dramatically.

Chloe is getting very sassy these days, Ruby thought as she willed her hands to help lift her head up from the couch pillow. Now in a sitting position, Ruby turned to see what she'd used as a pillow—a Smiley guy, whose button Ruby inadvertently pushed while getting up. It suddenly played the tune "Happy Birthday." It was way too early, or way too late, or way too happy for all that commotion this morning. Ruby gave it a fling to the other side of the room.

Chloe was giggling at the happy song and shoving her mother's clothes at her. "Hey, don't take it out on him!"

Ruby woke up while driving Chloe to school, and she realized the huge load of crap with which she had to deal upon returning. *No time for white mocha; just get back to the studio and loaded for bear for Jordan.* Was that her second reference to guns within the past half day? She managed to get the coffee burbling and gritted her teeth in opposition of revisiting the project. She checked for any tweaks she guessed Jordan would demand, modified the message, and reestablished her resolve to stand her ground.

It was midmorning before Jordan dared show his face and he was brisk as he entered the hallway to the studio. Ruby met him at the door for a mood check. This time he would be met with her assertive skills, claw-side out.

She had not anticipated that Jordan would arrive loaded for bear. Disarming as he was in good looks, it was the white mocha and bagels he swished under her nose with an equally disarming smile.

Thunk! Her resolve dropped two stories down.

To avoid any lengthy interaction, her backup strategy seemed to be to get the encounter over with. She thanked him politely for the white mocha, set the bagel aside for later, and sprang into explanative action.

Jordan was, in turn, disarmed by Ruby, but he allowed an indulgent smile for her gamely efforts. It was not easy dancing between hard-to-please clients and often eccentric artistic types such as Ruby. For all the hoop jumping, he highly respected Ruby's work. He simply could not come close to comprehending why Ruby would want to waste her life in Tepid Springs when Denver lay at her feet. As far as he could appreciate, Tepid was a place to survive rather than thrive. He shrugged it off because it's her life, but not without briefly entertaining the what-if of visiting Ruby when he was torqued with his spoiled wife had Ruby been in Denver. He sort of also knew that Ruby would most likely not consent to being a player in that arena, even if she was closer in proximity.

Ruby was totally invested in defending her original

position; Jordan was intent upon pleasing the clients. To bypass the impasse, they settled on changing Ruby's brilliance into mediocrity. Ruby said in her head, *To hell with it. Just pay me.* Jordan was ushered out long before his flight back to Denver would depart. Ruby plopped herself at her desk, cranked up the computer, and set to work on perfecting her idea and trolling for new clients—and a new agent.

She lingered over a blank, uncreative moment to suddenly ask herself, *Now, why did I choose advertising for a career?*

Then she thought longingly about her parents and their dismay in her choice of career. It was beginning to sink in how right her parents may have been about a career in advertising. It seemed like a good time to give them a call. *Whenever in doubt, call home!* She rang them up.

Dad was out golfing with his business partners. Mom was home from school—early dismissal for teacher in-service—but had a doctor's appointment. All was well, and busy. They had plans to come out and visit during July and watch Chloe march in the band. Ruby's heart ached to see them.

Back on task. On to productivity. Ruby did not realize how easy it was to find clients who wanted to advertise. There was a plethora of people wanting to pay her big bucks to design public messages for their sales departments, and it mean increased profits for her. She could be her own agent, she decided, and she sent out no fewer than a couple of dozen e-mails. She unexpectedly had to struggle with some ethics that apparently Jordan-as-agent had been absorbing for the benefit of Ruby. That illumination caused consternation for more than a little while. Ruby felt suddenly alone and vulnerable. Jordan may have protected her from a lot of schmuck from the very type of people she had always tried to avoid in life. What would she say or do if entities such as the NRA wanted her to make signs about toting guns around the country? In spite of thinking about owning a gun twice in the last twelve hours, she'd never believed that guns solved any problems. And those insipid, insufferable political campaigns! What if the abortion advocates requested her expertise in advertising? What if the anti-abortionists did? Where did she stand?

Ruby did not honestly know. She had simply been willing to get paid for her awesome creativity and graphic ideas for designing billboards. More and more and more billboards to shout to the public to buy, own, and accumulate. Was that the field she knowingly chose? Was that what she wanted out of life? Was it actually meaningful work? And did it jive with her world view, with the way she'd been brought up? Ruby had always loved art and creativity. She needed money to raise her child and support her own dreams. She would never ask for financial help from her family, even though she knew they wouldn't hesitate to offer.

With all of these foreign, uncomfortable notions plaguing her, she needed a break. Why not surprise Chloe and sashay straight into the kitchen to make double chocolate chip cookies? She told herself that she and Chloe would have to get out on the bike trail for quite a few hours this weekend to work off their indulgence. In addition to exercising her own body daily, she wasn't the kind of parent who would allow her child to become obese or lazy about her health.

After sleeping for most of the day, riding a wild horse for a few liberating and deliberating hours, briefly experiencing the ranch life for a few days, and sleeping all night (complete with dreams—well, more like fantasies), Mark was primed to get on the road again. He planned to detour straight south through Wyoming and take a very sharp left turn back through the Black Hills and Tepid Springs. Why? Well, why not? But he hadn't asked Ruby for her permission. He also hadn't yet devised a natural or authentic reason for doubling back. He did not wish to encounter the law, so why risk it? But still, how could he possibly not?

Mark knew his Kansas City home base needed his attention ... as did a certain woman who filled up his senses like a Montana meadow. His friends were questioning his every move, and Dan was mutely anxious to get his own cell phone returned in order to terminate the unspoken cover-up. Dan never questioned him, never refused to help, never judged, and never pestered him about changing phones; he simply conducted their alliance strong and silently. Mark figured Dan's philosophy was that if he never asked what Mark did on his mysterious jaunts, Dan would never have to testify against him. In fact, Dan gave him much latitude and approval toward his goals, often agreeing with him about signage being entirely too excessive in this beautiful land of tacked-up America—but always and forever, they mostly communicated nonverbally.

Mark flipped open the phone and dialed Dan.

"Hey, what's happening?"

"Mark, KC police have been all over your place, along with the media and their antics. I drove by a couple days ago to check on things like you asked, and it was a three-ring circus. I kept driving. The neighbors reported you went to Montana. Sorry, but that's about all I know. When are you coming home?"

"Soon, Dan. And that brings up a favor I might need. I'm not sure yet. Things are pretty complicated right now ..."

"Oh? Who is she?" quipped Dan.

Mark chuckled. "Maybe, but I might need you to pick me up at a tiny little airport in northwest Nebraska."

"Sure, anything. Just be careful, okay?" The way the law was always nipping at Mark's heels, Dan wondered how long his activities could safely continue.

Mark had called Dan on a disposable cellular to avoid the

question of why Dan would be calling his own number from Montana. Mark would drop the disposable it in a gurgling stream, break it in half, and deposit each half in different trash receptacles.

Mark appreciated Dan more than either of his other two friends for Dan's wordless, lecture-less acquiescence and support. Sometimes Mark even exchanged cell phones with Jim and Greg for the same reason Mark exchanged phones with Dan. Although Mark would never implicate his friends in this or any other scheme, technically they were all probably accessories by association or some other loophole. He regretted that threat immensely and did everything in his power to erase any evidence pointing in their direction. But he knew throwing the law off was not sustainable. One day soon, he would need to retire from his political activism.

Mark inhaled the clean air, fresh woodsy fragrances, and mostly unadulterated environment as deep into his soul and mind as he could stuff it, in order to take it back with him as the most memorable and stimulating auditory, visual, and kinesthetic souvenirs one would ever need from a short vacation. He was already dreading the smog, noise, busyness, and drone-ish activity of Kansas City.

After prying Julie's clinging arms from his neck and hugging everyone for the tenth time, Mark jumped in his truck and roared south, waving until the lovely people behind him were nothing but specks. His final glance in the rearview mirror was that of a lazy column of smoke from the fireplace rising up between the patient, antediluvian pines.

Chapter

10

MARK'S FAITHFUL OLD truck sputtered and gasped a peaceful demise; luckily it was near a junkyard southeast of Great Falls. Mark knew it was past time with over three hundred thousand miles on it. She'd served him well, and he grieved the loss. But he also knew it was getting crucial to dispose of it too. The owner of the junkyard didn't look like he'd seen civilization for at least three-fourths of his lifetime, so Mark figured the truck and any incriminating evidence would be properly disposed of through the dealer's own severance with humankind. Just in case, however, Mark wiped down the steering wheel, dropped a few unidentified hairs around the driver's seat, emptied the cab and bed of all his questionable belongings, and lovingly patted her weathered side good-bye. Mark loped down the main street and bought a secondhand economy car. The wreck of his pickup was already completely forgotten and parted out by the junk dealer. The town, straight out of an old western, had an unforeseen, outdoor *working* telephone booth. He slipped inside, dialed, and took a long, anticipatory breath.

Ruby's cookies were delicious. She had mastered the art of chocolate chip cookie making in college while whiling away her study time drawing, planning, sketching, and designing on the campus computers. Her sorority sisters teased her relentlessly about earning a degree in baking CCCs and playfully calling her *Stooie Ruby* but they devoured her cookies regularly. Whenever anyone was sad or stressed, or had broken up with a boyfriend, cookies were the magical cure. She reminisced about her college days. What a free time in her life!

Ruby absentmindedly picked up the receiver of the phone to call her mother and ask for the specific reason that she and Dad had suggested she not choose advertising as her major. Why was she second-guessing it at now of all times, after she'd worked in the field for fifteen years? Ruby did earn an elementary teaching degree as a minor, but she had no wish to teach, and she certainly did not want to mentor any budding artists. Ruby did not care for discipline, pure and simple, and it took the fun completely out of teaching for her. During her student teaching semester, she'd failed miserably at behavior issues, and she'd suffered the embarrassment of her evaluations reflecting her difficulty in classroom control.

The question of, "Why wouldn't I choose advertising over teaching based on those miserable evaluations—she who never received a grade less than an A in her entire elementary, middle, high school, and college years?" was on her lips to ask her mom, but the phone line was already live.

Ruby then heard someone saying, "Hello? Ow, you're hurting my ear!"

"Oh, hello? I just picked up to dial the phone, and someone was on the line."

"That would be me. Just a sec while I get the ringing out of my ear."

Ruby knew that voice. "Okay," she replied as a pleasant smile radiated across her face.

"Darlin'?"

"Yes, Mark?" She dropped the pretense of not knowing his name.

"Hey! You recognized my voice!" Then like a teenage boy, he added, "Wicked awesome!"

Ruby was chagrined that she had so quickly acknowledged him. *Really playing hard to get, aren't I?*

"Wow, I just dialed your numbers—I mean, number and there you were! They say great minds think alike!"

"Numbers? I only have *one* number."

"Yeah, and I've got it!" He chuckled, much to her double chagrin.

"What's that supposed to mean?" inquired Ruby, suddenly full of questions more than smiles.

"It's my own private little joke, darlin', which I shall be most happy to share in due time."

"In due time?" Now she was piqued. He was suggesting a future. She glanced at the clock and noticed that Chloe would be home any minute. She did not care to explain any unusual telephone calls to her daughter's impervious little mind. The oven timer rang. The cookies that were *never* overbaked—the absolute secret to perfectly chewy, moist cookies—were due to come out immediately.

"Mark, where are you?" She obviously wondered, based on last night's news, whether he was in Montana near the most recent arson site.

"At your alley entrance door," he teased playfully, to test her boundaries.

Ruby panicked and quickly gawked in that direction, secretly (and insanely) hoping. But she should have known better than to wish him at her back doorstep. "Mark!" her scolding voice exclaimed as she sucked in her breath, contradicting herself. She could also hear Chloe talking with Ashley right outside the front door. Time was fleeting. The front door opened, and mercifully for Ruby, Chloe hung in the doorway, still chatting. Ruby's heart slowed down by a few beats.

"Okay," he drawled. "It's just where I *want* to be." He had nothing else to go on, and so he listened intently for tone-of-voice clues as to how she felt about him being at her back door.

There was no immediate rejection, but no immediate acceptance either.

"Mark, my daughter is coming in from school, and I have to go. Sorry." Chloe was still lingering, and it sounded like she was wound up into another drama. Ruby kept concentrating on Chloe so she could hang up before she got completely inside. She chastised herself repeatedly to hang up, but she did not want to let Mark go. She bit her tongue to prevent herself from inviting him to call back.

Mark picked up on the clue and took a wild risk that she might be slightly receptive. "Darlin', I know you must go. I will stop by in the next day or so, but I will call first, okay?"

Ruby's heart sped up again and fluttered over his words. She barely whispered, "Okay."

Then he said, "Bye, Darlin'," and was gone.

She stood at the phone with her hand still on it.

Ruby's logic asked, *What the hell did I just do? Am I allowing an arsonist to visit me at my home of all places?* But her heart neither said nor did anything of the sort. Ruby's shallow breathing hardly sent oxygen to her brain, and she released her grip on the phone to twirl around innocently to greet Chloe.

Chloe squealed delightedly over the cookies. She'd hitched a ride home with Ashley, no note needed; apparently, safety was not an issue for extracurricular activities on Fridays when there was no school.

"Mom, what fun things are we going to do for the rest of the day?"

"What would you like to do? Maybe take a bike ride down Mickelson Trail from Deadwood?"

"Cool! But there might still be some snow up in the hills."

"You're right. Why don't we take the city trail in Rapid?

Then we can afford ourselves a shopping spree and dinner at Olive Garden?"

"How soon do we leave, and how many cookies can we pack?"

"Lots!"

Ruby and Chloe were on their way north in less than half an hour, with bikes loaded in the pickup, cookies packed, and Ruby's MasterCard ready to slide. After all the cookie dough she'd sampled while baking, Ruby needed a good, long workout, especially if Mark was going to stop by in a day or so.

Chloe was confused by her mother's jubilant mood. She chalked it up to the Smiley guy singing "Happy Birthday" earlier this morning. That had been the last good thing Chloe knew of her Mom's day.

Ruby was thankful not to have to explain anything about her sudden interest in a complete stranger. Mark had respected her request to keep her daughter oblivious, at least for now. Ruby had no expectations or desire for a relationship—and especially not with an arsonist, if he was one—but she did want to see him badly, as crazy and dangerous as it may seem. Ruby and Chloe did not have many secrets, which was how Ruby wanted it to be, especially when Chloe entered the guaranteed roller coaster ride of the teen years. However, for some reason she decided to withhold this new encounter from her precious, innocent daughter. She wholeheartedly embraced the bike ride and the vitally necessary exercise for her body and soul.

Mark felt like a highwayman hitting the road again: adventure along the way, and a special sweet someone at the end of the trail. *Whenever you're not looking for someone, there she is.* Mark had dusted Great Falls hours ago and set his GPS for Billings. Sometimes it was necessary to mix and mingle with larger populations, keep his ear to the ground about what locals were saying, and try to appear anonymous. If he camped or stayed in smaller towns, it seemed like they had sharper memories of his presence there. He had been questioned, harassed, and stalked, by more than one small-town law enforcement bunch. If anything permanent developed with Ruby, Mark would tell her everything, but for now it was in her best interest to *not* know and therefore not be implicated on his account. For him, hurting Ruby would be like setting fire to a national forest. So far, he had been careful *(or lucky)* that none of his projects had burnt even more than a couple dozen feet around the detritus he had 'waste-managed'.

He was in a heightened state after talking to Ruby, his eyes steady on the road. He dodged wildlife, his coffee sloshing in the cup on the console of his new crime-scene beater. He combed his hair through his fingers and noticed a lopsided grin in the rearview mirror. He wouldn't have been able to go to sleep if he'd been lounging in his favorite hammock at home. Thoughts of Ruby hit him regularly, nearly every thirty seconds, and he wondered if it was possible to die of longing to know more about someone.

This was very atypical for Mark. He was not looking for a girlfriend—they usually came to him and dallied until boredom moved them on. But what was it about Ruby? Mark had laid low in Montana for only a few days, but it seemed like Ruby had been on his mind for his entire life. However, from past experience with women, he'd set his jaw knowing that laying his heart out there was a sure way to get it stomped on, and he'd steered clear of many sticky situations.

Now he knew she had a daughter, almost a teenager. The track record wasn't so good on step-parenting these days. Even as those issues from previous experiences rolled around in his head, he gave a deep, longing sigh for Ruby's beautiful face, and for her eyes that shone with intelligence, mystery, and passion. She was femininity from head to toe. Mark replayed the sight of her lightly bouncing across the street between the blaring roar of those emergency vehicles on the way to his private Fall River barbecue. That morning last week, his heart had actually skipped a beat for her safety. But when she entered the cafe—now precisely eight days ago—she'd landed her at first flustered—then self-possessed, gaze directly on him. What a picture! He would never get that picture out of his mind as long as he lived—and he wouldn't want to. Initially, he sized her up as being a snob, thinking, *Couldn't touch that girl with a ten-foot pole.* He guffawed over the cliché in the hope—no, the resolve—that he would soon be much closer to her than a pole of any length. Dusk fell and along with it, always, an invitation to more danger, aka, his career.

Ruby and Chloe hopped on their bikes after effortlessly unloading them from the back of the pickup. The trail was smooth, inviting, and devoid of fellow patrons; mother and daughter could chat freely, which they did. Chloe was nonstop prattle about school, Ashley, Rodney and what would happen to him. It caused Ruby to think of Mark and his whereabouts— as if she needed any prompting. Ruby listened and reminisced about her early years in young adulthood. Ruby rode bikes with her own mom many times; both of her parents were active and kept themselves in decent shape. She missed them so. After divorcing, leaving Denver, and settling in Tepid Springs, Ruby dreamed that they would move to live near her and Chloe. Maybe someday it would happen. She loved the Black Hills and the West. She could never move back east, even to be near them.

Her parents were the happiest married people she knew, and she often wished to emulate them. Nobody her own age came close to the respectful companionship her parents had attained. Her friends were divorced, dysfunctional, and compromised in so many areas of their lives. Ruby's life was difficult enough without wishing to be and have a significant other. However, she wanted nothing that would contribute to any heart-wrenching troubles. *Are there any good men out there?* After listening to friends get in and out (and in and out) of relationships, and given her own lifestyle being so manageable, secure, and safe for Chloe, she was practically convinced there were not.

Once in a while on the trail, a biker, a man, would whiz past them, usually saying hi. It was always men—there were so few women bikers. Ruby would ride a bike out in God's beautiful country any day, rather than pound a boring indoor treadmill hour after insufferable hour.

After ten miles and not even breaking a sweat, they still felt clean enough to dine in their favorite restaurant. Chloe loved Olive Garden after being treated like a grown-up by an indulgent waitress, who brought her a wine glass of Sprite with a cherry in it; Ruby enjoyed a few ounces of red. Chloe scouted for that same waitress every time they came to town—not completely understanding at her tender age how quickly people changed jobs; her hero was probably a student working her way through college. They sat for two hours enjoying hors d'oeuvres, entrees, and dessert. Ruby loved spoiling Chloe, who sweetly basked in the attention. Actually, Ruby thought the longer they stayed at the restaurant, the less time they would spend shopping. She loved spoiling Chloe with shopping, as well; but alas, bills had to be paid first. It was difficult to tell Chloe no, at times—back to the forever nagging discipline thing.

Ruby glanced past Chloe's sweet, ecstatic face to notice a very good-looking man staring at her. She quickly looked away and then back. She was almost certain she'd seen him in Tepid Springs. He was similar in build and looks to the too-brief of an assessment she'd gotten of Mark. The stranger blatantly stared at her now and nodded in a tip-the-cowboy-hat kind of way, and they locked eyes briefly. Ruby's mind was so freshly on Mark that she surprised herself by allowing the eye-lock; in her mind, she wanted it to be Mark. Then she blinked and refocused on Chloe. She dared one more sweep his direction and observed a lady coming between their mutual stares and sitting familiarly at his table. *Oh, my god. Such two-timing creeps!* She felt sorry for his date, and she was so disgusted she abruptly cut Chloe's sentence off and got up to exit.

"Uh," was all Chloe had time to utter. Ruby quickly swiped her credit card, feeling his eyes continuing to follow her, and she ignored any accidental contact by turning her back toward his direction. She immediately conjured up *pervert* in her mind—but she was wryly annoyed upon remembering she'd thought the same of Mark. Was she too suspicious? Or paranoid? Or just plain bitter?

Once out the door, they headed to the mall, where they spent a much shorter time. Soon they were back in the purple machine, speeding south under the radar. Chloe fell asleep at about Hermosa. Ruby allowed her relaxed head to bob against her shoulder, kissing it and whispering that she loved her; and what a huge responsibility weighed down her mind. *Just plain crazy,* she thought. Rhett's Scarlett might probably have picked this moment to burst into fake tears. Not Ruby. Not that kind of drama. But she laughed at the screwy analogy.

A golden football uprights sign came into view. With all the humanitarian acts McDan's had done for charity, including the Randy McDandy house and much, much more, Mark knew they had maintained an industry for decades that also generated millions and millions of tons of garbage annually into rivers, waterways, landfills, and ocean garbage dumps. In fact, they were leaders in mass production of high-fat content food in the nation—reminding him immediately of his gastrointestinal friend, Jim. They, among other fast-food chains popping up all across the land, were the main focus of styrofoam studies informing the public that it required thousands of years for the products to decompose. Mark had been fascinated with the concept back in fourth-grade science. He loved science, and he loved his science teacher, Ms. Merfeld. All the boys loved her long, straight hair that smelled of clean, fresh, flowers or something very unboy-like. Ms. Merfeld told them she made her own hair rinse from an herbal recipe. Mark laughed and wondered where Ms. Merfeld was these days; he figured she'd be about two hundred years old by now. Realistically, she could probably still be teaching science somewhere to some little love-struck fourth-grade boys.

The golden sign read, "Sorry for being so awesome," complete with a sizzling charcoal burger, a dripping-cheese look, crisp lettuce, juicy tomato, and a toasted sesame bun. Mark braked after seeing the slogan. *Of all the egotistical, competitive, fake apologetic drivel!* Mark was indignant.

This kind of advertising was an insult to human intelligence, in Mark's biased opinion. First, the word *sorry* in this context was a bold-faced lie. They were not sorry in the least. That kind of use of a vital word (and action) like *sorry* was simply a smokescreen for bragging. Second, who decided if a product was awesome? Consumers, of course—not producers, and certainly not advertisers! To self-aggrandize was one thing, but to insinuate it came from the public and to couch it in an apology ... really! *Are you really sorry? Don't think so. You're goin' down!*

He pulled to the side of the road and quickly assessed the situation: a deserted highway. The poles for this billboard were metal, and so this job had to be a hit and run—a splash, flash, and dash. Easy. But he still had around seven hundred miles to go in order to see Ruby by tomorrow, and he knew he wouldn't be staying in her little cattle-drive town for very long. Thankfully, the law would still be on the lookout for his truck, and he might be able to slide through Tepid Springs without questioning because of his new low-profile vehicle. Normally, there would be a definite plan for his program. Being interested in Ruby really complicated life on the run.

He chastised himself. Then he considered, *If she's half the woman I think she is, she'll understand me being late one day. If she doesn't understand, case closed.*

Mark first set his jaw—then set to work.

Chapter

11

RUBY TRUNDLED CHLOE into the house and into bed, and she crashed herself after watching a bit of TV. No more fires; nothing about the most recent fire. Ruby hoped it would rain cats and dogs all over the land so no fires could be set, intentionally or otherwise. She mused over whether or not she could influence Mark to not to do this anymore—if indeed he was doing it, and if he was interested in her. *Why couldn't she get it through her head that he was absolutely doing it?* No, she refused to believe it until he came out and told her himself. But would he, ever in a million years?

Ruby said to herself, *I am just dog tired and heading to bed.*

But she did not drift off to sleep without anticipating his words: "I will stop by in the next day or so."

Mark could not use the slow-igniting fuse or a slow-burning process on these metal poles. He usually used those on the billboards with wooden poles, which was the specially designed method from Jim's ingenious chemical recipe. As usual, he could only destroy the advertising part, not the structure, which always created a massive flash of a flame, drawing huge amounts of attention before the classless advertising would be consumed. In the dusk, he could not see any nearby residences lighting up for evening activity; they were usually the first reporters. It gave him very little time to sprint to his car for a quick, clean getaway; he never risked parking his vehicle near the potential scene of the crime. He hid it safely concealed behind a wall of baled hay, with the exit route going out the other end of the pasture and onto an alternate back road, trailing back to the highway. Thank goodness for his GPS. With car tracks to modify as well as other logistics he couldn't omit—such as safety equipment and disguises—he was tremendously slowed down. Even if he risked getting caught, he would have been proud to destroy that obnoxious advertising.

At this point, Mark ambiguously realized that instead of taking a whack at big, rich corporate capitalism, he might possibly be hurting the little guys who make their scrapping living from honest thinking, planning, creating, printing, and installing the ideas that take shape on billboard sign—the Rubys and Chloes of this world. He thought, *Maybe my career in activism is coming to an end.* He couldn't think of a better reason than Ruby as he threw a match onto the splashed gas on the face of the sign, which he'd siphoned from the car gas tank. Then he charged into the dusk toward his car over two miles away. He carefully drove out on newly cut rows of hay on the opposite highway, leaving tracks but no telltale tire treads. When he hit pavement, he sped up to normal speed. While ten miles down the road, oncoming fire trucks met him and shrieked past, barely noticing the commuter driving in the opposite direction. At least, that was what he hoped.

Ruby was up early the next morning, diving into the waiting project on the drafting table. The coffee was percolating, and knowing that Chloe would sleep in until around noon, Ruby smiled and entertained herself with thoughts of him.

Now would be a great time to call, Mark! she thought at him. *I'm waiting here, completely free to talk for hours!* She continued to tantalize her mind in this fashion while truly making a valiant effort to concentrate on advertising. Miraculously, the phone obeyed.

"Hi, sweetie!" chirped her mother. "How's my precious red Ruby jewel this morning? I hope I didn't wake you."

"Oh. Hi, Mom," answered Ruby, concealing a speck of disappointment. "No, I've been up for a while." Ruby was always happy to hear from home; it was just that she was anticipating someone else. *Oh, well.* She perked up for her mother's sake.

"How's my baby Chloe?"

"Not quite a baby anymore, Mother. She might be mortified if she heard you say that."

"Mortified?"

"Yeah, it's all about drama, Mama," giggled Ruby, tacking the rhyme onto the end of her sentence.

"As opposed to Obama?" quipped Ruby's mother back at her. They both howled with mirth.

"I suppose we could go so far as to address the drama with Obama's llama, Mama." Ruby climbed into a much better mood after going over the top with more rhyming.

"Oh, shoot! Ruby, she'll always be my baby, my one and only granddaughter, my little jewel in the midst of three diamonds in the rough—y'know, Jake's three young sons. So how's work going?"

"Problematic, convoluted, and ... Anyway, Mom, I've been meaning to ask you an important question.

"Anything!"

"Oh, it's not so important, really ... But I've just been wondering just recently, why you and Dad discouraged me from going into the advertising field as a career."

"Goodness, Ruby. That was so long ago, and pretty much irrelevant now that you've achieved such success in advertising and are doing what you love. Art and creativity has always been your calling, you know, and that's what is important to us now! Remember, we grew up in the sixties, when the least hint of capitalism and affluence was bad.

Goodness, everybody was antidisestablishmentarian! As true rebels without a cause, we burned everything: flags, bras, draft cards, cars ... I think once we lit up an old couch from the dorm just to get attention. But why are you wondering after all these years, dearie?"

"You did?" Ruby was incredulous. She knew crazy things went on in the sixties, but she never dreamed her parents could have been in the middle of the upheaval. They always acted so normal and predictable! "You burned stuff?"

"Well, yeah. But please don't tell Chloe, hun. We don't want her to lose respect for us. We're not exactly proud of getting arrested, among other—"

"Arrested? For arson?" interrupted Ruby.

"Oh, good heavens, no! Arrested for disturbing the peace! And arrested for participating in sit-ins and walk-outs and demonstrations and marches. It's all in the past and mostly, forgotten. At least, it would be better if it were forgotten! Nobody cares anymore, anyway ..." She trailed off.

Ruby tried to digest this covert information about her parents. "Geez; I guess I don't know you people as well as I thought I did. Well, I never thought I'd ever get bored with art or designing or anything; probably, it's more about trying to please difficult people, I don't know ... Just second-guessing myself, as usual."

Her mother said, "Well, don't! We all go through perplexing junctures in life. What do you think it's been like, being in special ed your entire teaching career? This, too, will pass. Whatever it is that you're questioning, Ruby, you'll handle it and undoubtedly get it resolved to your satisfaction. But only if you remember the comma ... in the drama!" She laughed after bringing it back to their previously enjoyed nonsensical amusement.

"Oh, Mom. You always brighten my day!" Ruby thanked her for calling.

After a couple more exchanges, they worked out the logistics for her parents visiting during the Fourth of July week.

Ruby held on to the receiver after letting her mother go, just in case it rang again very soon from someone else. It did not.

Ruby sipped coffee, smiling over the call from her Mother. *What would I ever do without her?* Ruby refused to think about being without either of her loving, supportive parents. The project had stagnated hopelessly as Ruby thought about everything else. Then her mind drifted dreamily down a beautiful, tree-lined, flower-sprinkled lane as she walked arm in arm with Mark, smelling flowers, pointing out species of songbirds, and looking into his handsome face, which barely concealed luscious mischief ... and maybe, just maybe, love. Was it possible? Was romance in her future? Was Mark in it? How could she go off on these fantasies if he wasn't in her future?

Ruby immediately chided herself for being so uncharacteristically dreamy. She probably had limited time to work while Chloe still slept soundly.

The layout on the advertising idea was catching, appealing, and succinct. It read,

You *will* have Perfection in Production with

Monopolo-Santo!

This Product is ridiculously easy ... ridiculously effective.
Health, wealth, and happiness is yours
in 90 days/one season!
Just call 1-800-Dip-Sh!t or
Go online to <u>www.monopolo-santo.com</u>

Since her flare-up yesterday with Jordan, she'd calmed down and decided to get through this melee, placate the clients and her boss, and get paid for her hard work. She could look for more amiable clients (and bosses) later. In fact, independent advertising, or freelance, was her goal for the future. She'd always wanted to work as a consultant. Life had prospects, options, even *excitement* for the future. She smiled over another one of the many frequent "Mark intrusions" into her mind. She assessed the disorganized project in front of her and mentally gave herself thirty minutes to rectify it. She determined to present it so well that it would be irresistible to Jordan and the finicky clients. *All I have to do is play their game*, thought Ruby. *Then I'll be done with them. Easy!*

If only the rest of her life was as easy. What would she do about Mark stopping by in the next couple of days? When would he show up? Should she get involved with him, knowing full well that he was breaking the law? She wished she could bodily set her heart aside while she mentally sorted this out. *But then, her own parents had participated in nonviolent resistance of societal issues!* That was the sixties. Most of them were potheads, weren't they? Ruby conceded that she didn't know enough about the sixties to fill a thimble, let alone really *know* her very own parents. Wow, if she'd done those things as a college student, they would have throttled her. Naturally, she would never tell Chloe what her grandparents did in their college years. At least, not until she got Chloe nurtured past that roller-coaster age!

Mark was chewing up the miles between him and Ruby as fast as he could, within the law. It was not a good time to get stopped for breaking the speed limit! Hills, wide-open spaces, and pastoral scenes blurred past. The Powder River basin sprawled and wound lazily through the scene below. Mark's appreciation of this pristine land was automatically compared with his cramped quarters at home. His house was big enough; it was the city and neighborhood itself: gridded streets, platted lots, cul-de-sacs with no outlets, malls on every corner with accompanying parking lots, and too many people. Kansas City was a great place to be from, but he never could quell the desire to be a small participant in the present expanse before him now. Nature was a power to be recognized as sacred—the web of life, the ultimate denominator of everything. Nature had a purpose! *Why doesn't anybody ever seem to recognize the value of Nature? Why do human beings always use nature to the ever-living end of its usefulness? Are humans ever going to realize what they are so quickly destroying?*

He'd spent hours with native peoples, listening to them speak of the old ways, the ways of their elders, the ways of the Great Mystery. He read and researched hundreds of books on the original inhabitants of North America and how they respected and revered nature. He'd recently read a book about taking a walk on the Appalachia Trail and learned of all the flora and fauna that have become extinct from the human species in the last century and a half.

His portable GPS said he would reach Tepid Springs by early evening. *Perfect!* His overactive mind, at least in regard to Ruby, began to invent scenarios for when he would be at her back door in exactly 6.75 hours. What would she be wearing? Would she be surprised? How would she react? The only thought he could mentally articulate that would not be too painful was that she would be radiantly anticipating his arrival ... and his arms!

Ruby was finished with the advertising prep and was almost unconcerned as to its presentation. Jordan had not left a clue as to when he'd return, and whether he'd be with or without the clients. She mulled over Mark's words that he would stop by in the next couple of days, and she continually questioned whether she was making the right decision. She got busy with the usual Saturday morning chores: laundry, dishes, cleaning. The morning zoomed by; still no word from Jordan. Maybe he was going to wait until Monday, or for her to cool off.

Ruby's weekend jobs were done. Chloe still snoozed, so Ruby picked up an unfinished novel and sank into a comfy position on the couch.

Words jumped all over the page, and she could not concentrate. She pulled the afghan over her and tried to nap. She allowed her imagination to lead her down a primrose path during a beautiful summer season, with companionship and romance—or was it more? Ruby did not think she drifted off to sleep, but someone was impatiently pounding at the front door. Her mind was foggy, and with her eyes blinking, she threw the afghan back on the couch behind her, ran her hands through her hair to fluff it up, and opened the door.

"Hi, Jordan. I thought you were going to call," Ruby drawled, still straightening and smoothing herself.

"Good morning, Ruby. Sorry. I just hopped in the car and set off. I have to get back to Denver today—didn't mean to be inconsiderate. What have we got?" Jordan was full of himself as usual, in an impossible hurry, and stressed out. He started in the direction of the studio without an invitation, and Ruby had no choice but to follow.

"Come on back," Ruby said, sarcastically, by now wanting to get it over with so she could go back to her pseudo napping and disguise her daydreaming about Mark.

Ruby soon caught on that just about any project would please Jordan because he was so anxious to get back home for some odd reason. She decided to try to detain him by telling him all about how the project developed, her vacillating idea process, and detail upon detail to irritate him. It was difficult to contain her smirking over his discomfort and need for haste.

"Ruby, I don't have time for all your issues ..."

"I just want you to know the amount of effort I invested in this project, and—"

"I know, I know. I just can't stay long. I've got to get back. We've had an incident at corporate. The project is good, it's all good. Thank you. The clients will be happy, thrilled. Gotta go, okay? Wrap it up—let's go! And ... thanks. You do good work, Ruby."

She did not get him at all. The proofs were wrapped, insulated, placed in protective cardboard, taped, and handed over. Ruby had even made a CD that could be accessed on their computers. Still puzzled, she ventured one more attempt at finding out what was wrong. "Uh, Jordan, if there's any problem or change needed, you know I will do my best to—"

"Yeah, yeah, I know! We'll be in touch." Out the door he jetted.

Ruby would not let him go without asking, "You're acting weird. Whatever is wrong?"

Jordan fairly leaped into his classy rental and shot back, "We've had a fire at corporate. Vandalism, arson. Don't know anything yet. Later!"

She was left aghast and standing on the street corner as Jordan zoomed south out of town, ignoring the one and only red stoplight on Main Street.

Ruby went back inside. Chloe was sleepily rising for the day and stepped out of Ruby's way in the hall. The phone rang. Ruby was still a little too shocked for her feet to respond to the sudden activity. *Fire at corporate? Arson and vandalism? Is Mark still in Montana, or is that a lie? Is he in Denver? Kansas City? Where?*

Chloe slowly grabbed the phone and said, "Hullo?"

Ashley wanted her to attend her slumber party that

evening. Chloe was still only one-eyed from sleeping so late, but she asked politely if she could go.

Ruby spaced off, so Chloe yelled, "Mom!"

Ruby turned to her in a daze and half-heartedly said, "And leave me all alone to fend for myself?" They both laughed, knowing that Ruby would take full advantage of the peaceful opportunity and rare pleasure of vegging out and catching up on some leisurely reading, now that the project was on its way to Denver. And perhaps a luxurious bubble bath ... Her mind really had no false hopes, but it could not help reverting to thoughts of Mark.

"Of course, honey. Spend the night trying on each other's clothes, poring through magazines with the latest styles, and putting on makeup. And eat a load of junk food! Are you ready for some brunch?"

Chloe tightly hugged her Mom and whooped. "And gossiping! You're the best, Mom. Thanks!"

Chloe took the stairs three-at-a-time and plunged into the daunting task of packing for overnight. The bag was always excessive and almost heavier than she and Ruby could lift together.

Soon Ruby noticed she was ready to go. "Did you remember to pack the kitchen sink?"

"What?" Chloe furrowed her brows.

"Just an expression, hun. Do you want a little brunch or lunch before you take off?"

"No. Ashley's mom is going to make her world-famous vegetarian pizza. And she always makes enough for an army, so we'll be eating on it all afternoon and evening, up until we go to bed for the night—I mean, morning! Gee, I feel bad that you won't get any. Why don't I have Ashley's mom call you and invite you over too?"

"Oh-ho! No! I'm not going to pass up a golden opportunity to kick back and spend some time alone, sweetie. But thanks anyway! I could stand to drop a few pounds, and this way there'll be no cooking tonight. I'm gonna love having a little solitude!" Then for the hundredth time that day, her mind drifted to Mark. After Chloe bustled out the door, the afternoon began its excruciatingly slow pace.

Mark turned on the crackling radio, which basically didn't work, thinking that he may be able to decipher any information coming through about his most recent job. The miles flew by. He estimated he was no less than three hours from Ruby, and his stomach was beginning to knot up. Or maybe it was that quick bag of chips and buffalo jerky that didn't set well. Not knowing whether or not the tracphone would operate, he dialed Ruby's phone, knowing it would be the last time he'd use the trac. Always, Mark completely dismantled every removable part on each phone and disposed of them in different recycling containers in different towns and cities. He always used fabric gloves because rubber gloves sometimes left fingerprints or DNA.

Ruby walked to the phone with her face still buried in her book and absentmindedly answered. She had not heard from Mark, so she'd decided to blow it off and do something— anything—productive, like getting caught up on a little reading ... but only after spending a good share of the early afternoon pacing and watching out the window, just in case. After hearing that Jordan had skiffed out of town because of a fire at corporate, she figured Mark had in fact, been in Colorado rather than Montana, creating havoc there. Therefore, he might have found it necessary to circumvent Tepid Springs altogether. *Oh, hell*, she thought in a deteriorating mood. *You win some; you lose some.* She slammed herself into a self-deprecating funk. Instead of her luxurious bubble bath, she had dashed through the shower an hour ago, and then resumed her historical novel while munching on carrots and drinking chai tea. She ignored the thump at the back door, at first thinking she'd forgotten to feed the feral cats. The phone shrilled obnoxiously.

"Hi, darlin'! I'm here. What are you wear— I mean, doing?"

Ruby's heart skipping a beat was the answer to the voice she'd been anticipating but had given up on. She sucked in a shallow breath and shyly whispered, "Hi. Uh, you said ..."

"I'm at your back door. Will you let in a stranger who thinks that you're one in a million?"

Chapter

12

DISBELIEVING AND WITH phone still in hand, Ruby shuffled to the back door knowing she had not yet locked it for the early evening. She turned the knob, swung it open, and uncharacteristically melted into the arms of the man she denied—at this point—that she had already begun to love.

Mark's strong hands followed around her waist, pulling her close and dearly. He inhaled the scent of her hair, closed his eyes, and held her just tightly enough that her ribs didn't crack. Ruby had not felt such a safe, delicious embrace for a very long time. Her mind raced and repeatedly scolded her responding body. She began to sputter all the right questions and concerns. *But just a little too late, girl!* Mark quieted her questions with tender kisses to her forehead, neck, and mouth. Soon their bodies, lips, and minds were locked into each other's beings, totally and irrevocably. There would be no going back, no more hesitation, no second-guessing for either.

"Ruby, you are an exquisite creature!"

"Oh, Mark. Thank you, but I have to know ..."

"Have to know what?" Mark's mouth hungrily found Ruby's face and lips again and again. Breathing short, heavy gasps, Mark came up for air long enough to say, "Darlin', I cannot stay but a few minutes. Can't let anyone see me here— just could not pass this close to this state without seeing you."

"But ..." wailed Ruby, her heart audibly pounding.

"No buts. I gotta go. I'll call!" Mark grabbed her body close to his for another long, satisfying kiss and released her. He backed into the dusk, blew kisses to her, and slunk into a pile of metal in which every nut, bolt, and movable part creaked on his way out of Tepid.

Ruby stood watching in shock and seething arousal. *He came!* He blasted into her life and thoughts and emotions out of nowhere ... and then he snatched her heart completely out of her chest. All she could do was gawk after that rolling pile of rusty metal.

She could not will her mind to make sense of such an encounter. How could he have timed that so perfectly? Arriving after Chloe left, and in the near dark to avoid nosy neighbors, when she would be home alone ... Ruby could still feel the warmth and taste of his lips, his muscular arms holding her against him ... It was so fast! Plain and simple, it was cruel!

It was so daring! Ruby stumbled backward into her apartment as Mark rolled down the street with tail lights still off. She watched them until his brake lights flashed momentarily and disappeared into the dark.

What just happened? screamed her head. *What is he trying to do? What am I, of all people, doing? Did he know whether or not Chloe had been in the house?* She expected him to respect that she had a young daughter. He didn't even come in. Why did she fairly leap into his arms like an addled female? She was revolted at her behavior, asking *Why?* to every thought, feeling, and question that went through her spinning head.

She resolutely locked and double-bolted the door, still shaking her head. The phone was jangling off the wall. Ruby grabbed it, angry more at herself than him.

"Hello?"

"Mom, Ashley and her mom want you to come over for pizza. What's wrong?"

"Nothing." Ruby tried to calm her uncontrollable heaving and breathing.

"Oh, okay …" Chloe was clearly puzzled. "Can you get over here before we start the movie?"

"I've just locked up for the night. Why don't you guys just enjoy? I'll be fine. Talk to you tomorrow, okay, sweetie? But please tell them thanks!"

"Okay." Ruby's sweet daughter hung up.

Ruby pushed down on the receiver while hugging the phone piece. She leaned her head against the wall, sighed, and shook her head back and forth in shame. But as shameful as she thought of herself, the one thing for which she'd never apologize was how incredible she had felt in Mark's arms.

The rest of the night was spent restlessly reliving and relishing every short second of Mark's presence at her back door, from the odd phone call to Chloe's miraculous absence, to actually going to the door and finding him there, to the ensuing deliciousness of standing against Mark's athletic body. She had tried lamely to resist. *Yeah, sure!* Would that be before or after she'd nearly knocked him down by leaping into his arms? She had to find a way to reconcile her pitiful heart and her nagging mind. Why did both of those body parts insist upon being total opposites? She had a right to be happy, didn't she? She had a right to love and be loved. Oh, why was she talking about love? Three or four minutes of passionate lust did not amount to even the sparsest beginning of love. Or was it ten or fifteen minutes?

Get your head in the game, Ruby, before it's too late! She marched into the kitchen, grabbed a rare bottle of wine, and tanked it. The next thing she knew, it was past midnight, and she was uncomfortably hanging over the bathroom stool and purging.

She got up from the floor, tried to drown her face in the sink, splashed water on, and mused that the only thing

Murphy could offer at this pounding head moment that hadn't already gone wrong was an obnoxiously loud noise. Which he perversely did—the sonofabitchin' phone was ringing! Ruby's mind said, *No way!* At this time of night, it could only be a wrong number. It mercifully stopped, but then it mercilessly began again. Ruby was ready to swear as she grabbed it without saying hello.

"Hi. Sorry to call so late. I'm home."

"You're home? You're *home*? Well, isn't that swell?" Her voice dripped with sarcasm.

"I hated leaving you tonight, darlin'; I wanted to take you with me. I wanted to—"

"Mark, uh, next time you blast into town unannounced—oh, yeah, and *uninvited*—please tell me so I can at least comb my hair." She slammed the phone down so hard the whole unit fell off the wall. Ruby crashed onto the couch and did something she detested in so many other women: she burst into tears.

Mark was not surprised at her hang-up. What he did was a classless trick and was beneath his sense of chivalry. He was trying hard to avoid getting Ruby implicated in any of his activities. What with surveillance, cell phone records, cameras, forensics, spy equipment, and computer technology as advanced at it was, no method of communication could be underestimated. He knew it would be risky to go a hundred miles out of his way to see her, although he was more than pleased at the reception he received, knowing now that she liked him at least a little bit. But at the same time, he could not resist seeing her, could not resist the inevitable introduction, could not will the car to go the direction he should have taken. Seeing her even for just a few minutes—and it was precious few—was vitally important to him. Mark had destroyed relationships before because of his activism, and Ruby was too important to him to make that mistake again. He would have to think of a way to make it up to her.

How Ruby got through the rest of the night—morning, really—she did not remember. Nevertheless, morning came. So did a pounding at the door. Ruby was livid, and her first thought was, *There's no way in hell ...*

Her friend from the flower shop was at the door.

"Ruby! Got a delivery!"

Ruby was in no mood to be trifled with, and in no mood to get flowers. Her friend must have had other deliveries to make and left the bouquet on the front step. *Thank goodness. No raised eyebrows, No probing questions.* Ruby glanced up and down the street; nobody was up and about. She quickly brought the flowers inside. She felt slightly better than she had last night, but she still wanted to give the vase a fling right back into the middle of the street. That petulant act would result in more unwanted attention (and gossip), which she obviously did not need. She brought the picture-perfect dozen red roses, accented with lavender and baby's breath, into the kitchen and indifferently checked the card.

"Whenever you're not looking for someone ... there she is!"

Even though her anger had abated, she wanted to rip all the petals off the roses one by one, and torturously so. Simply put, they were too beautiful. Ruby was not a destroyer of nature or beauty, and neither was she vindictive. Everything must have hit her wrong yesterday. She'd had such high hopes for finding someone like Mark; she should have known that unlike the card stated, he was not out there. She tucked the message away in her desk drawer, and deep into the dungeon of her heart to forget about sometime later. *But, oh, such a kind, gentle feeling to let go of—gentleness and passion that Ruby wanted.* Could she really let go? She arranged the flowers as a centerpiece on the table. What would Chloe think or ask?

Ruby determined to hide the reason for the flowers *and* the person behind them from Chloe.

The torturous weekend passed on to Monday morning. Ruby was thankful to hit the new week at top speed and put the past three days and long week-and-a-half of longing behind her. Chloe asked endless questions about the flowers all weekend long. Ruby had heard not a word from him. There was uncharacteristic miserable weather to guarantee putting one in a funk. So, yes, Ruby welcomed Monday morning. Chloe, not so much.

However, unlike most school children, Chloe never wanted school to get out at the end of the year. The week would prove to be loaded with end-of-school activities: field days, picnics, field trips, incentive parties, graduations, and the like. It was too busy to think about the possibility of love, —which apparently didn't exist for Ruby anyway. The school year slogged to a close; and this was the exciting time of year when Ruby and her sweet daughter celebrated together. They had planned a vacation to visit relatives. Chloe had a few weeks she spent with her dad, and Ruby found all kinds of ways to spend her time when Chloe was gone. Life truly did go on. Ruby looked forward to her parents visiting and Chloe playing in the school band in the Fourth of July parade.

Still, as vehemently as she acted, deep down in her soul, she honestly treasured the brief encounter she'd had with Mark—as insane and wrong and sordid as she knew it to be. Ruby had never felt so strongly about a man.

The summer hit full throttle with mother and daughter going to plays in the Hills and at the Fort, and swimming, canoeing, and kayaking down the Cheyenne and the Niobrara. They went swimming at the water parks, biking on the Mikelson, camping at the lake, and hiking to Harney. They attended the Volksmarch at Crazy Horse. Ruby and Chloe enjoyed powwows at the civic center and shopping for Indian jewelry. They topped off their fun by going to farmers' markets, Thunderhead Falls, spelunking, and local tourist attractions.

Summer seemed to rush by, but Ruby's mind was never very far from the tiny snapshot she'd experienced with Mark in May. Three weeks had passed since their brief rendezvous, and she'd heard not a word. The flowers had long since shriveled; their heads hung reddish-brown, dried, and almost as sad as Ruby's heart. The *Star* made a huge deal about a certain "Mark Smythe, Suspect in Arson, Returns to Tepid" for further questioning. *So what?* said Ruby's resolve. *Big deal!*

By the middle of June, Chloe was off to Denver for a visit with her dad and step-mom. Jordan had been extremely unavailable, but the flip side was less stress for Ruby. It also meant less money. Ruby had done a trifle more hacking to find clients and freelancing, but she was reluctant to follow up some of the leads. After Chloe departed, life seemed to slow a bit, and other than getting off the merry-go-round for a breather, it allowed more time for Ruby to reminisce about Mark.

Mark smoothed into his familiar life, connecting with friends, catching up on mail and e-mail, working, checking in with family, and trying to pretend he hadn't been gone. All the time, he was convinced he wanted to do nothing except hear Ruby's sweet, playful, teasing voice. *And much more.* He longed to be holding her as he'd briefly enjoyed embracing her three weeks ago.

Never did he expect that Ruby would be so receptive to him stopping by. He'd hoped and prayed for it, but he'd had no illusions because he recognized how extremely careful she needed to be in her dating boundaries while raising a young daughter. Normally, he would not entertain stopping by a lady's residence so soon after meeting for the first time—and it couldn't actually be called a meeting, as brief as it was. However, for the first time, he absolutely could not stop himself. The night was so perfectly calm, the stars had been shining, the moon was bright, and he was driving within less than a hundred miles of Tepid. How could he go straight past? But realistically, he should have; when one is absorbed in covert activities, one must constantly be on alert. He regretted it, except that Ruby's beauty, her response, her immediate reaction to coming into his arms, her smile, her kissing—everything about her was so perfect, so desirable. What warm-blooded man could possibly resist? This warm-blooded man certainly could not!

Since then, he had not been able to wipe the smile and pleasant look off his face while around his friends and family. They knew his mind traveled to pleasant parts unknown. No matter how they cajoled him and brought up the subject, he revealed nothing. No matter how they commented about him being elsewhere, he resolutely denied all. This was not the average kiss-and-tell relationship, not the normal talk of conquest. This was something far more valuable than how many notches were on the conqueror's belt. Sooner or later, Dan would have to help him out; he knew Dan would oblige whatever he asked.

One day out of the blue, the call she'd been expecting, hoping for, finally came. The phone had been plastered back on the wall and as a result, didn't work as well, but Ruby kept the old phone just so it was not necessary to give out her cell number to everybody. She did not recognize the phone number.

"Hello?"

"Hi, uh, I have a message for you. Is this Ruby Jewel in Tepid Springs?"

"Yes."

"My name is Dan Dawson. I'm a close friend of Mark Smythe." Ruby's heart skipped as he continued. "I am very sorry to contact you this way, but you see, Mark's life is extremely complicated, and it is absolutely necessary for him to reach you through a third party. I hope you won't be uncomfortable talking with me. Mark desires very much to see you. Do you wish for me to continue this conversation?"

Ruby stuttered out, "I, uh ... Mark? Uh, I fail to see why Mark can't call me if he wants to. Well, go ahead, continue."

"That's the confusing part. I am not exactly free to speak for him. All I can do is make the gesture and take your answer back to him. Really sorry it has to be like this."

Ruby thought, *How do I know this message is from Mark? I've never heard of a Dan Dawson. What if this is a prank of some kind?*

"Then I guess I will have to pass up this wonderful opportunity. So, sorry. Thank you very much." Ruby hung onto the receiver after replacing the phone on its cradle. *What in the world was that all about? Geez, the world is full of nuts!*

But, could it be possible? Did she just pass up an opportunity to see Mark? How could *he* possibly think that she would communicate with him through a third party, a stranger? He was a stranger himself, and then to expect her to communicate through yet another stranger? It was insane! But wasn't the whole prospect, from beginning to end? Maybe he was a pervert, just like she thought the first time she'd seen him lounging against the historic sandstone building across the street, surreptitiously watching her. Ruby wished she could get a grip on her heart and mind. She kept telling herself, *Give it up! He's a loser! Give it up, girl!* The next second, her mind had herself right back in his arms, wishing she didn't know what she knew in her heart to be the truth.

The phone rang again.

If they're calling back to harass me, I'm calling the cops myself. Ruby snatched the phone again in a steam.

"Hi, Mom!"

Relieved and thrown off, Ruby sighed, "Oh, hi, sweetie! How's Denver these days?"

"Good. Well, boring. But I called to tell you that Jordan's Advertising offices got burned down. They were totaled! He's the guy you work for, Mom!" As if Ruby didn't recall for whom she worked.

"Good gracious, Chloe! Is everyone all right? Is Jordan okay?"

"Yeah, everyone got out before the smoke choked them."

"No, I hadn't heard that." Her mind was calculating that if Mark had been in Denver, he couldn't have lit a fire in Montana. Then she solemnly considered that perhaps if he was not busy in Dakota lighting up the night, he ostensibly could have been in Denver doing the same thing there. These mind games attacking her day and night were monstrous.

"Chloe, do they have any idea why the building was burned?" Ruby was trying to think rationally, almost for Jordan's sake.

"No clue."

"Well, what else is new.? Is there any good news, honey?"

"Yep. Dad and I are going to the butterfly pavilion ... Did you know monarch butterflies eat milkweed?"

"No, I did not know that." Ruby thought, *How could Chloe possibly switch gears so fast?*

"Mom, I would like to build a home for monarchs. Could we do that when I get home?"

"Most certainly. Let me know what materials we need, and I'll have them on hand, okay?"

Chloe was thrilled. She loved doing learning projects with her mother.

"Chloe, tell your father to take you to the hardware store to buy some pink hand tools of your own."

"Great idea, Mom. Gotta go. I love you. See you soon!"

"Love you, too, baby. Bye!"

So had Mark been in Denver? Was that where "home" was? How could this arson be Mark? He was kind and gentle; a look into his eyes would reveal integrity.

Ruby tried putting the thoughts of Mark to the back of her mind as she planned Chloe's homecoming, along with her parents visiting around the Fourth of July.

She flounced onto the couch and blasted on the mindless TV in an effort to keep him in the back of her mind. There hadn't been much in the newspaper, but the TV said when police were finished processing the scene, a certain Mark Smythe, a tourist from Kansas City, may be considered a person of interest.

The phone began blasting away in the background again while Ruby leaned forward, straining to listen to the television bulletin.

The TV was reporting that a certain Mark Smythe would soon be charged and tried in Tepid Springs for arson. *What? Then it is true! Undeniable! Why would they charge a person who wasn't guilty?* Her heart sank as low as it could go.

The phone continued interrupting. Finally, she rose simultaneously snapping off the TV. She answered the phone, which she presumed was her mother. Caller ID was a puzzle.

"Hello?"

"Hi." The kind, the familiar, the resonant, the irresistible, and the desired voice for which she pined.

Her brain scoffed. "Oh, it's *you* ..."

"Yeah. I bought another disposable with very few precious minutes on it in order to contact you. You could not have known my best friend, Dan. Sorry. I'm the one who put him up to it so I could hear your voice and get in touch you."

"Yeah, I was wondering."

"Really, really sorry, Ruby. I do not like clandestine interludes—so risky for the innocent party—but it really is necessary right now. I want ... I want to see you so badly and continue where we left off ..."

"Mark—"

"Please don't say my name. I would like to explain everything, but I will absolutely not implicate you. Please try to understand ... and be patient."

"I cannot risk my daughter. Did you do it? Did you burn down an advertising business in Denver?"

There was a long pause. "I will tell you everything you want to know. Will you let my friend Dan, pick you up and bring you to see me? It's the only way I can ..."

"I don't know... I'm not sure. I just ..."

"Well, in about thirty seconds, this phone is gonna die. Maybe you could ...? Ruby, I've gotta go. I don't know how this is possible, but for the first time in my life, I think I lo—"

Click.

Chapter

13

RUBY, SAID, "HELLO? Hello? Oh, *please* don't go *now!*" She held the phone to her heart, hoping it had not disconnected.

She thought the disconnect would break her heart, but, in the end, she knew she had to give up this man for Chloe's sake, and probably her own.

She wandered through the house, trying to sort out feelings, questions, nonanswers, and parts of their short conversations. She tried to decipher and replay and make sense of them. Was Mark trying to say he loved her? What was that last word? She could not think of any other English word that started with *lo*. Or maybe it was *laugh*, or some other word. She could not imagine what else he could have wanted to say.

But wasn't it too soon? What were her boundaries for a man telling her he loved her? Should it be weeks, or months? How long had it been since she'd first encountered him casually leaning on the wall across the street? Maybe seven or eight weeks? She'd known people who had gotten married in shorter periods of time. Then she also remembered that those relationships didn't have the best track records.

Ruby finally decided she needed a pain killer—not necessarily for a headache, but maybe it would work for a heartache, too. She tidied the flat and decided to head to bed early. She wandered into the studio and, on auto-pilot, sized up her next project, which was for a hybrid seed company. At least she would be making graphics of plants and nature—something she loved. She opened the drawer of her drafting table and saw the card from Mark. She picked it up and read, *'Whenever you're not looking for someone, there she is.'*

At that, she slowly climbed the stairs to bed, glancing at the calendar to verify the number of days it would be when Chloe came home. *Six, long, impossible days!* Ruby guessed she was simply lonely tonight, and surprisingly she crashed into bed with all of her clothes on, sleeping soundly. She dreamed long and satisfyingly of a handsome man who would love her, be faithful, and be true, and with whom she found incredible happiness.

Eight hours later, she awoke suddenly to real life, where no such thing as true love existed unless a person was thinking of soap operas—which she would not even consider. At any rate, someone was pounding the door off downstairs.

She sprang out of bed, realized she was still dressed, fluffed down her hair, and checked her face for sleep drool and smeared makeup; she didn't have time to actually decide whether she looked okay. She opened the door to Jordan, who was in the usual big hurry and was all business.

"You look like hell, Ruby! What did you do, sleep in your clothes or something?"

"Well, you look like you spent the night in your car!"

"I *did* spend the night in my car … thanks to corporate being destroyed by an arsonist, along with my entire list of clients and business associates, and a pile of cash that nobody knew I kept in the place."

"Geez, sorry. Why would you keep cash at work?"

"To keep it away from my wife. She spends money like we've got a successful counterfeit business in the basement."

Ruby tried very hard not to be amused. She had only met Jordan's wife one time at a company party—or should she say, his arm candy—and she could see that the woman spent every last dime she got her hands on. But the fact that Jordan had lost thousands trying to hide it from her (and knowing how little he paid her for her awesome advertising skills), she found it irresistible to jab at him.

"Really? Sounds like there's trouble in paradise! Why did you spend the night in your car?"

"Well, the first motel I found out here in god-forsaken-ville wasn't fit for rats—in fact, you could hear them mating from outside the office door!"

Ruby giggled. "Surely, you exaggerate."

Then he said, "The second place I went to, nobody would answer the door. Just as well—it smelled like garbage. Let's just get in and discuss the next project, okay? Do you have any coffee?"

"Sure." Ruby got the pot bubbling.

They went into the studio and put their heads together over the hybrid seed company project.

"These people are rabid, Ruby. We have to please them unequivocally."

"Jordan, I am not sure I want to bend over backward for dopes like this anymore. And anyway, I'm sorry for the fire at corporate. Do you have any idea who did it? Any clues left behind? Any suspicions?"

"We know it's the environmentalists! They hate advertising, they hate corporations, and they hate everything that isn't love, peace, and pansies!"

That sent Ruby into gales of derisive guffaws. "You've got to be kidding! Why would environmentalists care about your little advertising company?" She wickedly thought, *If it was Mark who did it, hooray for him!*

"They are investigating Greenpeace, among others. They say advertising companies are wasting Mother Earth's resources, chopping down trees, blah, blah, blah. They just can't stand it when businesspeople make more money than they do. I don't know their reasons. They are just stupid, illiterate, evil people!"

"Jordan, that is a very unkind thing to say. How many environmentalists do you know?" Ruby thought fondly of her parents, knowing they were not misguided or evil.

"None, and I'm going to keep it that way! I don't like perfectionist sorts who interfere in other people's livelihoods!"

"Okay, enough already. Let's just get to the project." Ruby wanted no more of Jordan's opinions, right or wrong.

For half an hour they discussed, vehemently argued, and brainstormed over the advertising project. Ruby could at least get it started without any more directives from Jordan, who was flying out of town anyway. He let her know again that he never cared for her moving away from Denver into this little backwoods conurbation of a town. Ruby thought it was charming and historic, and *safer* than Denver. After every encounter with Jordan, Ruby was mentally exhausted. He was one of those types who continually drained one's energy. She knew she'd made the right decision for both her and Chloe. And knowing his growing disenchantment and distrust for his wife, she did not care to be available to him in case he wanted to compromise his wedding vows. Ruby bolstered her decision to find her own clients and freelance for a change.

Now that the morning had so abruptly begun, Ruby took full advantage of the time to dive headlong into the next task. After a couple of hours, she noticed the Redrock Cafe getting busy for lunch and later. She needed a break. She tidied her makeup and hair, slipped into a crisp blouse, and jaunted across the street. Wonderful smells of buffalo burgers frying and greasy onions greeted her nostrils. She sat down to a man-sized cheeseburger with all of the trimmings.

Soon the sheriff and deputies joined her—practically surrounding her with pulled-up chairs turned backward and leering gazes. She took a huge, sloppy, dripping, unladylike bite and wiped across her mouth while gulping a cherry Coke that was soon to be belched out, just to irritate them. Unfortunately, she knew she would pay for that act with heartburn for half of the afternoon.

Ruby ignored them until they fidgeted, watching in disbelief as she continued devouring her three-inch-high burger. The sheriff finally spoke. "Well, Mistress Ruby, have you seen anything lately of that there gentleman a few weeks back, who looked at you like he was going to do to you what you are presently doing to that sandwich?"

Ruby was inflamed and immediately defensive, but she necessarily hid it well. Why should she feel like she had to defend Mark? But these a-holes were so crude and insulting that she wouldn't have given them any clues if she had despised Mark.

She smiled sweetly and put a manicured finger to her mouth to gesture that they had to wait until she was finished chewing. Then she took an inordinate amount of time chewing and swallowing to keep them waiting—also, to further irritate them. When she had laboriously finished swallowing every little bit of food, she dabbed at the corners of her mouth with her napkin, took a second drink of Coke, and again dabbed her mouth corners. Then she said, "No."

They were trying to hide their irritation and impatience, because they descended on her so overly confidently to grill and squeeze info from her. The sheriff dumbly repeated, "No? That's all you gotta say?"

Ruby continued with the charade of making them wait from another outlandish bite, pampering her defined lips and mouth with her nappie. She said, "Yes."

They decided then to heave their behemoth bodies, testosterone, masculinity, egos, and barely concealed lust all the way back out the door, cussing, accusing, and 'promisin' to keep an eye on her.

Ruby wished she could reach Mark and warn him. But why? Oh, lord, she was confused. But alas, she had no way of achieving it, so why waste time thinking about it? After those two humongous bites, Ruby had lost her appetite—not because of the burger, but because of the chauvinistic men who would ramshackle their little town under the guise of keepin' the peace. Then she thought of her sweet little daughter, who would have been mortified watching her mother eat that slab of animal. Ruby decided to set it out for the feral cats tonight, and she asked for a box to go. She ordered a white mocha and trotted back to her studio fully charged to submerge herself into work so she and Chloe would have some mother-daughter time when she got home. She made a mental note to buy materials for the butterfly house.

She could hear the ringing of the phone from outside the building. She fumbled with her keys and tried not to hope that it would be Mark. She raced to the phone and checked the caller ID; it was not familiar. She breathlessly answered.

The sheriff drawled, "Listen, li'l sweetie. If you change your mind about any info about that dude that hit town, don't hesitate to call."

You idiot! Ruby's mind silently screamed. "You just bet your woody knockers, I will!" mocked Ruby, instead of saying what she wanted to say.

"Hey, little lady. This here is the law yer atalkin' to!" growled the protector of the city, which could probably do without his style of protection.

"Certainly. Good-bye," she dismissed him, rather than allowing him to dismiss her. No sooner had she dropped her hand from the phone than it rang again. Expecting it to be the sheriff again, she hissed out a rabid "Hello?"

"Wow! I sure don't ever want you mad at me!" teased the warm, sensuous voice of Mark. "I bought another disposable and only have another few minutes, but I just had to hear your voice. Is everything okay, darlin'?"

"Uh, no. The sheriff accosted me this afternoon at the Redrock and wanted to know if I had heard from you. Mark, will you please tell me what's going on? I can't take this anymore, wondering and wondering, speculating and worr—" She caught herself before she completed the phrase.

He reminded her to not use his name and then teased, "Worrying? Was that what you were about to say? Worrying about me?"

She rolled her eyes and bit her cheek. *Busted! Damn!*

Mark continued. "That's why I want to see you, darlin'. Will you please agree to get picked up by my trustworthy friend and let him bring you to me? I would hand my own mother over to Dan."

"Okay, okay. He sounded nice enough. It's just that I ..." She trailed off.

"Yes, I know it must have come as a bit of a shock, but ..."

"But, I'm probably not in the least prepared for the next shock, now am I?" she tested him.

"You got me there, darlin'. Now, with only a few seconds left on this phone, here's what we'll do. Dan comes by tomorrow evening, near dark, picks you up, and drives you to a designated place far from town. We join up together. Okay? It will work, just trust me. And leave the lights on at your house so no one thinks you're gone. Okay?"

With Chloe coming home in only a few days, how would she explain her absence to everyone who knew her schedule? Her Mom, Jordan, Chloe, the neighbors, the cafe?

Ruby was less than enthusiastic for obvious reasons. She sighed, vacillated, and stammered. With only seconds left to talk, she mumbled out, "Yes, uh, I'll figure something out. Uh, what does Dan look like?"

"He looks like a perfect gentleman, darlin', and he is. He

wouldn't hurt a fly. You'll be safe, I prom—" The phone went dead.

Now what have I done? It just goes from bad to worse to worst! She heaved a sigh for the daunting task of the invention of lies, deceptions, and covertness. *How could I get caught up in this? How could I not?* "Well, let the games begin," she mocked herself.

Ruby excitedly bounded up the stairs for the more daunting task of packing a hurried overnight bag. *He did intend overnight, didn't he, if Dan is picking me up at night?* Was she presuming too much? Maybe they would hide out for a quick dinner or something, somewhere off the grid. Maybe they would ...

Off went her mind into wild, crazy imaginations and impossible expectations. Sheesh! Why in this ever-lovin' world did she agree? She knew she would get no sleep tonight, worrying and thinking. She lost count how many times she told herself that she was precariously wading into uncharted waters.

Surprisingly, Ruby did sleep. She was too mentally exhausted not to. When she did wake in the morning, she flew out of bed to face probably the worst decision she'd ever made in her life, with the exception of the ship anchor. She buzzed around the house doing chores, making sure all was nice and ready for Chloe to come home. She watered plants as if it might be their final drink and finished tasks that had languished over the weeks Chloe had been gone. The agonizingly long day at last slipped into early evening. Ruby was ready to face this man who refused to stay out of her mind. She resolved that she would know immediately and unconditionally if she could love him, and if he could reciprocate. She had to stop comparing every man to her ex. She had to stop doubting herself and just live. And she probably had to stop hating. Ruby was ready to love again. He had said to trust him, and she would sincerely try, but maybe she had to develop a little trust in herself first.

Dan called. "Hi, Ruby. Are you ready to go?"

She took a deep breath and, hesitating, with slight misgivings, nearly whispered, "Yes."

"Good. I'll be there in about fifteen. I'm wearing a black T-shirt. See ya."

"Yeah, see ya."

It seemed like less than fifteen minutes, but Dan quietly walked to Ruby's back door and lightly knocked. Dan caught his breath but said nothing when he met her. He completely understood Mark's passion over this woman named Ruby. The woman was exquisitely beautiful.

Ruby had purposely left a lamp on in the back of the house so it looked as if she'd already retired for the night.

They shook hands, and Ruby followed Dan out to a waiting car. They drove for almost an hour and arrived at a small airport south of Tepid. Dan, the pilot, had a plane ready to go. Without saying any more than was necessary, Ruby climbed aboard the light airplane and buckled herself in, praying again that this adventure would turn out okay after making such an uncharacteristic and nitwitted choice. After takeoff, tensions leveled out emotionally and conversationally.

Dan spoke first. "It's nice to finally meet you, Ruby."

"Nice to... meet me?" Ruby burst into uncontrollable laughter. *Meet me? You are a complete stranger, you whisked me out of my house, and you are flying me to god knows where. And you say it's 'nice' to meet me?* Dan's innocent attention to manners got the best of the incongruence of the situation. He was bewildered, to say the least. Ruby often expressed nervousness by sudden outbursts of laughter. Ruby did not need a butterfly pavilion—she had a colony right inside her stomach.

"This may seem pretty strange activity, Ruby, but Mark

and I have been friends since high school. I would bet on Mark with my own life."

"Thank you, Dan. 'Nice' to meet you too!" Ruby's outburst was finally subsiding; it was more about rattled nerves than humor.

"I try not to get too involved in his activities, but I trust him explicitly. You will too; I guarantee it. Mark is quite taken with you—I've heard nothing but Ruby, Ruby, Ruby for weeks. I can assure you I have not heard him speak those words about a woman for a very, very long time."

Ruby thanked Dan again and began to relax. Dan was a nice man. And a gentleman. *And* a nice–looking gentleman who did not seem to be attached. She smiled and sighed a bit of relief. They cruised for two hours or so, getting to know each other better with every speedy air mile, and soon they began laughing like old friends themselves.

Soon it was time to land. Ruby had sort of forgotten to mention she was afraid of flying, but she had not communicated this to Mark or Dan. Of course, she hadn't known that she would be flying to wherever it was that Mark was waiting. Dan noticed her nervousness, took her hand for a few minutes, and squeezed gently. Then he concentrated with both hands on the controls to land them safely. It was an easy landing with a very experienced and competent pilot. Ruby appreciated Mark's friend, whom she felt would also become her friend.

When they disembarked, Mark came out of the dark from nowhere, and she was at last in his enveloping arms. After Mark reluctantly released his embrace on her, Ruby looked around to see if she could identify where she was. Not a clue! And... not a care! Not only did she fling all caution to the wind in every aspect of this venture, but she could not have called anyone to rescue her because she didn't know her location. Ruby nervously thought what her mother would say, all the while knowing exactly those reprimanding words. *Really credible ... Help, help! Come rescue me! I have no idea where I am!*

It didn't matter. She trusted both Mark and Dan. Suddenly, she trusted herself. She was in the company of two very trustworthy, upright gentlemen—two dashing gentlemen—and she determined to enjoy herself. *While it lasts,* remnants of her cautioning conscience tagged on.

Chapter

14

OFF THEY SCURRIED toward the beckoning city activity of considerable size. Ruby avoided asking which city; Mark avoided saying. Dan stayed with the plane. Mark opened the door of a snazzy little BMW for her to flounce herself down into. Lush, comfortable leather, easy, and safe—much like Mark. Mark strode to the driver's side. Ruby watched his lithe, gallant, masculine movements as he slid into the seat with the ease of a panther. Before starting the engine, he leaned toward her and smiled irresistibly with perfect teeth and, she imagined, a special look reserved just for her.

"Ruby, I'm so glad you made this happen for me. I think I would have died if you'd said no."

Ruby could only beam right back at him. She knew she was crazy, but somewhere in the air, all reservations deserted her. This was a rare evening out that nothing was going to destroy. Mark took her hand for a second, kissed it passionately, set it carefully on his thigh, and started the powerfully rumbling car to life. He concentrated on driving in the city while squeezing her shoulders closer to him. He seemed to be looking for a predetermined destination, and at every red light he nestled his face into her hair with a devilish smile that Ruby already loved. She never moved her hand from where he had placed it. Ruby would have been happy to drive nonstop like this for the next four weeks with Mark, in order to never break the spell.

Too soon, they arrived, and Mark jumped from the car to open her door. When she stepped out and looked up into his face, Ruby knew she had never known a man like him. He pulled her against him and softly pressed his lips to hers, his hands caressing her back and surrounding her waist. Even though it was dark, Mark would never allow himself to get frenzied and carried away in a public place—not for his sake, but mostly for hers. Ruby admired him for such consideration. He took her hand and led her through the back of a building he seemed to know well.

Waiters and workers greeted him pleasantly, shook hands, nodded, and acquiesced. They were ushered to a lovely table set for two: china, crystal, and silver on a dazzlingly white tablecloth amid the privacy of plants, art, statues, and a quietly gurgling fountain. Ruby thanked herself that she'd decided to wear a casual skirt and a silky, feminine blouse instead of jeans; she would have been sorely under-dressed for this classy establishment. She noticed that Mark had on slacks rather than jeans. Whew! Still, she wished she would have taken a little more pride in getting ready.

As she patted the wrinkles out of her skirt and smoothed her hair, Mark bolstered her confidence by whispering that she looked ravishing. That was a stretch, obviously, but she still appreciated the compliment. Then he bent next to her ear and growled, "I mean it. You are a unique creature, my darlin' Ruby Jewel!" The passion in his tone of voice both convinced and surprised Ruby, and she forgot everything else except enjoying an incredible evening with Mark the billboard burner.

Dinner seemed to last for three aching hours of anticipation. For the most part, workers left them alone to talk, tease, banter, get to know each other, laugh, and remain in the privacy and safety of not being observed or incriminated. Waiters never stopped bringing food, however, and in the space of a very short hour, Ruby could not eat another bite. The food was superbly delicious, the servers were wonderful, the ambiance was perfect, and the company was indescribable. Both of them languished in each other's presence until they slowly sauntered, attached, to the exit. Neither could help noticing they were the only ones remaining in the restaurant, which was well past closing time. They laughed and joked the rest of the way out. For Ruby, this evening had been so comfortable, so compatible. It was a brand-new feeling for her.

Mark was deliciously watching her enjoy herself. He had already deducted that Ruby sacrificed much of her freedom, fun, and social needs for the gift of a consistent, safe life for her lovely daughter. *Wow, how chaste and decent.* He loved her more for it—that she considered her child before her own goals and desires. He wanted more than ever for her to have a memorable weekend with him—presently, and definitely in the future. Mark was wise enough to know there was rocky territory ahead concerning his activities.

The manager was politely loitering at the bar, waiting for them to finish. He and Mark shook hands, and Mark said he would settle up with him on Monday. Then he pulled a bill from his wallet for the servers. He steered her to the elevator, where they climbed to the tenth floor. They walked with Mark's arm around Ruby and Ruby's hand resting on the back of Mark's pocket to the door of room 1010. The door opened to a lovely sitting room furnished with satin chairs and a couch, TV, ottoman, desk, and miscellaneous other pieces of homey furniture. It also included a hot tub, floor-to-ceiling view out of windows, and sliding glass doors that invited a person to stare and marvel for eons. The moon was right on schedule to light up the room and balcony, where more cushy love seats beckoned. Ruby immediately wanted to step out onto the balcony. Mark stood behind her with his arms around her. The air was chilly and Mark's warmth felt delicious. Ruby swooned, leaned into Mark, and timidly mentioned, "Mark, you've never told me where we are."

Sinking into her hair, which intoxicated him with lavender, tea rose, and essence of Ruby, he murmured, "You are with me, and I am with you. That's the only place we need to be."

Ruby's soft laughter agreed, because that *was* the only place she needed to be, and the only place she could think of in the entire world that she wanted to be at this moment. They stood together, gently swaying, and then ultimately settled onto the love seat with Ruby plastered against Mark, who had both arms cradling her even more tightly against him. They talked and reminisced about that first encounter in the Red Rock Cafe. They shared childhood stories and foibles. They risked several long-forgotten dreams. Ruby truly felt like she was dreaming as she relaxed in Mark's circling embrace. Hours went by like seconds; seconds were mere flashes. Ruby thought she could spend the rest of her life in this loving embrace. What she did not know was that Mark was thinking the exact same thing. Both of them were exhausted from the stress, the risk of the trip, and the lateness of the hour. Neither knew how to ease into the subject of hitting the hay. They did not want to be too bold, and they could not pretend that they weren't interested in a physical encounter.

Finally, Mark murmured, "What do you say we get ourselves some rest—zero expectations?" Ruby nodded and slowly dragged herself out of the comfort of Mark's arms. He didn't go very far away. Soon they were in a standing embrace and a locking kiss as they moved toward the king-sized bed. Without releasing her, Mark pulled back the covers, and they both crashed in one heap, laughing and trying not to curtail any part of the physical contact of their bodies or unlock the prolonged kiss. As they provocatively peeled out of clothing and spooned into a workable sleeping position, Mark quipped, "See you in the morning!"

Ruby recognized a ploy a mile away, and with as little acrimony as possible, she said, "Okay, g'night!"

Mark laughed long and deep at Ruby's playfulness. He thought, *God, please never let this end. Please never let this woman get away from me!*

He easily flipped her over on top of him, with the waning splash of moonlight filtering through the sheers of the sliding glass door. In a rare moment of his senses leaving him, he said, "Ruby, will you marry me?"

She flatly ignored his comment, still in her playful mood. She allowed her hair to fall down onto his chest and tickle his face, and she said, "Yes. When? Tomorrow?"

Then he was completely serious. "Tomorrow is too late. How about tonight?"

Deciding to be literal, she glanced at the clock and said, "Tonight is already gone—it's after midnight!" Mark was shocked at how six hours could have evaporated so fast.

Then she stopped playing. "Mark, what are you saying? Don't trifle with me! I was just being goofy." She tried to slide off, but Mark didn't allow it.

"I know you are, and that's okay ... But I'm not."

She looked deep into his eyes. He was definitely serious ... and irresistible. She knew now it would be impossible to get a wink of sleep.

He continued. "I know when I see the real thing, Ruby, and you are it. Take your time answering. I've got the rest of my life to wait."

Mark feigned pushing her off him so he could turn over and go to sleep.

She shrieked, "Oh, no, you don't, Mark Smythe! You aren't going to sleep if I can't!" She battered at his back and ribs until he burst into heightened desire and laughing.

He rolled back toward Ruby, brusquely snatched her against him, and murmured her name over and over. Ruby felt comfortable and loved like she hadn't ever felt in her life. Her mind was surrendering to the caring strength of this handsome man, her body burning yet waiting shyly for his first move. Mark gently pulled her curvaceous body toward his own and began kissing and caressing like he might never stop. Ruby certainly did not wish him to. The night was long, sensual, and satisfying, melting two yearning hearts into one with a permanent sealing of a guaranteed happiness and future.

Morning came and went. The two lovers could not pry themselves away from each other. They slept, made love, slept, made love, and talked. Hunger ultimately drove them to breakfast (which was waiting on a tray outside the door), but not from each other's arms, not from one another's blissful tangle.

Soon Ruby dashed through the shower. Upon coming out, she was amazed because Mark set a steaming white mocha in front of her. His wicked smile revealed that he'd not forgotten one detail about their first encounter.

"Thank you." She glowed with happiness and went straight into another embrace. Both began to doubt whether they would get to breakfast at all today; it was nearly noon already. Ruby had never had such a wonderful evening, night, and morning with a man. She never wanted to leave this memorable place.

Chapter
15

THEY LUXURIATED IN breakfast out on the balcony and watched the busy city come to life on this exquisite, sunshiny, perfect day.

"What shall we do today, darlin'? I mean, besides the obvious, which we will continue to do throughout the day, uh, anytime you want to ..."

Ruby blushed. She loved it when Mark tried to be discreet, failed miserably, and then ended up stammering a revelation of what *he* actually wanted to do. She could only laugh non-stop. Ruby was deliriously happy. Mark completely enjoyed her happiness.

"I don't know. Uh ..." Somehow after hours of long, passionate, fulfilling, wonderful lovemaking, it was difficult to think straight, to come back to reality. Both had loved with total abandon, and both wanted the same thing. Each never wanted these incredible moments to end. Neither wanted to move on to some external bustle and risk destroying the ambiance of last night and this morning *(and apparently anytime during the day, if she was so inclined).*

"Maybe I will just surprise you, Ruby Jewel. Maybe I won't tell you! Maybe I will kidnap you so you can never go back! *Maybe ...*" teased Mark.

"Sure, Clyde!" retorted Ruby, enjoying the utter astonishment in Mark's expression.

"Clyde? *Clyde?*" Mark's voice was so high it cracked, and Ruby laughed even more. "You cute little imp!" he exclaimed, grabbing her against him, kissing everything in the vicinity of his lips, and loving every second of Ruby's teasing. Mark intended to take every opportunity available to pull that woman against him; he loved it, and she reveled in every gesture of his. He loved her more for it. In fact, he had not often found women who enjoyed or responded so positively and actively to some of his gestures. Ruby did—foreplay, after-play, and in-between play. Ruby was truly an exception to every woman he'd known, and to everything and everyone he'd experienced.

As crazy as Ruby knew it to be, she suddenly didn't care in which city she was. She was thrilled when Mark said he would spirit her away from it all. For this weekend, this rare time warp, she wanted more than ever to be taken away, and she would not ask again or even try to guess the locale.

After another significant segment of time, both hurriedly got into some clothes and came to a united decision on the two dozen or so suggestions to go out on the town for the afternoon. They buzzed around town in the Beemer, stopping whenever and wherever Ruby wanted to stop. They strolled through parks and farmers' markets, made wishes from bridges, sneaked behind obstacles to make out, and managed to hit at least fourteen major shopping malls, or so it seemed. Mark had mentioned going dancing, and he took her shopping to try on dresses. While she was posing and flouncing and parading in gown after gown, he slipped into the main mall to an exclusive jewelry store. He was determined to get a ring on her finger before the short weekend was up. In between stores, going back and forth to see how she looked in the twelve outfits she'd picked to try on, and carefully choosing a gift that he hoped Ruby would like, Mark was kept busy running. When she finally decided on a becoming navy lace and silk, full-skirted mid-calf-length dress, which she would not allow Mark to see before tonight, she presented it to the cashier for payment and wrapping.

Ruby left the store just as Mark, looking sheepish, sauntered over the threshold. She asked, "Where have you been, Mr. Smythe?"

"Oh, just around the corner spying out rings, Mrs. Smythe!" Mark hoped the actual truth would deflect any of Ruby's suspicions.

She punched him playfully and said, "Oh, quit teasing me about rings! You and I both know better than to dream that far ahead!"

"Okay, enough about rings. But please don't make me stop teasing you. You are simply a delight to tease!"

They found a small, private nook in a coffee shop, where they could plan their evening and exchange more intimacy. Mark was resting his heavy hand very firmly on Ruby's thigh, which was as close to Mark as clothing would allow. It seemed that for every moment of the past two days, these particular lovers had had some part of their body touching the other's body at all times. Ruby loved that kind of intimacy, closeness, and safeness. Mark would not have been able to keep his hands off Ruby, anyway.

Mark continued their conversation about how much he loved teasing Ruby. He described in detail how her eyes got a wanton look, and he knew that not for a minute was she serious about him stopping. She loved it, he knew it, and she knew he knew it. Furthermore, he knew that she knew that he knew she loved it! He went on to describe how her dimple showed when she tried to look serious. It was not long before the talk, the day, the afternoon, the banter and fun, the running around town, the verbal exchanges, and everything surrounding these two led them wishing to return to the privacy of the hotel.

Mark stood and said, "Let's get out of here." Ruby demurely

took his hand and followed. The next two hours were spent satiating physical desires and mutual, irrepressible love. They enjoyed each other, slept, and woke up refreshed and ready to go dancing.

Another shower and quickly drying hair. Ruby looked smashing in her dress. The happiness on her face made her ten times more beautiful than she was on a very good day.

Mark *ooh*ed and *aah*ed over every detail of her immaculate style. He said, "Where did you ...? Uh, I never saw that dress on you."

"You were out purchasing rings, remember?"

"Oh! Well, wow. It's beyond beautiful, and you are extremely attractive in it. I'd better handcuff you to my belt!"

Ruby slinked up to Mark and breathed, "Thank you, Mark. It's been a very long time since I've been out." Her smile matched his passionate compliment.

Mark was dressed in light tan slacks, black-and-white mobster shoes, a white silk shirt with the chest open, and long sleeves rolled up. He very closely resembled a *GQ* model. "Ready, Mrs. Smythe?"

At first she mustered a stern look for rebuttal, but then Ruby switched quickly so as not to spoil this magical evening by disagreeing. She raised her head high and said, "Indeed, I am, Mr. Smythe!"

He beamed and agreed approvingly, "Indeed, you are, Mrs. Smythe!"

He held out his left arm for her to put her hand through, and they strutted to the elevator like the beautiful couple they were—or perhaps, as in both of their fantasies, as husband and wife. Who would know the truth except them? More than a few people looked them up and down in admiration. The 'Smythes' gave each other knowing looks and read the love secrets in each other's eyes and minds.

Mark seemed to know all the great places in town to dine,

dance, and meet people. Ruby liked the places they went together, and she would never forget this weekend as long as she lived. The music was romantic and from all genres and decades. Mark was a superb dancer: easy to follow and very tender. He knew when to hold her closely, and when to make space between them. They danced so very professionally that most people didn't catch on that these two were heading toward crazy in love.

Dan showed up to find out the plan. His and Mark's contact was limited to business phones. He did not want to bother Mark; in fact, knew better than to bother his friend when he was in certain situations, and Ruby gathered this was one of those situations. She didn't even want to think about leaving.

Dan asked Mark if he could dance with Ruby. She thought Dan probably out and out delayed asking her in order to respectfully to ask Mark first. When he finally did ask if he could have the next dance, Ruby took her cue from Mark, who nodded. She noticed he took out his phone to make a call. *How dare he conduct business on a date!* Then she got distracted by Dan elegantly leading her to the dance floor. Dan danced very well too. He was a perfect gentleman and shortly returned Ruby to Mark. Somehow or other, they telepathically communicated a plan, and Dan reluctantly departed.

Mark stated they would dance a final one, and then it would be necessary for them to go. Mark pulled Ruby close, almost like a captive, and in her heart she truly could have been. She gladly would have given her permission without hesitation. Mark said he never wanted this weekend to end, and that this short interlude was really only the beginning. He also said they would talk when they got back to the suite, because he had a promise to keep, and he would always keep his word to her.

The last dance ended in a swirl and a swish of her lovely dress wrapping around Mark's legs. He held her tightly and tried to burn his lips onto her forehead forever. Ruby's heart skipped several breathless beats. They solemnly left the club and sank into the comfort of the BMW. Mark was smiling a sad smile because within several short hours, he would be relinquishing the woman he loved over to his best friend and pilot.

It seemed Mark chose the longest route back to the hotel. Ruby had no care where she was anyway. Soon he slowed down and pulled into the familiar driveway of a high-end residence. The house was modest but nondescript, with no special color, no style, and no identifying features. There was a car already in the drive and a light on in the foyer. To Ruby's surprise, they scuttled into the house in a New York minute, where Mark proceeded to engulf Ruby in his arms once more.

He stated, "We are not home-home, but you are at my house. I just wanted your sweet presence here before you had to leave, darlin', so I can bear the long hours when you cannot be here."

"We... We're... in K-Kansas City?" Ruby queried gingerly.

A devilish smile broke across Mark's face, and he retorted, "So you've been doing your homework, my innocent little Ruby Jewel!"

She did not like getting caught spying on Mark, and shot back, "I've been watching TV, you ... You ...!" She dangled.

"Come on, spit it out! Were you going to call me a criminal, my adorably sweet Ruby?" coaxed Mark with glee.

"I ... I was going to ..."

"I'm waiting, Mrs. Smythe." Mark wanted to maintain the couple momentum from the earlier part of the evening.

Finally, Ruby finished lamely. "I ... could never call you a criminal, Mark. I hope you know that."

Mark's answer was a long, final squeeze. He murmured, "Now that I've got you here, do you want to see the rest of the place?"

She gaped around a little and then said, "Not yet, not tonight. It's lovely, but ..."

"Fine, darlin'. Let's go where I know we can kick back." With a quick sweep, they were gone, and none too soon. As they were departing, red and blue lights appeared in the rearview mirror. Mark's Kansas City home was quickly surrounded by cop cars and FBI. A camera flashed somewhere off to her right as they sped off.

Chapter

16

RUBY OBSERVED HOW tense Mark's jaw was. "Wow, *that* was too close for comfort. Glad you didn't want a tour!" He laughed a nervous laugh and said, "Just call me Clyde!"

It wasn't that Mark was afraid of the law or being arrested. He would have gone peacefully without incident. It was simply that he did not wish to be arrested with Ruby anywhere near him. He didn't wish for that type of humiliation to happen.

Ruby sadly wondered how she could allow herself to get caught up with this character when there was no future in sight. Her heart ached, cried, and screamed. She sadly removed her hand from Mark's thigh and placed it in her lap, and there it stayed until they reached the hotel. They entered through the garage unseen and slipped up to room 1010. As they changed into comfies, Ruby wondered how she could possibly get any sleep that night.

Mark dashed through the shower quickly before settling in to explain to Ruby what needed explaining. She waited patiently but anxiously. She made coffee, stared out the windows, and chided herself for getting so carried away. Then two strong arms reached around and enveloped her tenderly, caringly, and intimately. Mark's strong body was against her back. She knew she couldn't stop now—she loved the man, and he loved her.

They sat down wrapped around each other, and Mark began the sordid explanation that he owed her. He prefaced the information with the warning that if anybody, anywhere, for any reason asked her about him, she was to flatly deny everything—except that she'd barely met him on one occasion. That was all. He'd been hired by an activist group to destroy advertising moguls who blatantly lied and touted their products as the best, the only, or the common-sense choice—and then ruthlessly stabbed consumers with hiked prices. They paid him to take the risks to get the job done, and they would provide the resources for him to skip town, leave the country, disappear, and defend him, if need be. He got paid very well. Their main goal was to negatively impact affluence and greed; their mission was to support the local mom-and-pop companies who struggled to put food on their humble tables, and their objective was to create a smaller footprint on Mother Earth. The group abhorred greed, CEO bonuses, obscene raises, and monies sacrificed that screwed the (real) free enterprise system—the monopolies, and bigger-than-life companies who made conscious decisions to drive out the little guys. Part of the group's mission was to level the playing field for the small businesses so that they had a fair chance of being successful.

"I'll just give you a little time to process that info, darlin'. It is the truth. I know it must be a shock, but I've told you as much as I've told my own mother." With that comment, Mark stepped out onto the balcony to contemplate Ruby's reaction—or more likely, let her grapple with it on her own, among the many feelings and wild weekend she'd had with him. It could go either way. Ruby could detest him and want to get back to her life and responsibilities, as well as her mundane job with Jordan's stinking advertising—which believed in trashing the scenery with detritus in the form of signage. He did not set Jordan's corporate headquarters afire, but he was pretty sure he knew who did. He'd specifically asked not to be a part of that job, because of Ruby. He never wanted to have to look into her eyes and lie.

Ruby was shocked—well, somewhat shocked. She wasn't stupid; it had begun to add up, and she did not like the sum. She'd seen the evening news from Sioux Falls with pictures of Mark, burned billboard signs, his home in Kansas City, an FBI mug shot, and incriminating reporters across five states. Why had she turned on the TV those weeks past? She never wasted much time watching TV, and yet there he was in all of his arrogance, luxury, trouble, and charges! There was no denying it now. Ruby had felt once again she'd picked the wrong relationship—a doomed prospect from the start. What was wrong with her? Was she a sucker for punishment? She remembered her ex being all about arrogance and superiority, and it was a ten-year segment of her life that she swore she would never repeat.

Now, here she sat with one leg crossed over the other, bouncing her foot and watching the silhouette of broad shoulders standing against the railing of the balcony (somewhat vulnerable), his set jaw (somehow indecisive), and striking profile (absolutely irresistible). She'd never been happier with a man. He was so raw, exposed, and honest when telling her of his swipes with the law. It was true that his group protected him; but how long could they, or would they? When would he make a glaring mistake? Everybody made mistakes, and it was bound to happen sooner or later. Could she get involved with someone who might jeopardize her baby? Mark was a smart man. Would he jeopardize them? She honestly couldn't visualize Mark taking such risks. Ruby thought, *Bonnie, it's now or never! You're either going to trust this man, or you never again will trust—let alone find a man like Mark as long as you live!*

Ruby strode through the glass doorway and thrust her arms around Mark from behind. He turned around, took her into his arms, and carried her into their last evening together. The night was short. Ruby thought of a million more questions to ask him—but tonight was not the night. She hoped she'd have one million more days to ask her million questions.

Mark had been awake for some time. He wanted to record forever in his mind the picture of Ruby sprawled against him, hair splayed all over her face, neck, and chest, and arms in tangled, obstinate curls. Over the past two glorious days, he'd noticed Ruby's impatience with controlling her out-of-control tresses. He smiled at her innocence, her passion, and her decision to trust him. A fleeting thought whizzed through his mind about a contract somewhere about never marrying again. Like the romantic he was, he fantasized that it might be lost, but he knew for sure that that particular contract was null and void. He would never let go of Ruby. No, not ever.

Usually, Ruby was a quiet sleeper and woke up in the exact position in which she went to bed. This night was an exception. She gave a deep sigh—wishing with all of her heart that last night was not over. She looked up into Mark's face. He kissed her on her forehead and said, "Good morning, my darling Mrs. Smythe!"

Ruby noticed the subtle inflection from *darlin'* to *darling*. She'd never felt so cherished and affirmed. Mark had never felt so appreciated and loved. For a few precious moments, they could do nothing except get lost in the love in each other's faces. A light tap at the door signaling coffee was ready brought them back to reality; they dragged themselves to the shower and a quicker-than-quick daily routine. As they flounced on the couch to enjoy coffee, white mocha, and croissants, Mark predicted what lay ahead for him and the magnitude of his involvement in the conspiracies.

"Don't know for sure, but I may be subpoenaed for a trial before summer is gone. My lawyer is working to prevent that as we speak. I am never going to embellish any of this information to you, my love ..."

Ruby looked aghast. Maybe she'd still made the wrong decision after all!

"If these guys work like they always have, there will be a trial."

Ruby visibly swallowed. "A trial?"

"If there is a trial, I will not risk you getting caught up in it. Do you understand? That means no contact, Ruby. It's going to kill me—but it's the only way to protect you from being compromised. I just can't believe the timing of this thing—it could have happened anytime during the past ten years, but no, it had to happen now, right after I finally found the woman of my dreams!"

She was shocked but helplessly nodded.

"Darling, this has happened before, but I've never gotten this close to court. It's somehow always been eased under the rug. I am so sorry. Just when I find the perfect woman, all my past begins to catch up with me. The only way we can communicate is through Dan. Please try to understand, and be patient. Okay?"

Ruby seemed to have lost her voice and could only nod. *Yeah, just when I've found the perfect guy.*

Dan came by in Mark's Beemer to drive them to the airport. He and Ruby would be jetting out of Kansas City as soon as the plane was fueled and checked. Ruby would be arriving home less than three-four hours before Chloe would arrive home from Denver.

The trip to the airport was solemn and heart-wrenching. They clung to each other hungrily as Dan turned and busied himself with the controls, knowing these were the last remnants of an incredible weekend together. They knew that there may be long, dry spells of not seeing each other, or even being able to access any kind of technology to circumvent the media. Their final squeeze was spent nonverbally but with unfathomable commitment to each other. Mark climbed the ladder to the small plane, helping Ruby, and he remained waving on the platform until it disappeared toward the north.

Ruby chilled all the way home from the mere fact of not being in Mark's arms, or within two inches' proximity of him. She watched him standing where she'd left him until he was only a speck. When they touched down south of the 'other Nebraska', Dan rented a car to whisk her back to Tepid. Dan was a comforting presence. He talked slowly and caringly, and he seemed to anticipate her pain, even when she could no longer hold back her tears. Dan said, "Anyone could see you two were meant for each other a mile away." He chuckled. "Oh, boy, is that boy in trouble!"

Ruby swung her head toward Dan, concerned. "What do you mean?"

"The contract!"

"Oh!" Ruby laughed through her tears, knowing of the contract the four friends contrived among themselves to stay single. She also knew it couldn't possibly work, if Mark was honestly expressing himself to her and she was trusting him with all of her heart.

Dan was still shaking his head at the scorn that would befall Mark as soon as the others knew. He swore, "I'll never tell! I'll never have to—they'll see it all over his face!"

Ruby was pleased and amused. But she already missed Mark so much that it ached. Dan soon led her to her apartment door, which seemed pretty ordinary after her incredible weekend, and set her backpack inside. He left as quickly as he'd delivered her and made an urgent call to Mark, letting him know Ruby was safe.

Ruby checked the clock and saw how soon Chloe would be home. From exhaustion, exhilaration, or both, she made the decision to get some sleep. It would be non-stop talk from Chloe for at least six hours after she would bomb in. Ruby thought it would be best to unpack before Chloe got home, to avoid any inquiries about her hiatus while Chloe had been absent—which she would flatly refuse to discuss. She tore through her bags, throwing most of it in the laundry, and soon after she was in never-never land.

Downstairs, people were yelling and banging and trying to wake the dead. Ruby woke in a complete daze. Where was she? Where was Mark, who'd been no more than four inches away from her for more than forty-eight hours? What was going on? She heard thundering hooves coming up the stairs, and Chloe piled on top of her in her bed.

"Mother, I'm home! Why didn't you answer your phone? Where have you been? What have you been doing? Daddy's downstairs, waiting to talk to you," and as soon as she'd crushed Ruby getting back up, amidst ohs and ahs, she raced back downstairs, yelling, "Daddy's downstairs waiting to talk to you!"

Ruby was chagrined that she'd gotten caught off-guard, and succumbed to snoozing oblivion. She'd meant to greet Chloe at the door, all smiles, sunshine, and normal. She slipped into her flip-flops and headed to the inevitable scrutiny of Jashawn.

"Hi."

He said, "Hi ... How're you?"

"Fine," Ruby lied, not being able to avoid comparing Jashawn to Mark and quickly calculating that they were complete opposites.

Chloe hugged her dad, and clung to him longer than Jashawn was comfortable. He was in a big hurry; his second family was waiting impatiently in the car for their real vacation as a family. They were anxious to deliver Chloe and get on with their camping trip in the Hills. Ruby felt sorry for her innocent babe, but she was relieved that Chloe did not seem to notice as she said her good-byes.

Ruby was second-guessing her wild weekend and near-promised future with Mark as she closed the door on Chloe's departing father and half-brothers. *Wow! Life certainly gets in the way of our fun!*

"Well, hey, sweetie. What shall we make to celebrate your homecoming? Fudge oatmeal cookies, chocolate chunk cookies, Bishop's Ambrosia Pie?" teased Ruby.

Chloe smiled rather sadly. "Mom, I met a boy."

"Oh."

"He's really nice, Mom."

"I'm sure he is." Ruby was both dubious and alarmed that her too-young daughter was already seeing the romantic side of boys. "Tell me more."

"Well, he's cute, and smart, and I got kissed ..."

Oh, dear! thought Ruby. She asked, "Uh, does your dad know all this?"

"Nope."

She ventured, "What is this young man's name?"

"Oh, he's not a young man, Mom. He's nothing but a boy! Marcus likes computers, and he's going to e-mail me! He lives next door to Dad and Kaitlin's new house. He babysits his younger sisters." Chloe continued telling Ruby every detail about Marcus. Ruby knew she was in for an all-nighter ordeal, and she began the process of making some junk food for the two of them. Soon she relaxed. She and Chloe chatted, shared stories, and were talking like old, reconnected high school girlfriends. They ended up staying up half the night and watching movies. It was so good having her back home, and being at home herself—even though *home* was pretty unglamorous in comparison. It certainly lent to feeling normal again. Still, her heart ached.

They both gave up around 2:00 a.m. and headed upstairs. As they trudged up the steps, Ruby marveled at how life continually grabbed one by the throat. What were the chances of Chloe's little puppy love having nearly the same name as her new relationship with Mark? Life was crazy.

Chloe flopped on her bed with her clothes on, and Ruby tried to kiss her goodnight.

"Mom! Not on that cheek ... the other one!"

"Why?"

"'Cause that's where Marcus kissed me!"

"Oh!" Thankful now that it had been on Chloe's *cheek*, Ruby tickled her and laughed.

Then she slipped around the corner to her own bedroom, knowing Chloe was near asleep. *Such innocence!* Ruby adored her.

As she was pulling back the sheets and preparing to crash in, she wondered more about Chloe's kiss. Could an eleven-year-old girl, nearly twelve, be so interested in boys? She never had been before. She would rather climb trees, bike, take hikes, read, or do just about anything else. It was the downside of giving her up for weeks at a time unsupervised, and her father not seeing the innocence he needed to protect in his precious daughter. But then, he had other children to consider now.

Ruby thought, *Would Mark be as nonchalant about boys kissing Chloe?* Ruby could not prevent her mind from wandering to unfamiliar niches and recesses that she didn't care to wander into. It was so much responsibility raising a child alone, and so much worry! She got back up and softly tiptoed downstairs to make tea. The pot was soon spitting bubbles. Ruby poured herself a cup and settled into the armchair with her feet pulled underneath of her jams. She continued thinking about Mark and missing him. She hadn't remembered if she'd taken her car keys with her when she took off with Dan three days ago. Knowing she would probably need them sometime tomorrow, she reached for her purse. She spent a little time digging around for keys and came across a package she did not recognize.

What? Where did that come from? Puzzled, Ruby carefully opened the unsealed flap to a card with two children, a boy and a girl, cutely dressed like old-fashioned adults; a Kim Anderson; a thick letter ... and a ring box. Ruby gasped and instinctively, moved to close the living room shades, which were always open. She carefully peeked in to see a beautiful, flawless ruby ring. Ruby was still gasping over the magnificence of the ring. She was beginning to learn Mark might actually be teasing her with the truth when he was distracting her by pretending to lie, joke, tease, or something else. She recalled the banter about the ring when she was trying on dresses. What a load of surprises he was! What an enigma! The thought of Mark shopping for a ring while she was busy with other minutiae excited and thrilled her. He was so thoughtful, so temptingly full of surprises.

The rulebook of propriety glided into her demeanor, and she knew she could not accept a gift this expensive this soon. She should probably not accept a gift at all. *Oh, hell,* she thought, Why is life so full of buzzkills? She added Chloe's new teen term to her vernacular. She'd think about it later. *Right, Scarlett?* Ruby, Scarlett, the color of her cheeks right now—what was the difference? Right now she was drawn to the fire in that perfect, incredible ruby stone. The gold band alone was expensive enough to trade in for a car. *Goll, how can I take this, keep this? I can't! I must get Dan on the phone immediately, or tomorrow—no, it is tomorrow—and get this blasted trinket returned.* Cheeks still aflame, Ruby turned to the adorable card.

The caption in the card said, "When we grow up, will you marry me?" Ruby could not erase the smile that that simple sentence brought to her face. Maybe it would never be erased. She unfolded the letter and began reading.

Dear of all the Dearest, Mrs. Smythe,

By now you are home, my darling Ruby, and I cannot describe the joy and fun and love I feel about our past weekend; I also cannot describe the bereft sadness of your absence from my empty arms. They don't seem to know what to do without you in them. Thank you very much for our time spent together; it meant the world to me. I sincerely wished it would never end, and some incredible future day, it will be a reality as well as a magnificent dream come true.

Of course, I knew you would never accept the ring I bought for you—which is why it had to be delivered in this way. I would much rather have placed that precious stone on your precious finger myself, darling, while we were engaged in lovemaking and other unmentionables, and being able to watch your futile refusals to accept my gift. Yes, that would have been most enjoyable! Hmm, I'm fantasizing about it right now!

Ruby was laughing uncontrollably and blushing. How could Mark know her so well—that she would probably refuse his gift? How could he know so soon how she would react? She was amazed over and over at this man called Mark. There was more to amaze her.

Unfortunately, I will be left to the devices in my own mind about how you found it, reacted, and made the decision to return it pronto, as any true lady would. But I implore you, at least try it on and think of me whenever you wear it, because I will be thinking of you. In fact, please never take it off—unless, of course, you need to read again and again the words I send to you that were first and are permanently etched on my heart. Please know that in this small gesture (and the imposed noncontact for a time), you are constantly in my heart and thoughts and mind and life, Mrs. Smythe.

I am presently and eternally yours, my darling Ruby.

All my love,
Mark
P.S., Perhaps you've already guessed by now, but from the very first time I watched you in your studio from across your street, my heart and soul knew you were the woman for me. I've always categorically refused and scoffed at love at first sight, but now I am convinced it is genuine. "Whenever you're not looking for someone ... there she is."

Ruby was stunned. She felt complimented given how he thought of her as a lady. She must have read the letter eighty times, and she was still looking at it—not seeing the actual words he wrote, but seeing Mark's kind and handsome face, devilish smile, and intense, twinkling eyes as he mercilessly teased her all last weekend and presently within the words of this letter. She replayed every gesture, move, situation, and conversation that happened each day and hour of the weekend, and she physically ached that it was now a surreal memory—still pleasant, still delicious—but, nonetheless, a memory. Ruby imagined his muscular arms pulling her close to his heart. Mark had given her a lifetime of memories and an anticipated future in three very short days—yet it was not nearly long enough.

Light was filtering through the closed shades in the living room, and Ruby realized she had been up for hours; morning was dawning. She was so happy but also suddenly exhausted, and she trundled up the stairs in the hopes that Chloe would sleep in on this day of all days, in order to try to steal a few more Z's herself.

This impossible situation would always have to be a secret she could never share with another living human being—for everyone's protection. In the upcoming weekend, her parents would be visiting. She and Chloe had so much for which to prepare.

Chapter

17

SATURDAY SCURRIED IN. The week had been spent squeezing in hikes and bike rides between spring cleaning and getting ready for company. Ruby's mother and father loudly dragged suitcases, food, gift packages, and traveling paraphernalia into the small apartment living room. They dropped it all and smashed into hugs and greetings and nonstop gabbing.

"It's so good to see you two!" exclaimed Lollie and Rory in unison. "You look so good ... You've grown up, Chloe ... My, you've lost weight, Ruby. are you feeling okay? Well, just look at you ... You're radiant ... Oh, what a trip ... What beautiful country ... It is so humid in Omaha right now, after all the rain ... Tell us, what have you been up to lately? Glad school's out, Chloe?" The chatter continued a full fifteen minutes.

"Yes ... no ... yes ... no ..." was about all Ruby and Chloe could get out. After a while, the greetings died down, and they began talking of serious matters, then lunch, then where they would tour first. The chatter reignited. It seemed they could not settle on settling down. Finally, Rory exclaimed above the din that they should go over to the coffeehouse for a buffalo burger. All agreed.

They sat in a booth, ordered, and continued the catching up. Soon Marcia, the waitress, locked on to a target and sashayed to the table with the newspaper in hand.

"Well, hello, Ruby! How's it going? Haven't seen you for days!"

"Fine, fine. How're you? These are my parents, Lollie and Rory."

"Nice to meet you! Ruby comes in every day for white mocha and ... Oh, hey, Ruby. Have you ever heard from that guy in Kansas City who came through here several months ago? He's in the news constantly for arson or something." She dropped the headlines in front of Ruby.

"Uh, don't know what you're talking about ... Uh ..."

"Read it for yourself, dearie. The sheriff should have slammed him in jail while he had him in his clutches! There have been a half dozen more fires!"

Lollie and Rory were staring wide-eyed at Ruby, who had pinked noticeably while the food was being set down in front of them. Ruby was not prepared for this shock. There on the front page was Mark's Beemer, speeding away from the scene of his house with the back of *her* head, and her hair cascading everywhere, in full view!

"Why, Ruby, that looks like you from behind!" exclaimed Lollie. "Whatever is that Marcia person talking about, honey?"

"Mom, I have no idea. Obviously, she doesn't know either. She's the town gossip, and I really don't pay much attention to anything she says."

Chloe was inspecting Ruby's flushed face. "Mom, it kind of does look like you from the back ..."

"Nonsense! Let's eat!" and Ruby jawed into her buffalo burger. Her father agreed and asked to have the ketchup passed.

An uncomfortable lunch ensued. Ruby had to nearly choke down her food to feign hunger, act normal, and dismiss the newspaper. She wondered to herself, *How could that shot have been taken?* She did not remember any cameras flashing. Could the press find out who the woman in the photo was? Her mind took off in a spiral. Just when Mark had told her the importance of being anonymous, there she was in full regalia! Had he noticed the photo too? Would Dan contact her? She thought suddenly she would bob off her hair, or dye it, or straighten it ...

Lunch was near its completion, and she wanted to get them out of the restaurant before Marcia came back to stir up more controversy. She allowed her dad to pay, and she scooted Chloe and Lollie out and across the street.

"Hey, let's go on a hike this afternoon, okay?" Ruby lilted superficially.

"Sounds good, honey, but ..." began her Mother.

Rory was jogging across the street, and Ruby had an idea to get them all away from her home. She said, "I want to take you guys on a tour! Grab a change of clothes, and let's go!"

Her parents were always ready to adhere to an adventure. Chloe looked rather blank but grabbed some extra jeans and a shirt. Soon they all crammed into Ruby's truck; the back seat wasn't all too comfortable, but Chloe hopped in the back along with Lollie so they could converse. Ruby didn't even grab a map; they would simply drive. The Hills were alive with the sound of cycles heading to Sturgis; the scenery was spectacular. They soon traveled into Wyoming. Everybody wondered where she would let them rest, and the farther Ruby got from Tepid, the more free, unburdened, and fun-filled she felt. She began to relax a bit. She had not a clue how Dan could possibly contact her, if he or Mark even thought it would be necessary.

Without really planning the trip and the serendipitous idea to get away—in the mayhem of packing—she had totally forgotten to remove Mark's ring! There it glared, sparkling, obvious, and glittery on her hand on the steering wheel. *What am I doing? Where can I stash it while we tour so I don't misplace it or lose it?* It would only be a matter of time before precocious little Chloe or perceptive, inquiring Lollie would notice. She slipped it off while steering and distractedly talking. Then she undid the clasp on her necklace, ran the ring onto the chain, and refastened it around her neck. It fell into the caressing cleavage between her breasts. She sighed in relief, closed her eyes for a second, and thought Mark would like it there. Wow! How many more close calls before getting busted? She had to prove Mark could trust her by not revealing this bombastic secret. *Whew!*

In Montana, more than fifty miles distant, rose Devil's Tower, outlined on the horizon like the sacred laccolith that it was. They marveled at the site. It would be another couple of hot, dusty hours before they arrived. Soon enough, they began the hike looping around the base of the tower.

Ruby's mother had been paying attention. She knew her daughter well, and read body language like a pro. That was what special ed teachers did, after all. When Chloe and Rory took off ahead, Lollie stopped Ruby as they rounded a breathtaking scene which only a postcard could boast.

"Sweet child, whatever was that gaudy red jewel on your finger earlier? It was also on your left hand, indicating something, or someone, very special ..."

Ruby sighed. It wasn't that she couldn't trust Lollie; she absolutely could. She simply did not want to implicate her parents or Chloe in any mix-up she'd gotten herself into. "It's complicated, Mother," she nearly whispered.

"You've met someone, then?"

"I have. Mom, he is so kind, so loving, so ..."

"I know all about it, dear. Tell me about him and what is his name?"

"I can't, Mom. I will not lie to you, but I simply cannot tell you anything... He's not local, and I just can't ..."

"What that broad in the cafe said about him being in jail— is that true? She seemed to imply something... or accuse you of knowing him or whatever?"

Ruby knew her Mom would pick up on little details, clues,

and nuances to drag the whole sordid story out of her. "Don't worry, Mom. I am happy. Isn't that enough for now?"

Lollie began walking again, and Ruby kept pace. It was not like Ruby to avoid her. It was not like Lollie to pry. They put their arms around each other and walked together for the rest of the mile around the base of the tower, amid a view of surreal perfection: trees, rocks, blue sky, the far horizon, eagles, wildflowers, and peace. Ruby's heart was bursting with love for her family, and she also missed Mark. It even seemed more in the past than two weeks ago could possibly have been. She had not heard from Mark or Dan. Her mother smiled knowingly at Ruby, totally understanding the multifaceted feelings of life and love.

They found a quaint motel, stayed the night, toured the Battle of the Little Bighorn, traveled through the Bighorn Mountains, and zigzagged back to Tepid. They laughed, shared, and made new memories. They landed late in the evening back at Ruby's apartment, talking about their fun, pictures, seeing each other again soon; and the next morning, Rory and Lollie bade their good-byes. The place quieted down, and Ruby was glad to be home. Hopefully she'd dodged the newspaper episode, and it was forgotten. Ruby and Chloe had a little cleaning up to do, unpacking, washing the truck, and washing the smelly camp laundry.

Life once again seemed to settle down into near boredom. Ruby threw herself into her work and planned to finish several projects. Her computer was littered with e-mails from Jordan, suggestions, new clients, and promising new tasks. Chloe had piano practice, cross-country, gymnastics, sewing projects she'd attempted with her grandmother, reading to catch up on, and friends to squeeze in who'd missed her while she'd been gone with her dad. The Fourth of July parade was next weekend, and Lollie and Rory would be bussing back over for the festivities.

Chapter

18

MARK WAS FANTASIZING about Ruby. He could not stop fantasizing about Ruby. Here he was, in the middle of the predicted court battle, with the prosecutor asking him who the woman was in the photo taken by the paparazzi. His lawyer jumped up and said, "Don't answer that question!" Mark wasn't even on the witness stand, but the arrogant prosecutor was trying to goad him into some sort of irreversible reaction and disclosure. He innocently looked up at the prosecutor and shrugged, as if his own lawyer had given him no choice. He knew better than to incite a prosecutor. His lawyer asked for a recess, which was granted.

When they entered the back room of the court, Zane hardly let the door close before blurting, "What's wrong, Mark? You're not tracking, boy! You act like you could care less about what is going to happen to you. Your head is not in the game!"

"Oh ... I'll try to do better. Uh, what do you want me to do?" Mark tumbled out.

"You've got to act indignant! You've got to be pissed that they are accusing you of such atrocities!"

"Oh, sure, I can do that. I, uh ..."

"Get it together, then!" barked his defense attorney. "Now, I've gotta go piss."

Dan and Mark stood in the room after Zane had gone. "Geez, can't get my mind off her ..." confessed Mark, helplessly.

"I know," sympathized Dan. He was the only person sitting

behind the defense table (Mark had refused his parents' request to attend) and had more or less allowed himself into the back room of the courthouse without permission to speak to Mark. They walked separately from the room. Dan went out an exit before reentering the courtroom in order to deter anyone who may be watching he and Mark collaborating.

Nobody had thought it would come to this. Mark's company had always stood behind him and retained the best lawyers, but even they had not anticipated this event making it to an actual court trial. His lawyers had used every trick in the book to get him to settle—that is, pay a few damages, apologize, and go free. However, this judge, like a true anti-environmentalist, had decided there would be a trial. He was green and eager to throw the book at someone, anyone. He bent a few rules (and ears) to get this trial on the docket.

Mark still wasn't worried. He thought the group would handle it, and he thought constantly of Ruby and their flawless weekend together. Everything probably would have worked out if not for that damned picture. Dan had no idea who was in the vicinity taking pictures in the neighborhood. Dan stayed at Mark's house most of the time to produce the appearance of someone living there, and also to watch the place and deflect suspicious nose-poking. Neither had a clue who had taken the photo of Mark and Ruby driving off—and ostensibly sold it via the Internet. Both of them bolstered their determination to keep Ruby out of it.

Mark cocked his head toward the prosecutor, trying to look interested, and he inadvertently dredged up a humorous situation with Ruby. He bit his lip to cover the humor. *How I love that woman! How I want her! How I wish I could listen to her sweet voice right now in my ear.* He bit harder and tasted blood. He could not for the life of him get her out of his mind. He reached down on his thigh and gripped with all his might to cause enough pain to wipe off his smile, and he coughed to stifle the pain, drawing looks from Zane and the entire court. Then he pressed his hand to his forehead as if in deep thought. It worked ... for a few seconds. What would he do for the next two-plus weeks of this ghastly trial? He'd work on Dan getting him some pills of some sort. Maybe if he was sleepy ... No, he needed to be alert. *Oh, hell!*

Now the prosecutor announced a witness from Tepid Springs. It was the damned deputy sheriff. The deputy glowered at Mark as if saying, *You're gettin' yours, buddy!* He stepped up to the bailiff and swore on the Bible to tell the truth and nuttin' but the truth, so help him gawd ...

The prosecutor asked if he'd seen Mark before. The deputy went into extraneous detail about how Mark had first entered the Red Rock Cafe.

"Did he smell like smoke?"

"Nope, he just looked guilty, like he'd just committed arson somewheres, Your Honor."

"Did he have soot or ashes or burn marks, as if he'd been near a fire?"

"Nope, he just looked like he'd committed arson somewheres, Your Honor."

"Well, did he have matches on him. or reek of gasoline when you questioned him?"

"Nope, he just looked like he com—"

"Objection!" roared Zane, leaping a foot off the floor. Mark pinched off his smirk. Dan got up and eased out of the courtroom to guffaw in the men's room. "Yeah, yeah, Mr. Deputy. Will you please refrain from saying what you think he looked like? We're trying to establish the facts here, okay?"

"Yep, Your Honor."

"Also, deputy, I am not Your Honor. The Judge is."

"Yessir."

"Did you check his hands for residue of any accelerants?" continued the prosecutor.

"Yep, sir. I think so, sir ..."

"And?"

"There weren't none, sir."

"What *did* you check him for?"

"We just interrogated him, sir, and he just looked like he'd committed arson—"

The judge whacked the gavel. "Deputy, if you use that phrase again, I will hold you in contempt!"

"Yessir, Your Honor, sir."

The prosecutor said, "No further questions."

Zane stood and said, "No further questions, but reserve the right to call witness again." He then turned to Mark and whispered, "Whatever in hell were you doing in such a dipshit of a town?"

"Lookin' for love in all the wrong places ..." He was unable to resist another easy invitation Zane had just offered him, to drift to thoughts of Ruby.

The judge called a recess for the day. Court would resume at 9:00 a.m. Thursday, and then they'd recess for the weekend. Mark sighed in relief that the day was over, but he ached to see Ruby. His group was covering the costs for a secluded condo near downtown and the courthouse. Still, he was certain he was being surveilled, so he could not call or contact her. Dan departed too, and Mark was left to watch mind-numbing TV for another long, insufferable night. His computers had been confiscated; he was glad he had never mixed business with pleasure on those machines. The group had managed to maintain his reports at his work computer, because he always signed in under an alias. It would be nearly impossible for prosecutors to track him through that avenue.

Dan had an idea. Whenever one of the four friends ached, they pretty much all ached. He thought he'd call on Jim and Greg to help him create a diversion. Although the friends had never discussed Mark's activities, they could put two and two together and surmise the nature of Mark's profession. In order to sound plausible, if they were ever legally questioned or if it became necessary to bail him out, it would be easier to claim innocence if they hadn't specifically known of his missions. Why not cause some confusion? Dan dialed Jim first, and then Greg. They had "friends" ...

Chapter

19

RUBY LONGED TO hear Mark's voice, and she wondered how long this no-contact crap would last. She thought about him day and night and could not motivate herself to do anything productive. She felt herself sinking into some sort of female fit of self-chastisement for the wild, crazy weekend she'd recklessly enjoyed. It had been two whole weeks! In her mind only, she'd confided to her mother a half dozen times. She figured Mom knew anyway, but she could not bear the reality of the humiliation by sharing her secrets. She knew her mom would never say "*I told you so,*" but, still ... Ruby dialed the phone.

Lollie answered. "Hi, sweetie! We had such a great time visiting you and Chloe, touring, and seeing how well our favorite girls are doing! Chloe is getting to be such a beautiful young lady ..."

"Mom, I think we're coming down to visit you and Dad for the weekend. Are you busy this weekend?"

"This weekend? Again? Heavens, no! We'd love to see you, and we could take Chloe to see the prehistoric museum in Lincoln! But is everything all right?"

"Oh, yeah, sure! Sounds great! Okay, we'll see you in a couple of days, Mom. Thanks!" Ruby's mood was beginning to improve.

Lollie, being the perceptive mother that she was, slowly replaced the receiver and thought, *Uh-oh.* If they were coming down for a quick weekend, they would have to be back in

Tepid for the Fourth by Wednesday! *It sounds like Ruby has gotten herself in deep schmucky-schmuck!* Lollie pondered the recent questions Ruby had asked about her advertising career, among other subjects. What could be wrong? And who was that new man in Ruby's life? That was probably the real question.

Greg and Jim knew Mark was in court. They decided to meet that evening to brainstorm Dan's idea. They hadn't been together for several months and needed to reconnect anyway. Mark's defense team allowed short walks to alleviate the claustrophobia of the condo, but someone was always on his tail. Dan couldn't even come for a visit to help pass the time or be seen with him; Mark was certain the people following him were housed next door and most certainly had devices to eavesdrop. He kept the television loud, the radio blasting, and the toilet flushing. Sometimes he sang off-key, just to irritate and screech their amplifiers. Now and then, he knocked something against the wall to give their ears and brains a good rattle.

Many times Dan would have called Ruby on Mark's behalf to report the progress, but he could not chance the phone being answered by Ruby's child. He decided to write to her advertising company because the address was listed, and he'd make it appear to be business correspondence. He'd simply gave Ruby the telephone number of a disposable cell, which he would have for only one week. Then he'd write again and give her another new number for yet another disposable. It was all they could muster in the way of communication. He could not send the letter via any method but regular mail, in order to avoid attracting attention. Dan was from a very small Iowa town, and knew the ramifications of gossip and the rumor mill.

It was four days before Ruby got his number, and in fact, it was the day Ruby and Chloe had already left for Omaha.

Dan waited impatiently for Ruby to call, never guessing she may not be there. When the brotherhood finally met to collaborate, Greg and Jim were quickly filled in on Mark's troubles, women and otherwise. They began the debauchery of rescuing Mark from his funk. At first, Greg and Jim knew nothing of Mark's infatuation with a new relationship who lived out in the middle of nowhere... *the Dakotas?* They were stymied over Mark's most recent clandestine activities. Now, apparently, there was a beautiful woman in the mix! Just when things could not get more complicated! They'd certainly been out of touch; but part of that old contract joke was a sketchy romance loophole in which none of them would or could seriously interfere. At least, they all remembered that they'd agreed not to interfere. But perversely, they also included a rather archaic and chauvinistic belief that none of them would allow women to impact their resolve to maintain bachelor status or continue their sporting fun. Life was a mind-boggling paradox.

Actually, Dan had two ideas. First, the three friends would create a confounding travel plan that would facilitate getting Mark out of town for the night so they could at least reconnect, be brought up to speed, and be able to communicate beyond the long reach of the law. Plan B could only be discussed when they were all together and safely out of the city. Jim and Greg readily agreed to both plans and rearranged their schedules to help their buddy. They deluded themselves into thinking they were helping to fulfill the obligatory *'What are friends for'* issue. In reality, they were thrilled by the challenge of participating in a trifling, negligible fracas with authority. The friends' mantra as kids had been to thrive on the "boys will be boys" cliché and milk it for all it was worth. However, at this time of early middle age, they humorously and wickedly tweaked it to *'men will be boys'.* Growing up under a strong TV influence of the *A-Team*, they celebrated whenever a plan came together, and with glee, jumped in the ring. It was Friday night, and each craved an exciting game of cat and mouse.

The miles flew by down Highway 20 toward Omaha. Chloe slept, played her Nintendo DS, read, and hooked up to her music, which gave Ruby much-needed concentration on her recent fun and foibles. Billboards blurred past with all of their insipid messages and drivel. With every single one of them, her mind left its senses to dream, relive that weekend, and hope for quality time and a future with Marc—all the while interrogating her brain about the asinine craziness she could possibly be considering, in addition to questioning her career choice. She missed him terribly, and her heart flip-flopped. She sighed deeply. She yearned for the normalcy of Mom, Dad, home, and big-city life.

What was wrong with her? Just then, a sign crept by that touted something to the effect that all Americans deserved new cars every year. *What? A new car every year? Do they have any idea where all of those pieces and parts of old cars end up, and how many landfills it would take to dispose of the old models?* Ruby had over two hundred thousand miles on her truck, and it was still purring along like a kitten; she faithfully changed its oil every three months. She loved her truck and had no plans to trade it in any time soon. Outraged, she briefly entertained the idea of burning down the sign. Then she looked over at the innocent girl sitting in the passenger seat, smiling at her. She trashed that idea.

Her mind drifted back to Mark. *What possessed the man to start in that vocation, anyway? And how did he do it? How did he keep getting by with it?* Even thinking about arson led her thoughts to Mark—as if she could ever get him out of her mind for two whole minutes! *Drive on, girl, and just try to breathe!*

Chapter
20

MARC SAUNTERED OUT of the condo and heard a door behind him open and close. The feds were on his tail for sure. Without looking over his shoulder or acknowledging in any way that he knew he was being followed, he put on a good show of warming up for a long jog. Then he suddenly sprinted down the block between traffic—jaywalking—going in one store and out the back, moving into another store and out the front, and staying enough ahead of the suits to tantalize them. Suddenly, a car careened around a corner with Jim in the driver's seat. As Jim slowed down, Marc dove into the back seat. They were gone, *whiz-bang*, just like that. The hapless G men had not anticipated a trick like this, and they were not in the least prepared with a chase vehicle. They immediately crackled out the license plate and description of the car on their devices for a car to take over.

However, the friends had planned well. They quickly slipped down an open alley and switched vehicles. Now Greg was in the driver's seat, and all four of them were in the same car. The pickup car had only been a rental and would be retrieved by the rental company. If the rental guy got stopped and questioned, he'd been paid some hush money; he would be most happy to share info with the chasers: he knew absolutely nothing, and certainly not where that bunch of guys were headed.

"Great planning, guys. *Love it when a plan comes together.*

Let's go have some fun already!" scoffed Mark to his amazing friends.

For five minutes or better, they laughed and jeered at the men hired to report on Mark and said, "You should have seen the look on that guy's face when he stood there gawking that his captive had escaped!" Unfortunately, the detectives had been lulled into the notion that because Marc had no visitors, no family, and no contacts, the only activity he did was go out to jog. It was hilarious, and all of them felt like partners in crime who were ready to divvy up the spoils. They almost felt sorry for the poor guy, because he'd be required to answer to somebody higher up.

It didn't stop there. For yet another fifteen minutes, they created spoofs and entertained themselves by imagining the look on the detective's face when he discovered the get-away car safely returned to the nearby rental lot.

They hit Interstate 29 and got lost in the anonymity of traffic. They had freedom and fresh air. This adventure, however short, was so good for Mark. How could he thank his incredible friends for this bombshell? Wow! Not a word was mentioned about court, Mark's mission, or anything about the long-drawn-out trial and consequences. If he was truly going to be free for a number of hours, conversation about the situation was banned. They laughed, connected, bonded, celebrated, and enjoyed the present moments and evening ahead of them.

As far as Mark could ascertain, they were headed to Omaha and their "good old boys" college club. Dan was pleased how well this came off. He only regretted that he'd not heard from Ruby and could not get the lovers together; otherwise, this trip was perfect. Dan then passed the Cuban cigars around, and they continued down the easy highway with smoke drifting out of every window.

The closer Ruby drove to her childhood home, the shakier

her resolve became. How could her mom offer any advice if she didn't know what she was advising about? But she would not, break her promise to Mark. Ruby fondled the ring on her necklace; she ached to see Mark and find out what was happening with him. This no contact was much more difficult than she could imagine.

The miles clicked past. They hadn't gotten a very early start, and Ruby was not too happy about getting there toward dark. The trip was at least seven hours, and they probably needed to stop for a late lunch; knowing her Mom, there would be food, snacks, desserts, and many other excesses to greet them, so she did not want to hit the consumption too heavy.

Her thoughts were continuously in turmoil, and usually not far from the subject of Mark. But finally they turned into the long, tree-lined driveway where Rory and Lollie lived just outside of Omaha, and where Ruby and her brother had grown up. Chloe loved visiting her grandparents. They had redecorated her Mom's old bedroom to be Chloe's—the house being quite an old Victorian monstrosity. Chloe had explored every nook and cranny of the old homestead, including the barn. Jake's bedroom and Ruby's bedroom, now Chloe's, connected into a beautiful, bright, spacious upstairs solarium, which the entire family loved. Lollie had placed fresh lavender to perfume the place; growing flowers was one of Lollie's various hobbies. Rory was on the back deck, grilling up steaks and veggies in the near dusk.

They hugged all the way around time and time again. One would never believe this family had been together only one and a half weeks ago! Chloe and Ruby felt welcomed and special. They only had time to eat, clean up, and unpack before everyone was ready to crash for the night. No uncomfortable questions, silences, subjects, or anything. Just to bed for much-needed rest and relaxation. Breakfast promised to be another smorgasbord of Lollie and Rory's cuisine. Chloe could hardly wait; Ruby was already dreading the weight gain.

When everything settled down for the night, Ruby heaved a huge sigh of relief. She guessed that tomorrow would be one miserable marathon of pouring her heart out to her mother. Emoting about it was not the best way to relax, and finally exhaustion overcame her physically. She drifted off with thoughts, fantasies, and dreams of Mark being right beside her.

The men easily found their old clubhouse near the campus—not associated in any way with the university, but nostalgic just the same. Nearly the only choice for food and drinks were pizza and beer, which they plunged into without care or remorse. Talking continued far into the night; it was never about the court business, but that subject was always present in the background. Dan truly enjoyed seeing the load shed from Mark's shoulders, even if it was temporarily. Mark came out of his shell, joked, laughed, blew off his predicament, and demonstrated through his enjoyment of the evening his appreciation for their daring efforts to entertain him. What cool guys!

Ruby was never far from Dan's mind either. It was obvious how much Ruby and Mark belonged together, and Dan truly felt he'd let his friend down by not contacting her before this anticlimactic hiatus. His plan B involved getting them together, but it necessitated him being very cautious about reaching her. Dan smiled at Mark as he conjured up ideas in his head to achieve his ultimate goal.

The friends ate, drank, gabbed, reminisced, and told stories of long ago college days. They would not let the night close. When the bar closed, they took it to the next bar, and the next, always giving enough time between their drinking to recover before the next round. Finally, around four o'clock they'd experienced quite enough freedom and catching up, and they landed in their adjoining rooms in the hotel to sleep it off. Mark, who had to stay alert, did not get quite as soused as the rest of them, and he spent the remainder of his night—which was really morning—pining for Ruby.

"Pancakes! Homemade maple syrup! Real churned butter!" Rory was shouting from downstairs, which immediately woke up Chloe. She scrambled down the stairs knowing the incredible breakfast they would soon be enjoying.

Good mornings were exclaimed all around and the day was promising picture-perfect weather. Ruby descended a little less enthusiastically and queried whether there was coffee yet. Soon everyone was happily devouring the incredible pancakes and fresh fruit that Lollie had prepared for the loves of her life—her beautiful daughter and granddaughter. Breakfast was stretched into midmorning, and Rory tempted Chloe to check out the barn with him, feed the horses, and gather eggs. Also, they would crank up the four-wheeler and take a tour of the farm, leaving Lollie and Ruby to their mother-daughter time.

Ruby languished a while longer, appreciating her parents and their home. Then she joined the ritual of cleaning the kitchen. "Mom, you always do so much work whenever we come to visit!"

"Oh, that's no problem. We enjoy treating our girls to our specialties!"

"I just feel so pampered and lazy here, and you and Dad slave after us." Ruby was a little less stressed than when they'd arrived last night.

"Honey, I would go to the ends of the earth for your comfort and safety."

"I know, Mom. You're the best ever! I'm so lucky to have

you two as my parents, but especially you!" Ruby was humbled by her parents' care.

"Now, while Chloe's off somewhere, tell me what's gotten you so upset."

"Mom, it's going to be some time before you can meet him. Things are so horribly complicated right now, but hopefully it's being resolved as we speak. It just hurts sometimes to be in love ..."

"I was more than suspicious that that was what was going on, dearie. Yes, it does hurt. But if it's meant to be, then the two of you will find a way to accomplish it. Does Chloe know anything about this new man in your life?"

"No! I can't let her know. But I will tell you, she's got a man in *her* life, too!" Ruby and Lollie giggled.

"Love is so simple when you're eleven, going on sixteen!"

"True." Ruby knew how children in one-parent homes could become responsible so much earlier.

"Honey, just promise me you'll be careful, okay?" Ruby nodded. "And for what it's worth, if he's worth waiting for—and you say he is—you've waited this many years, so what will more waiting matter if it all turns out special in the end?" Lollie took Ruby into her arms for an encouraging and a caring embrace.

"Thank you, Mother. I knew you'd have the right thing to say to me. I love you so much!"

The women worked in the kitchen, cleaning up the breakfast meal, laughing, sharing, and planning for Italian cuisine for supper.

Mark and his buddies hung out at the mall on Saturday, went to a movie, and planned to find prime rib at a high-end restaurant for the evening before landing back at the hotel straight afterward, where they could most likely drink themselves silly in safety. Then on Sunday, they would mosey back toward Kansas City and drop him off near the condo where he could appear suddenly, jogging back to his room.

At one point during the shopping mall time warp, Mark had to get the question off his mind about Ruby. "Why couldn't you arrange for her to have been here with us—uh, me?" Marc looked like a sick puppy asking Dan that question, and it broke Dan's heart to tell him he had tried and it hadn't worked out. She hadn't answered his letter. Mark did express his appreciation for Dan being extremely careful. That was the single mention of Ruby, but it was definitely not the only thought of her. Mark's senses were consumed ruminating about his new squeeze and the only woman he would ever want for the rest of his life.

"Is there much of a chance of getting this trial over within the foreseeable future?" Dan asked.

"Sure wish, but not likely." Mark shook his head. "Seems like they are bent on bringing up the most confounding minutiae and rabbit tracks they can think of, to avoid the fact that there is no evidence!" They both groaned.

Ruby's brother and family showed up on Sunday morning to crash the party. Ruby was so happy to see him that she could not contain herself. They took a couple of walks around the farm, caught up on their families, and shared endearing childhood memories. This familial situation was a drug that Ruby needed in her life. Chloe and her younger cousins played throughout the big house and farm. The house was one 'big-kid' temptation for running—because of the bridge—which was actually a landing *and* quick getaway. The steps were configured to go up from the kitchen, across the landing, then back down into the living room, making for a constant carousel of kids chasing kids and having fun together.

Ruby and Jake hatched the idea to exercise the horses. As nature lovers, they had always gone to the Middle River, where it was shallow, rocky, and wild. Talk was not necessary; companionship was. Nature erupted all around: birds, wildflowers, trees, bunnies, and once in a while a den of foxes. Ruby filled up her soul with home, family, love, and memories. Hopefully, this would get her through some of the longing for a normal relationship with Mark.

On the way back to the farm, Ruby and Jake reminisced about their childhood, and how they loved nature and wanted to protect it. After reviewing this recollection and favorite part of her life with her brother, she opened a door just a crack in her mind and honestly grappled with the question of how she could have misguidedly pursued a career that was so diametrically opposed to her philosophy.

Jake simply said, "We've all been wondering," and smiled his disarming smile.

"Who's been wondering?" she upbraided him.

He gave her that little-brotherly eyebrow, to allow her to figure it out. The horses then required their attention, until they were brushed and fed. The siblings headed to the house with his tanned, strong arm resting on her shoulders. The entire family was gathered and greeted with to-die-for Italian waiting for them to appear. Everybody was in a jovial mood as mountains of food were consumed and enjoyed. They sat out around the patio fire ring, roasting marshmallows, making s'mores, and eating blueberry smudge pies. Jake's wife had brought sparklers for the kids. When they had all finally burned out, chaos finally resigned to peace and the comfort of crackling coals in the dying embers. Nobody wanted the evening to end. Ruby finally stood up and moaned as much from a full, satisfying meal as from everyone probably needing to go to bed so they could leave in the morning.

Lollie, who was exhausted by then, chirped happily, "Yeah, we've got to get cleaned up and packed to head back to the Springs in three days for the Fourth, and Chloe marching in the band!" Once again, hugs were exchanged and promises made to visit soon, and they all retired for the night.

"Ugh!" was Ruby's reaction to Sunday's early morning dawn hours. The weekend was over, and work awaited back in the Springs. There was the long drive back and much to do to get ready for her parents' visit in a few days. She stretched, briefly mused about what Mark might be doing, splashed through the shower, and hauled her stuff downstairs toward the aroma of percolating coffee and the noise of happy people sitting around the dining room table.

Lollie hopped up to grab a cup for Ruby and fill it. Ruby said, "No, Mother, you've done enough! Chloe and I will head out so you can enjoy the day with Jake; we'll hit the Starbucks near the gas station, where I can fill up. I think I rolled in on fumes two days ago."

Lollie hesitated. "Well, uh, last night Chloe told me she wanted to stay here and come back with us in two days?" She checked quickly for Ruby's reaction.

"Uh, okay, I don't see why not. Sure, she can ride back with you guys."

"She wanted to connect with her cousins; they had so much fun yesterday. Are you sure?"

Ruby laughed. "Oh, yeah, go ahead. Maybe I'll get some peace on the way back by myself!" Everyone said good-bye. Ruby threw her gym bag into the back of the truck and waved all the way down the driveway.

The "men will be boys" group thought it best to get back the evening before court, which was scheduled for 9:00 on Monday. A plan was rehearsed on how to get Mark back with as little observance as possible. They were gassing up, buying energy drinks, and preparing for the two hundred miles back to Kansas City.

Ruby pulled in behind them at the same gas station, next

to the Starbucks, to slip once more into the ladies' room. On the way in, she observed two nice-looking gentlemen leaning against a car and glancing at her. She thought, *Not a chance, guys. I've already got someone.* She chuckled to herself how it seemed as soon as she decided on one man, all sorts of prospects presented themselves. *How could they even notice me? I'm grungy and sure haven't taken much time with my hair or makeup."* They smiled approvingly anyway; she tossed her head and went in.

Mark and Dan moved from the refrigerator section to the front to pay for the gas and drinks. Then they went out to join Greg and Jim.

Ruby came out of the restroom and lingered at the checkout counter, looking at some fancy cigarette lighters.

Mark, who was constantly thinking of Ruby, noticed the SD license plate outside and fondly wondered, *"What the ...? What are the chances?"*

Jim and Greg were tripping over each other to describe to Dan and Mark the beautiful lady they had just lusted all over.

"Yeah, yeah, yeah! Sounds like one in a million!"

Jim said, "You'll see when she comes out! We're not lying! Maybe we can just sit over there behind the kiosk and watch ..."

"You guys are perverts!" teased Mark, and Dan totally agreed.

"Yes, we are!" Jim and Greg admitted unashamedly.

They drove over to the Starbucks a few hundred feet away, facing the station, and began disputing who was going to pay for coffees. Dan, in the front seat, saw her first. "Hey, lover boy, isn't that ...?"

Already tipped off with the license plate, Mark was in the back seat but jerked up from thumbing through his wallet. "Impossible!" For the next few minutes, he could hardly concentrate. The coffee attendant was patiently waiting for their persnickety orders: low fat, skim milk, no sugar, et cetera.

"Cancel the orders! Jim, drive over to that purple truck—quick, before she gets away!"

"Serious? Are you two sure that's her?"

Dan said, "Yeah, without a doubt!" Mark was frantic and ready to launch himself from the back seat.

"Wait! She's pulling around behind us!" He quickly ducked out of sight. Dan edged one eye around the headrest and confirmed it was Ruby, who pulled in behind them at the coffee kiosk.

Mark told Jim to order a white mocha double shot and handed over a generous tip for the gal. He said to give the coffee to the lady in the truck behind them, and to tell her it was sent with all his love to Mrs. Smythe. Mark could barely keep a lid on his excitement. "Did you plan this, guys? 'Fess up!" They swore it was a shocking surprise—even Dan the Planner! When they got their coffees, Jim pulled the car ahead fifty feet and idled.

Ruby drove to the window, digging in her purse and getting ready to order. Instead, she was handed a white mocha with the message from Mark. She spun her tires up to the waiting car and braked. Mark stepped out of the car like she could drive straight into his arms. She rolled down the window almost cautiously, and Mark leaned in and whispered, "Take a drink. I want a taste of white mocha." When he was finished, he added, "And you."

While he was kissing her, his hand reached in and opened the truck door to let her out and into his whole-body embrace. Neither of them cared who watched, honked, drove by, or guffawed from the Kansas City vehicle. The men in the car tried their best to look away, but they relished the happiness of their friend. Nobody was sure when or if the embracing would ever stop, so Mark's buddies emerged from the car to be properly introduced. Ruby shyly pulled away from Mark's kiss with all of his friends drooling, but she did not leave his side. The lovers squeezed hands tightly, and Mark's arm encircled her waist. Then he peeked down the front of her blouse and noticed, approvingly, the ruby ring clinging between her breasts.

"Where do you think you're going, Mrs. Smythe?"

"With you guys, maybe." They all laughed and agreed that she could go with them, stay with them, be with them. It was evident that Mark's friends approved of Ruby.

"This is so unbelievable! Impossible! Unfeasible!" Everybody continued exclaiming.

"Well, now what?" asked the pragmatic Dan. "Are we going to make it back to court in Kansas City?" He felt horribly responsible if they were unable to pull these two apart, in order to still have enough time to drive back to the city. No way would Dan jeopardize Mark's success in court. He would judge *himself* to be in contempt. Just couldn't happen.

A cacophony of ideas ensued. How late could they make themselves scarce and give these lovers as much time as possible together? Everyone wanted to fix the problem. Neither Ruby nor Mark wanted to leave each other's side. Ruby was so thankful that Chloe had stayed with her parents. At least, that embarrassing detail worked to her advantage. Oh, what would she have done? How could she have explained Mark to Chloe? How could she have ignored Mark in order to protect Chloe? That situation was beyond a simple solution.

Mark and Ruby were no help at all; it seemed all they could do was beam at each other in euphoric admiration. Mark was first to reenter reality.

"I don't want to delay Ruby getting home too late tonight, and I can't risk losing this trial if I hope to see her again," he stated sadly.

Dan had explained to Ruby that he would be contacting

her through snail mail and had tried to reach her before they shot out on this venture.

"That's not all. My parents will be monitoring my trip back home as well," she reported. "And even though daylight is longer now, I do like getting home before dark... there's a lot of wide-open country out there."

"Okay," Dan said. "I've got one day left on this phone, which I'll give to you, Ruby, and you two can talk all the way home. Then you'll have to destroy it somewhere on your way back, preferably, in two different towns, hours apart, with a hammer—no fingerprints."

"Or we can purchase two more new disposables ..."

"And get two extra phones so we don't have to wait until snail mail delivers the numbers ..."

Suggestions and plans continued. Mark and Ruby wanted to stay padlocked to each other.

One of the men offered that they could wait if the lovers wanted to get a room. Mark immediately busted that idea, "No—too sleazy."

Finally, Ruby said, "This amazing coincidence is enough—just being able to see you, touch you, talk to you, and know that our previous weekend together was real. This is going to have to be enough until you are cleared from these charges." She sighed. "I will be patient, and Dan can write to me."

"Babe, you are so sweet. Thanks for understanding. I want you more than the world, but for your and Chloe's safety, I have to get this debacle behind me."

She reluctantly agreed and wanted to get on the road before she burst into tears. It had been so incredible being held tightly against Mark's muscular body. The rest of them agreed. Dan sighed a deep breath of relief, thinking, *Wow! That was close!*

Mark picked up a borrowed phone and dialed the disposable. It rang in Ruby's hand. They all gave Ruby a hug good-bye and told her how perfect she was for Mark. She told them it was nice meeting them, even though she did not care for the initial *appreciative* looks they had given her earlier. They laughed and said, "How were we supposed to know?" She immediately forgave them. Then she answered the ringing phone and hopped into her truck.

"Hi, Mrs. Smythe!"

"Hi yourself, Mr. Smythe! Where have you been? I've missed you." Both vehicles took off in opposite directions. Ruby couldn't bear to wave good-bye, and she was drenched in tears as soon as she headed north. Mark was quiet and contemplative as they headed south. *How close they came to missing each other!* Now he needed to get serious and get this trial over with. Maybe he could help the prosecution by just confessing, serving his time, and getting on with his life. All he wanted in life was Ruby. He knew Dan would think he was stupid to do such a thing, but he wanted to be with Ruby, *authentically.* Within the space of three-four hours, after stopping for a quick bite of food outside of his jail, they were soon coasting up to a corner three blocks away from the court condo, hopefully undetected.

The conversation had continued between Ruby and Mark for many sweet miles, until the batteries in both of their phones expired.

Ruby was busy with another project. She had arrived at the offensive sign that encouraged every person to buy a new car every year, and unfortunately, she was in the mood to break the law—to wield a slashing strike against affluence—for Mark's sake and all the risks he'd taken. The highway was deserted—no houses visible, and not another human being for miles. *Why not?* If Mark could engage in removing useless detritus from the scenery, why couldn't she? Chloe was safely with her parents. *What could it hurt?*

She stepped out of the truck; gathered some dry sticks,

leaves, and litter; and slowly stepped down into the ditch by the wooden pole of the sign. She piled the kindling up around the post and lit it with her new pink cigarette lighter. The dry material flared and caught immediately. She sheltered her face from the smoke and backed up out of the ditch to her truck, where she took off in a gravel-spitting sprint.

All the way back to the Springs, she thought of clues she may have left behind: tire tracks, footprints, hair, DNA on the gathered bits and pieces, eyewitnesses ... Could anyone have possibly seen me? Had any cars driven past while I was crouched down in the ditch getting the fire started? Did they see my license plate number? With her heart pounding out of control, she could not accurately remember. What if Chloe found out? What if her parents found out? Geez, what if Mark found out?

Chapter

21

RUBY DROVE, NERVOUS and guilty, trying to justify her shame and crime! *Oh, what is wrong with me? Am I out of my mind?* Then, she belatedly wondered what Mark would think. She was surprised that she truly cared what he thought! Then she finally had to admit to herself that he would definitely not be pleased.

By the time she drove into the parking space at her apartment, she was exhausted, mentally weary, and didn't give a dog's damn. She went straight to bed with a bottle and three Advil.

Ruby didn't see Dan's letter until morning. She gave it a toss because it was obviously after the fact. *Time to get on with life ... time to get on with whatever!* Ruby made coffee, tidied her apartment; threw laundry in the machine, and slogged into her studio to the pile of work awaiting her there. She had switched on the light to make it look like everything was back to normal. The mailbox was full; the answering machine was full of messages. She doctored her coffee into a white mocha, not wishing to trot over to the café, and slouched into her chair to think about Mark.

Hours later, she was still there, thinking about Mark. Every now and then, she gave a great sigh and second-guessed herself. She knew that Mark would be in court right about now. She wondered when she would hear from Dan again. After one more string of profanities, she dragged herself out of her chair and into her studio—just as someone knocked on the door.

The post master saw she was home and ran a Fed -Ex package over to her as he headed to his lunch break. Ruby tore into it. She had two new phones, a letter from Mark, new phone numbers to call Dan, contact numbers for two new trusted friends—Jim and Greg—and a fake contract of bachelorhood torn in half! Ruby laughed until her face ached. She fantasized how the four of them planned to have a package waiting for her arrival home. Wow, how could this ever end? Never would she allow it to end.

Then she caught sight of one more item of great importance: an itinerary. Dan would pick her up, drive her to a small airport, and fly her to some exotic location again. This time, she would have time and the wherewithal to make arrangements for Chloe. With this optimistic information, she set herself to work so she'd be ready whenever Mark beckoned her, hopefully, when the trial was over.

Court recessed at noon. The entire morning was bogged down with the magnitude of Mark's errant absence over the weekend. Zane must have had a dizzying weekend as a result, because the feds had contacted him to locate Mark. Zane was definitely not happy and refused to speak to Mark. Dan had feared this all along. Zane appealed to the judge that because Mark was back on time, why did it matter? The judge was in no mood to be trifled with, and he was loudly affirmed by the prosecution. At precisely one o'clock, court resumed. The morning was wasted, however; it fell by the wayside for lack of being able to make a federal case out of his absence. Mark spent the next four stupefying hours committing to memory the delicious taste of white mocha from Ruby's sweet lips.

The defense dug up a procession of character witnesses for Mark: co-workers, neighbors, ministers, volunteer organizations, Greenpeace, golf partners, and more. They went all the way back to his Boy Scout leader. Then the prosecutors had their heyday. It seemed not too many people were all that upset or negative about Mark Smythe—a big disappointment for the prosecution. First day in court: done!

Mark slowly walked back to his condo, realizing that short interim with Ruby was a tantalizing taste of what awaited him and *how many more insufferable days of this miserable trial.* He flung himself on the bed and stayed there all night— no TV, no jog, no Ruby... just torturous thoughts of her. He didn't even flush the toilet. The only salvageable idea about this first evening back in the condo alone, and court today, was that next door the PIs might be seduced into thinking he'd given them the slip again because it was so quiet. Of course, they couldn't rap on his door, or else he would know he was being tailed. He didn't get up until the next morning. However, he did come to the realization that if he didn't take control, this dumb trial may very well last the rest of his life. He entered court with a purpose and a plan.

Later that afternoon, the newspaper whacked the door, and Ruby slipped out to pick it up. She brought it in, sucking in her breath at the headlines.

Arson Suspected in Small Nebraska Town

> A fire was deliberately started in a ditch just outside the city limits of Norfolk, Nebraska, on Sunday morning. Because of the rash of fires, lately the federal marshals have been contacted to help solve these hate/vandalism crimes. Near the scene was found a pink pearl cigarette lighter ostensibly, belonging

to a woman. However, officials have not ruled out delinquents or other parties. There is a case being tried presently in Kansas City. Mr. Mark Smythe, the alleged arsonist, could not have been the culprit because he has been under house arrest for months.

A reward is being offered. If you have any information regarding this new rash of crime in this location, please contact your local police department.

Ruby's heart skipped a beat as she instinctively searched for her pink cigarette lighter. She could not find it. *Oh, no! Was I that stupid that I left evidence so blatantly? Geez! Why didn't I just leave my business card? Well, if we both go to jail, I hope they'll allow us to be together.* Again, she questioned why she'd done such a crazy thing. She kind of regretted it, but she didn't regret the strike against corporate affluence. It seemed that this fire not only scorched the billboard into ruin, but it became a massive grass fire that went up and down and across the highway for miles due to the wind being an unfortunate factor. No other significant damage was done, but it did hinder traffic for hours, with cars trying to crawl their way through the heavy smoke. There were several fender benders, but nobody was physically injured. One crazed animal was struck—a bawling, wandering calf that had slipped under a fence.

Ruby asked herself, *Whatever possessed me?* She wondered whether she should just crash into the sheriff's department and confess, get it over with. She realized that she would never make a successful criminal—not with her nervous, overdeveloped sense of guilt!

Dan called. It was so nice to hear a friendly voice, and

she felt such genuineness from Dan. His tone was soothing, understanding, and reassuring. Ruby was vulnerable, lonely, and missing Mark, and she immediately confided in him regarding her lawless activities.

The phone was quiet.

"That was you?" Dan was thoroughly unreadable. "I ... I don't know what Mark will say ..." Then he was incredulous. "Oh, no. Dear Ruby, dear god, you didn't!"

Up to this moment, Mark, Dan, and the other two thought Ruby was flawless and incapable of wrong-doing. Ruby felt like she'd let Dan down, and probably Mark as soon as he found out.

"Ruby, I'm not going to pretend. I will be obligated to tell Mark. Actually, I saw it on the news already, and I would imagine he did too. But it never would have ever in a million years occurred to me or him, that our sweet darling would have done it! Oh, golly!"

Ruby became irritated at how Dan was acting like an errant schoolboy and seemed to be half scared of Mark. "Sorry I told you, Dan. I sure didn't want to implicate you in any of my illegal schemes."

"Yeah, that's okay, I guess. It's just that Mark and I have already had a discussion about it, and it will only be a matter of time before Mark finds out anyway. See, he already knows that his group did not authorize it. So either it was random, or was some kid playing around. But this I guarantee: you will never be able to keep it from him. Nobody can hide anything from him! I've never been able to conceal anything from him. He's got a sixth or seventh sense when figuring out people. Guess you've got to, in order to be in the clandestine activities that he is. Sorry, sweetie."

Ruby's heart was in her throat. She dared not ask how upset Mark would be. She was reasonably sure she didn't want to know.

"Listen, Ruby. I called for a different reason, but I'd better get this info to Mark right away, before he assumes it."

"But, please, Dan. Tell me how he would know if you didn't tell him."

"First, he had noticed and then mentioned that you had a pink cigarette lighter, knowing you don't smoke. Second, the fire was on the route you took to go home. Third, you didn't have your daughter with you. Fourth, he actually joked after he'd heard about it that maybe it was you, but he was *only* joking. One look at my face or yours, and he'll immediately know. Oh, I'm just so sorry!"

Ruby was nearly ill. This yanked her decades backward into the constant nagging conflicts of and in and around relationships.

"I'll give him a call, okay, sweetheart? I'll call you back in a jiff!" Dan hung up.

Ruby nearly threw the phone back at the wall. This would be the first test of their compatibility—or not. If he would condemn her for doing the very thing that he was being tried for in court ...

The disposable phone rang.

"He laughed!" Dan didn't even say hello. He simply reported that Mark had laughed himself silly. Both of them were extremely relieved.

"Oh ..." Ruby was clenching her chest. She could not lose this man whom she loved.

"Ruby? Still there?"

"Uh, yes, I'm here ..." Ruby rested her cheek against the wall to cool her feverish forehead. She would not be able to continue with a relationship built on conditional love. It had to be all or nothing the second time around. She did not wish to live with depression and never measuring up to expectations that were not even her own! She couldn't handle unrealistic expectations that *she* would never think of imposing upon another human being.

"Got good news too." Dan was trying to cheer her up. "Did you receive the mail?"

"Yes, I got your message!" She didn't know whether she was free to talk on the phone.

"Good! We're going to try to spirit him out of the city again, and we'll fly soon." Dan was also being extremely vague and careful. "I will call you as soon as I know, okay?"

"Sure!"

"Gonna let you go now. Don't worry about anything—it's all going to work out. I just know it! Okay?"

"Okay, bye."

Ruby knew all chance of sleep had gone out the door, and she dove into her work with a vengeance. By 2:00 a.m., she was weary to the point of rest—maybe not sleep, but hopefully rest. Ruby smiled at remembering Rory constantly saying, "No west for the ricked!"

With Zane ticked at him, Ruby now in shaky trouble (Mark may have laughed, but he was still going to shake her silly when he next got his hands on her), Dan absent with his own business, and Mark's own inability to concentrate, this trial promised to be the trial of this century. He had to get with some people to work out a deal. He beckoned Dan to get a meeting set up with his Group. Court was called to order.

The judge had a few words today. "Folks, I don't believe in wasting my time. Frankly, I don't mind wasting other people's time, but this case is going to have to proceed with significantly more speed, or I'm declaring a mistrial. I might even dismiss all charges."

Mark could only hope.

"This has been postponed and prolonged and sabotaged to the point of ludicrousity."

Mark and Zane looked at each other. *Was that even a real word?* So the greenhorn of a judge was also getting bored!

"I'm going to do something unconventional, maybe unheard of, and try to facilitate some relevant information. Prosecution and defense are both going to declare the extent of their evidence, and the court will decide if we even have a case."

Unbelievable! Why didn't he do this to begin with? Zane was about to ask to approach the bench and inquire, but he stopped himself. Wouldn't that action continue to prolong it? The judge said court would adjourn until one o'clock, so defense and prosecution could prepare to approach the bench. If they agreed, they would have one day, and only one day, to present their evidence. Mark knew he would be busy communicating with Zane and the firm, and the days would go faster. They hurriedly exited for lunch. Now, Mark would have a chance to tell Zane to throw in the towel: he'd confess, get the case over and done with, and move on with his life. Now, ironically, his life may consist of keeping Ruby out of trouble. What a delicious thought!

By one o'clock, after having skipped most of their lunch in lieu of arguing, Zane and Mark entered court and promptly ignored each other. Zane had nearly blown them out of the restaurant, yelling that he didn't take cases so he could throw in the towel. He took cases to win! Mark tried to appeal to him that it was Mark's life. Zane hotly retorted that if he wasn't smart enough to save his own ass, it was a good thing he had an attorney who would.

The best surprise of all, however, was that the judge adjourned court until after the Fourth of July, until the next Monday. Mark contacted Dan on the way out of the courthouse.

By Tuesday evening, Chloe and Ruby's parents had arrived back in Tepid, just in time for Chloe to set out for marching band practice for the parade. Lollie and Rory relaxed and talked on and on about their gifted grandchildren and the exhausting fun they'd had over the last two days.

"You know, it's not really so far a distance to travel out here—just the best part of a day."

"And it goes so fast with kids in the car, don't you think, dearie?"

"Of course, Mom. Chloe and I have a lot of fun traveling together." Then she winced, which only served to remind her of her recent bonfire. Ruby knew full well that it would never have happened if Chloe had been in the car.

"Just think: in a few years, she might be driving you!" All three enjoyed laughing (and scaring themselves) at the prospect.

More seriously, Lollie said, "I'd read a blurb about a fire along Highway 20 before we came north, and we actually drove past it on our way to your house, Ruby!"

One eyebrow quirked up in question as Ruby continued stirring the iced tea.

They decided to grill burgers rather than go to the Redrock. Ruby had no intention of exposing herself to whatever might be the most recent drama from that direction. She did wave whenever she spotted Marcia, just to look like she was not avoiding the place. Rory departed to pick up Chloe, and Ruby had a chance to mention to Lollie that she may need Chloe to go back home with them for a few days.

"Really, so soon? Well, fine, honey.! We'll take Chloe anytime you need us to!" She waited for an explanation, which wasn't forthcoming.

Finally, Ruby simply said, *"Him."* Lollie nodded knowingly.

The burgers were ready by the time Rory and Chloe returned home, and supper was simple and splendid. They sat together on the patio, knowing there would be no peace with all the firecrackers going off throughout the night.

The disposable rang at Ruby's house. Dan told Ruby he would pick her up late evening on Wednesday, and he asked whether she would be able to 'take care' of her daughter... finding a sitter. She said yes and then raised eyebrows again to her mother. She paused and explained that she would be back by Sunday evening. Lollie nodded in conspiratorial agreement.

Wednesday morning was all about the parade, getting Chloe ready, and heading to the parade lineup on time. In the process, Chloe almost forgot her instrument. Then Ruby and her folks arranged chairs and placed them right on the street where the parade would glide by. The parade went fairly fast when it finally got started, coming down the Veteran's hill, around the Plunge, and on to downtown. Chloe was adorable, marching and trying to ignore Lollie taking pictures. Ruby cringed when the sirens went by; their only contribution was splitting the sound barrier and her mounting stress headache.

How was she going to get everything ready that she would need in order to spend time with Mark? How their initial meeting was going to be after she'd petulantly disappointed him, remained to be seen.

Lollie, being complicit and sensitive to Ruby's plans, suggested they leave shortly after lunch. Chloe put up no huge opposition, because she and Grammie would be going to the mall in Omaha to shop for school clothes.

Ruby was left to take care of no one but herself. She relaxed in a hot tub of herbal bath oils. Then she stuffed clean jeans, a sweatshirt, several femmie blouses, and her navy dress that Mark liked into her overnight bag ... along with Mark's brilliant ring, now displayed where it belonged. Ruby had caressed her ring tightly in her fist and up against her lips many times as she dreamed and longed for Mark.

Dan had been in town all day and had watched the parade.

He calculated his part of the trip carefully to ensure there were no mistakes. He mixed well into the throngs of tourists and idled patiently until nearly dark. He knocked on her door and, like the gentleman that he was, escorted her to his rented economy car. They drove to the Springs airport. The plane was checked and ready. They took off without any glitches and hopped to another small airport nearby in Gordon. They picked up Mark almost in a touch 'n' go, and every detail was conducted smoothly.

Mark leaped up into the plane and grabbed Ruby without regard to Dan's presence. After embracing her in a long, passionate kiss, he suddenly took both of her upper arms in his strong hands and bellowed, "Don't you ever burn down another sign! Okay? Please, Ruby! I do not want you in that kind of danger again! Okay? Please, darling."

Chapter

22

STILL SWOONING FROM his hungry kissing, Ruby was then taken aback and shocked by Mark's brusqueness. She searched his face for answers to questions she was too discombobulated to ask.

"Lots of people despise environmentalists. They'd sooner shoot them than bother! Ruby, you must promise me right now!"

She managed to solemnly whisper, "Okay, but I thought you laughed about it. Uh, I thought you considered it funny."

"I did. I thought it was precious. But that doesn't mean I want you to do it ever again, okay? Do I have your promise?" Mark pressed her into answering and touched her finger tenderly to find his ring. He kissed the ring and then tried to gobble up three of her fingers. He looked very serious but slightly smiled.

"I don't know what got into me. I'll never plan to do it again. Sure, I promise ..." She choked it out and wondered if he had a tendency to be bossy or controlling like this all the time. Although she nearly fainted at his caring passion for her well-being, Ruby enjoyed her independence and would never surrender to any man the right to make her own decisions, right or wrong.

She could not bring herself to pull away from him. However, she said, "Mark, I am not apologizing."

Mark burst into wild, uncontrollable laughter. He

continued laughing at her expense for several minutes and spouting off about it to Dan.

"Oh, that is so hilarious! Oh, Ruby, you are a stitch, which is why I love you so much! Did you hear that, Dan? Oh, boy! She isn't apologizing! What a kick!" And on and on and on, the lovers bantered.

"Yeah, I caught that! Just for the record, I observed absolutely no remorse!"

Still, Mark could hardly contain himself, and he pulled Ruby ever closer. Mark growled deep down into her smooth, irresistible neck. "I know you did not apologize. And also for the record, Mrs. Smythe, I would never ask you to apologize!" Then he seriously added, "Genuine apologies are never forced or coaxed. Besides, I never said you did anything wrong. ... Well, *technically* the law says it's wrong. I don't happen to agree, but that's beside the point. I am simply begging you not to copycat this thing and mess up our future together. I don't want to waste another minute in court trying to prove anything right or wrong about destroying offensive billboards. I just want to be with you for every minute of the rest of my life. Now, do you get my reasoning? Because I am not apologizing either!"

Mystified, Ruby agreed and allowed him to continue kissing her. Dan was busy at the controls of the plane and ignored them.

Ruby wanted to pound Mark, but it was too delicious having him kiss and caress her. *Call me weak!* screamed her brain. She loved where she was at this moment, going who knew where with this incomparable man.

Literally and figuratively, she was flying high in Mark's arms. Soon he excused himself to assist Dan wherever he could. She hung between their two seats and held on to Mark's shoulder. He loved her touch and placed his hand on top of hers.

Several hours later, they landed on a small grass airstrip in the dark. The luminous full moon lit the strip enough that Ruby thought she saw the silhouette of mountains. Soon they were in a ranch house and were being introduced to some of Mark's relatives. He was describing how he'd escaped his house arrest again. Even with the late hour, all sorts of snacks and drinks were offered.

Ruby had had no idea how sleeping arrangements would shake out; but it was not long before her head fell against Mark's shoulder amid raucous laughter and talking far into the night. Without waking, she was carried into bed and gently covered. Someone removed her shoes.

The next thing she knew, brilliant sunshine and a gorgeous day lit up a pretty room with ruffled curtains, and she had a thick, homemade star quilt piled on top of her. A cool breeze drifted in the window, rearranging her hair across her face. She was sleeping alone and had no idea of the time.

Vaguely, she could hear the sounds of a busy household several rooms away. She got up, tiptoed to the bathroom, and discovered she was still in most of the clothes in which she'd arrived. She tidied herself, lassoed her hair into an uncontrollable do-flop, changed her blouse, and prepared to find the morning clamor—and strong coffee.

Mark was very aware of Ruby waking up. He'd been listening for her, and he brightly announced her when she peeped around the wall. "Hey, everybody, Sleeping Beauty is up!"

Ruby was embarrassed but joined them on the sunny porch with a sideboard of ranch breakfast and coffee. Julie's kids were up and out doing chores, her husband, Chad, was leaning back in his chair, and Dan and Mark were doing their best to relay the absurdities of the trial. It was comfortable, cozy, relaxed, and pristine.

The view out of the breakfast sunroom was postcard

perfect: rolling hills and valleys, flawless sky from horizon to horizon, purple mountains with snowcaps in the distance, and a clear, fast-moving stream several hundred feet from the porch. Evergreen trees grew in colonies to the left and right, in the near and far distance. It was breathtakingly beautiful.

"Is this Montana?" Ruby innocently asked.

Everybody simultaneously roared.

Mark, aided in her embarrassment, "No, it's heaven!" Then a second round of laughter and agreement ensued.

"Just pass the coffee, please," Ruby said, allowing herself to be the butt of their jokes. How could anyone be in a bad mood with this splendor surrounding one's residence? She marveled continuously and exclaimed accordingly. Deer could be seen in the distant trees. A little family of baby skunks played with the cats. An eagle's nest was visible, and several were soaring through a few small puffy clouds and around the skyline.

Julie said they would go visit her gardens and fill the birdfeeders. Also, they could take a hike in the woods this afternoon, if Ruby wished. Ruby was thrilled at the opportunity; she'd felt like her exercising regimen had suffered the last few weeks, with her trips back and forth to Omaha.

Mark was in the mood to tease her and laughingly said, "Julie, Ruby has been picking up some bad habits from me."

"Oh, no!" cried Julie. "Do *not* let my cousin suck you into breaking the law, dearie!"

Ruby watched the banter between Mark and Julie and marveled over their familial friendship and kinship.

Ruby ate until she was gorged and then declared to Julie how vitally important for her hips it was that they take that hike. The gals started the cleanup, and the men stepped right in to help. Julie tolerated their help for a little while, but then sent them packing; there were plenty of chores to go around—elsewhere.

Chad good-naturedly announced, "Off to the barn to muck out stalls!" It was a toss-up as to whether Dan or Mark groaned the loudest.

Julie did not very often get the company of another woman, and she was going to monopolize and relish every second. They talked and shared like sisters. When the kitchen and breakfast room were sparkling, they got ready to go have their fun—which translated—meant peace and quiet with a break from fooding.

Julie mentioned that Ruby could borrow anything that she forgot or did not bring. They were about the same size in everything, down to their long, curly, untamed hair. In a matter of twenty minutes, they were spruced and ready to tackle the hike. They would start out on the four-wheelers to get to the trail faster. They parked the machines and set off into the wild perfection of the Montana woods.

Ruby briefly recalled one of her and Mark's very first conversations, when he vaguely mentioned visiting his cousin in Montana. *So it was true! This is really special for him to bring me here! Almost like meeting the family.* She loved him more for it. Ruby turned around and around in circles, looking up at the wide, blue sky—true to the state motto. Then she sprinted to catch up to Julie.

They climbed the trail and went over logs and rocks, dainty white and yellow woodland flowers struggling for survival between grasses, bushes, and thickets. In the space of an hour, they reached a clearing and an overhang of rocks that had probably stood guard over the valley for eons. Breathing heavily, they lounged on the smooth part of the sun-warmed rocks to rest and ruminate.

"There are no words to describe this beauty, Julie," Ruby whispered reverently.

"I know. You just let it pervade your soul. I try to get up here at least once a week to reenergize and refuel."

Across the valley, they saw a mountain lion. Ruby thought it was sleek, lithe, and beautiful, with sinewy muscles that flowed when it moved. Had it been near, she would have liked to pet him. Oddly, it made her think of Mark and how much in love with him she was; he moved with as much fluidity as that lion.

It was then that she noticed Julie packed a .22 pistol. Julie saw where Ruby's eyes were focused. "Only if the cat attacks. A lot of people kill them as soon as they spot them, but we never do. We figure we are invading their habitat. But he's a long way away. I was certainly hoping we would see one in the wild."

"Just incredible, girlfriend. Thank you." Ruby mused over the undomesticated-ness of this wild place. Ruby did not relish the possibility of seeing a bear, even from a distance. There was no lack of wildlife all throughout their hike. The hills were definitely alive with the sound of nature and activity ... as it was meant to be.

Ruby chuckled while thinking about burning down the sign. Then she explained to Julie that the message of the sign was for everyone to have a new car every year!

"Bombastic! I don't blame you a bit for burning it. Sometimes we almost forget out here that we are still part of a greedy, backstabbing, affluent, spoiled-rotten society that thinks only of acquiring and accumulating and getting more. We all get so dependent on our creature comforts that we actually destroy what we're trying to achieve, which is peace, goodness, and love."

Ruby snickered. "We sound like the sixties, don't we? Let's go tie-dye something!" They both shrieked with laughter and started back down the trail, arm in arm.

The men, who were finished with various ranching jobs and were every bit as dirty and sweaty as if they'd mucked out the barn, were wandering around and listening to each other's stomachs growl. They heard the four-wheelers from miles away. Chad calmed Mark and Dan by grabbing a plate of cookies and making more coffee. The girls were near, the men chauvinistically smiled at each other. Lunch was on its way!

Ruby was blessedly tired but also revived by the exercise and jaunt into the cathedral of nature. After parking the four-wheelers out front, hopping off, and dragging herself up the three steps to the breakfast room, she practically fell into Mark's arms.

The men had been sitting back, watching the gals bounce off the machines, dusting themselves off, and shaking brambles out of their hair while the men silently admired their pluck and athletic ability. They also tried not to make it so lustfully obvious that they were proud of their women's strong, slim bodies—and tough—but feminine beauty.

"You boys look hungry," began Julie. "Maybe we should throw steaks on the grill."

Mark desired Ruby so much he wanted to be animalistic, and he uttered a deep growl, "Hey, Ruby, let's go charcoal a sign somewhere!" Ruby blushed because now she knew *everybody* knew. Dan was glad it was out in the open and they could playfully tease about it. Sometimes Mark overstressed Dan.

Food, consensually and communally, was prepared and consumed and enjoyed. They cleaned up amid joking, banter, friendship, fellowship, and love. The day languished into an amazing meal that lasted half the afternoon.

Julie dragged Ruby, who was looking forward to a lazy nap, out to the barns to see chickens, horses, gardens, and birds. Julie plucked a few weeds from her garden, and then gathered sprigs of herbs (rosemary, thyme, lavender, and basil) for a grilled pasta supper. She filled Ruby's arms with tomatoes, zucchini, onions, and garlic, all picked fresh from the greenhouse. They filled bird feeders; Julie's favorites were the western bluebirds. She had a butterfly cage in which grew the noxious milkweed. Monarchs would soon be flitting everywhere, alighting on each and every flower. Julie briefly described how the earth was losing its pollinators due to chemicals and loss of habitat. She pointed out the beehives way off on the back forty and shared with Ruby her dream of finally getting her year-round greenhouse constructed. Ruby was amazed at the scope of projects this lively, knowledgeable, petite woman was involved in, and she admired her all the more.

Their dinner was mostly vegetables on the grill doused with olive oil, tomato sauce, and parmesan topping the pasta. It was delicious beyond description. Julie's children entertained the adults during supper with their discoveries throughout their early summer vacation.

Strangely, these children did not think of helping on the ranch as labor; they simply appreciated being lucky enough to live there. They read books and chatted with school friends on the computer during the evening. The rest of their day was spent helping or doing what they wanted to do out-of-doors. Julie's middle child was a girl about Chloe's age; Ruby thought how incredibly well they would get along. Ruby had never observed children with so many hobbies and interests. Their TV sat for days without ever being turned on. These kids loved learning and experiencing hands-on style!

The weekend was coming to an end. Nobody wanted to leave this retreat; nobody wanted to return to reality. Mark and Ruby never really got any time alone because there was so much activity with Julie and her family. They loved every minute of the chaos, but still, as lovers ... They could not leave this land of perfection without spending some intimate time together! Mark wanted to take Ruby out to Chad and Julie's cabin at the lake. He simply had to get alone with her. She felt the same—not that they hadn't been joined at the hip or in each other's minds the entire time they'd been in Montana!

Dan suggested a red-eye flight at midnight. They could save several hours if they flew Ruby straight to Omaha, where she could rent a car to drive back home. With the plan cemented, Dan went to get some extra sleep.

Ruby changed into her lace navy blue dress, and she and Mark took off for the cabin right after dinner. Chad offered, "You guys go. I'll help Julie clean up."

The lake was small with a sandy bottom; the clear, cold water, was spring-fed from the hills. They had four delicious hours to languish in each other's company. Mark pulled Ruby as close to him as he could without her climbing into his clothes with him—which he would also embrace! They swayed in the moonlight, her lace dress gently flapping against his legs. They were on the dock, the stars looked almost reachable, touchable. They dangled their feet in the water and talked. Then they talked more—nonverbally.

Mark filled Ruby in on what had to be done. He said if the trial did not get over soon, he was going to go crazy without her. He wanted to confess his crimes, serve his time, and then get out of jail sooner than his sentencing might dictate, for good behavior. Ruby painfully groaned that Mark might have to go to jail. He took a moment to reiterate that she could also end up in the same situation if she did not keep her promise about burning down any more signs. She assured him that it had been the beginning and end of that particular career.

They held on tightly so the inevitable magic of this evening would not vanish. It would be permanently written on their hearts and memories.

Ruby was freezing cold from the water, but also freezing over the worry and uncertainty of Mark's future—their future. She wanted nothing more in the world than she wanted this man. And he wanted her. To keep Ruby from freezing to death, they went inside the cabin and remained there until midnight. Only the two people in love and the silent four walls would ever know the secrets of their short night in the cabin.

Chapter

23

DAN WAS WAITING in the plane, idling and unsure whether Mark and Ruby would show. He was extremely familiar with the concept that two people crazy in love often had their own time warp. They had said good-bye to the children at suppertime; Chad and Julie sleepily waited and waved from the doorway of their ranch.

Tears ran down Ruby's cheeks most of the way to Omaha. They landed at a strip outside the metro to have more anonymity, and Ruby and Mark could say their good-byes. Ruby was worried sick; Mark tried to reassure her, kissed her longingly, and was whisked away by Jim and Greg to Kansas City.

If Ruby had to be left with anyone besides Mark, she would have chosen Dan. He was a good guy in every way. He escorted her to his car and would deliver her to a car rental company, promising to keep her updated. She would easily have a little time to freshen up and compose herself somewhere before heading to her parents' house to collect Chloe.

Monday morning dawned. Ruby put on a brave face and drove down Lollie and Rory's long, tree-lined road. They were having brunch out on the back porch; apparently, there had been a slumber party the night before, and they seemed to be continuing the frolic. Rory was bent over in the garden, retrieving fresh cantaloupe. Chloe and her cousins were chasing around the yard with the dogs and Frisbees.

Lollie stood up and was shocked when she saw Ruby. "Honey! Did you drive all night? Whose car ...?"

"Mother, my friends flew me to Omaha. I rented a car to pick up Chloe and then go back home. We spent the weekend in Montana. Thank you so much for taking Chloe; I had a delightful time." Ruby was still so melancholy about leaving Mark, and her face and body language spoke nothing of delight.

"Ruby, are you all right?" A mother could always sense when things were not okay.

"It's just that I have so much on my mind."

A mother could also recognize when her oblivious daughter was deliriously in love.

"Come here, sweetie. Let's go have a coffee indoors; the kids can play outside with your dad to entertain them."

Ruby allowed the mothering and smothering, and she felt like spilling everything but knew she couldn't.

Instead, she sat with her mom and told her there was nothing to worry about. This situation would be solved within days, perhaps a week, and then she would gladly share it all.

Lollie simply had to believe that Ruby was more than capable of handling her own problems. Nevertheless, it caused her more than worry. "Honey, you could stay with us for a while ..."

"Can't, Mom. Gotta get back to work so I can get that son-of-a-bucking advertising job finished. I hate it all ... I'm thinking about going into teaching. It seems so simple compared to what I'm doing."

"Okay, dear. You know we're here for you. Why don't we come back to visit in a month or so?"

"That's all we've done this summer—trot back and forth between Tepid and Omaha!" Ruby slightly giggled.

"I know. But we love it, Ruby! We love seeing you two, of course, but we love the tourists, the hills, and even the tourist traps! Oh, go on, honey. Get back to your responsibilities. Everything will come out in the wash. Maybe tainted a different color ... but it will all come out! Just keep us posted, and please don't do anything rash."

Was her mother referring to the fire she'd set? Ruby tried to settle her palpitating heart.

Within two hours, Chloe gathered her entourage along with her new school clothes. Ruby's small bag was already in the car; the stuffing was quickly squeezed out of everybody, and then they headed northwest.

Ruby breathed a deep sigh of relief and turned to her daughter. "Well, fill me in on your last two days, sweetie!" Chloe said she wanted to sleep. That worked too. The trip back was uneventful, except for that little scorched patch just out of Norfolk that they had to drive past, bringing up horrors of memories and guilt for Ruby. She was settled in the fact that she would never try that operation again. She didn't know how Mark did it. It was too nerve-racking for her!

She briefly considered stopping in at the Norfolk Chamber, or someplace, to donate money for damages. Then she thought better of it; that may raise more suspicions rather than resolve anything. Mark did not need any more to worry about, and neither did she. On the quiet ride back home, she began to focus on how Mark might be handling court.

24

MARK SLAMMED HIMSELF into court in an attitude to get it over with. Zane was wary of him and instructed him to not speak.

The judge reiterated their purpose: both sides would give a quick, succinct inventory of their evidence, and then he would determine how they would proceed. He'd decide whether there was a case to be tried, or whether the defendant should receive a fine and be dismissed.

Prosecution ah-hemmed until the judge was near distraction. He smacked the gavel finally, and they began. "Your Honor, we have boot prints, cell phone records, fingerprints, DNA, and hair samples. We know the fires had accelerants, and we think we know the method by which they were set. Also, the arson routes follow fairly predictable roadways—easy to access and easy for getaways. We have a defendant who has the profile and connections to environmental groups, who also have a reputation for being engaged in suspicious and unlegislated activities."

"So, in other words, you have speculation?"

"Uh ... No, sir. Uh, circumstantial evidence—strong circumstantial evidence." the prosecutor stumbled lamely.

"This reminds me of that joke of a sheriff we were unfortunate enough to be subjected to, and that performance is not going to repeat itself! I do hope your 'evidence' does not include putting him back on the stand!" The judge directed the jury to leave temporarily.

"No, sir. We also have a picture of a woman making an escape with the defendant, and we suspect either that she was involved, or was party to the defendant's arson crimes." The prosecutors were deliberately wording each response incriminatingly.

"Then please explain why she has not yet been a part of this trial!"

"Your Honor, we have not located her yet, but—"

"How hard could that be?"

"We only have a picture of her, uh, ...of the back of her head. But we are confident—"

The judge cut him off again. "You have a picture of the backside of someone, and you are so thick-headed that you think that will be sufficient evidence? Are you trifling with me? I am losing patience with this circus!"

"Your Honor, we think that when we identify her, we may be able to flush out not just Mr. Smythe, but a cluster of these arsonists to get their activity brought to justice. It is costing millions of dollars in corporate advertising. Mr. Smythe, as we know, was not involved in the arson at the Denver Advertising Group because he was under surveillance at the time."

"Yes, and we all know how well your surveillance team works!" Apparently, the information of Mark's multiple escapes had reached the judge. He slammed the gavel. "Recess until 1:00, sharp!"

It was a good thing court was dismissed. At the mention of implicating Ruby, Mark was primed to jump up and confess. Zane shuffled him into the nearest private room and attempted to verbally tear off Mark's head. Mark had not filled him in on his romantic penchant.

Zane had a foot up on a chair and an elbow on his knee. He rubbed his forehead as if he suffering from migraines.

Mark quietly snarled, "Sorry, didn't mean to embarrass you. But there is no way she's going to be sucked into my arson affairs, Zane. I'm not trying to be oppositional, but it's just not going to happen."

Zane grumbled, "Go to lunch!" and stormed out.

Ruby and Chloe hit their doorstep, hugged each other, and sighed. They were happy to be home.

"Maybe things will get back to normal and mundane, sweetie!"

"Yeah, I'm bored already," Chloe said disparagingly.

"Well, then, throw out some ideas for some fantastic plans for Saturday, okay? Just you and me?"

Retrospectively, Ruby remembered they had not made the butterfly garden yet. Even though summer was half gone, they could still make it for next year. Chloe excitedly agreed. They started with a trip to the Circle B for fence, posts, wire, mulch, and more. Soon they were planning and laughing at their amateur building skills.

"Maybe I should have asked Dad's advice while they were here," Ruby said lamely.

"Yeah, maybe."

For the next four days, life did return to normal, except for Ruby thinking about and pining for Mark. Ruby willed Dan to call, but he never did. The end of July was approaching, and only weeks were left to the summer before Chloe started back to school. Jashawn had not requested any more visits with Chloe, and he knew that school in Tepid Springs started in the middle of August. Ruby thought, *If he snoozes, he loses!* She didn't want to spend her time thinking about her ex, anyway.

Ruby and Chloe managed to settle down to a routine; even calls from Lollie and Rory slowed down temporarily. Of course, they would be busy gathering the spoils of their garden, canning produce, and probably welcoming a much-needed break from all the entertaining.

The Redrock Cafe kept the arson info alive and well. Ruby

kept her distance, although she could not resist her daily white mocha. She would passively listen to the platitudes and tittle-tattle, and then she would go home and break something, pretending it was someone's thick skull. She heard comments such as, "Yeah, boy, that sheriff really showed who was boss down there in that there big-assed city," and, "That scoundrel is not gonna get by with his crimes he done," and, "Nosirree, they's gonna hear him out and git justice!" She had also been subjected to similar gossip at the lumberyard when she and Chloe had bought the materials for the butterfly pavilion. Now it was referred to as a pavilion, to sound fancy; Chloe retorted fancy was *appropriate* for monarchs.

Mark presumed Dan would be nearby, and he sauntered around the courthouse, trying to spy him out. They connected in a bookstore across the street from the courthouse. Mark relayed the short version of what was happening with him and Zane.

"I don't know what the man's gonna do. Sometimes I think he'd rather be the prosecutor and stomp my face in the mud. Anyway, they are not going to let that photo go away, the bastards!"

"Agreed," was all Dan could manage. They fell silent so as not to be overheard; but both were strategizing. Mark quickly grabbed a triple shot espresso and headed back across the court lawn. Dan would nonchalantly appear later. Mark was wary of Zane, who he thought looked surreptitiously too decisive, too overconfident.

The judge, all business, called to order and said, "We've heard quite enough from prosecution. What evidence does the defense have?"

Zane stood and, by rote memory, spouted off cell phone records establishing whereabouts, good character witnesses, police reports that did not identify any persons or additional evidence of arson, and more. Zane wanted to face the question of the woman in the photo, and he declared, "Your Honor, we can produce the woman in the photo and prove to the court that it is absolute nonsense to pursue her as an accomplice or otherwise."

Mark jolted out of his chair and shouted, "Objection!"

"Be seated! You are out of order to object!" hissed the judge smugly.

Now, with his devious mind entering the gutter of humanity along with his desire for his courtroom achieving national attention, they had the beginnings of a real trial instead of this he-said/she-said drivel!

Mark sat down without even looking at Zane, who was ready to smack a Tazer to him. Dan felt the necessity to exit the courtroom.

Nobody spoke for a full minute. It seemed like twenty. Clearly, the judge was silently—but actively—assessing the situation in his overly suspicious mind. This outburst reeked of subterfuge and deception, something this defendant, Mr. Smythe, wanted to keep hidden. The Judge thought, *Yeah, how could Mr. Smythe possibly not know the woman in the car with him?*

Zane still stood, shocked at Mark's reaction. For him, to sit down would be to lose face.

The judge said, "Court will proceed with this trial. The woman in the photo will appear as soon as she is subpoenaed." The gavel pounded, and court was dismissed for the day.

Zane was still standing, reeling. Mark was still sitting, reeling. Everybody else filed out.

"I never thought he would call my bluff," Zane murmured under his breath, trying to convince himself more than Mark.

"Your bluff? You jeopardized my life, and maybe my future wife's life, for a bluff?" Incredulous, Mark could have launched Zane upside down over the bailiff's bench. He walked out and headed to the condo. He had to contact Dan and figure out a plan.

The evening papers again ran the story, along with the incriminating photo of him and Ruby speeding away from the flashing cameras.

Lollie and Rory studied the newspaper. Rory said, "Wow, that does look a lot like Ruby from behind. They say this was in Kansas City. She's never been in Kansas City in her life, that I know of. Do you know of her being in Kansas City lately?"

Lollie decided to call Ruby immediately. "Darling, have you seen the evening newspaper?"

Ruby hadn't, but she got online and saw the odious problem. She wished Dan would call so she could stop worrying. She couldn't imagine how Mark may have been driven to distraction over it. All she wanted was to be in his arms this instant. There had to be thousands of ways to deter this inconsequential charge. Who in this world could possibly identify the back of a person's head? How could someone know it was her when she lived as far away from Kansas City as she did? Then she wondered whether Chloe would have to reside permanently with her parents while this mish-mash got sorted out.

Zane showed up with a six-pack at the condo to apologize. Mark could care less; the damage had been done. He and the Group had trusted Zane to handle this trial; Zane, who had a reputation for being tough and not cracking under pressure. But to think he had gambled with Mark's life and future, *and Ruby!* Mark would not forgive him for as long as he lived. As soon as he could contact the Group, he was going to get Zane fired.

Mark sat on the couch, glaring at and loathing Zane. Zane popped open two bottles to get the party started and guzzled the first beer in two minutes. Then he began the second. Mark grabbed one, took a couple of sips, remained silent, and watched Zane. Maybe he could hold back and let Zane drink the whole six pack; then Mark would sneak out. Mark took another sip, as Zane finished his second beer. He belched loudly and obnoxiously and then popped the third. It was apparent that he came to assuage his own conscience rather than help Mark. After devouring the fourth beer, Zane was getting sleepy and lounged back on the bed.

Mark slipped out to make a call to Dan, who had dropped a fresh disposable in his suit pocket for Mark, but he couldn't use it in range of the goons next door. Mark had him on the phone easier than expected, and Dan said to watch for a black pickup in a five minutes on the opposite corner from where they had grabbed him the week before. It worked, and as they whisked him out of downtown, the friends were able to talk freely.

Mark asked if Dan had called Ruby. Dan said he thought he should wait until they talked first, but he promised that he would as soon as possible.

"Please tell her not to be concerned. This will blow over. They think they've got a case, but they are in for a bolt from the blue."

"How long can we maintain this anonymity and avoidance?" Dan asked.

"As long as it takes."

"Then I guess my real question is, how long will this whole fiasco take?" Dan sounded, uncharacteristically, anomalous.

Mark peered at him. *What is the guy thinking? What has changed?* Something was up with his faithful friend—Mark instinctively knew it.

Dan colored.

"Man, what's going on?" Mark fleetingly wondered where Dan spent all of his free time, and where he'd been flying.

Maybe Mark didn't know his friend quite as well as he thought he did.

"Don't worry about it. You've got enough on your mind."

"Buddy, don't give me that load of crap. You have something, or someone, on your mind!" Mark never failed in assessing other people; he could read them like open books.

"Okay, okay. I want to go see someone," he confessed lamely. "In Montana."

"Dan's been hustling behind our backs," teased Mark, and he tried to incite Jim and Greg to get in on the interrogation, "Wow! Just when you think you know someone. Who is she? 'Fess up, bro!"

Dan said he 'got around' during the times Mark was busy with Ruby and his cousin's family.

"Congrats! Two-fourths of our man club has bit the dust! I hope we never find that blessed contract!" In spite of his troubles, Mark was truly happy for his friend, and he thanked him for all the favors and unconditional support.

Dan assured him that he'd be available until the trial was over, but he was restless. He also disclosed that he embraced the wide-open Montana space.

"Ah, so you're going to meet someone in Montana, eh?" The brotherhood enjoyed flagrancy.

Mark said he was going to have to make connections with the Group and demand emergency intervention. At that point, they dropped the subject and sped Mark back to the condo, where he found Zane gone and the room littered with beer bottles.

Dan went straight away and called Ruby. Chloe answered the phone, but Dan disguised the call by asking if this was a graphics arts company, and whether she was Democrat or Republican.

Chloe sweetly said, "Oh, just a minute. I'll get my mom."

Ruby grudgingly came to the phone, and then she quickly slipped outside when she recognized Dan's voice. "What's happening? Is Mark all right? Are they going to find me?"

Dan reported, "A lot, yes, and no!" to her series of questions.

"Oh, sorry. I've been beside myself with worry and wonder."

"I'm sure, Ruby. But his Group is responsible for protecting him. He told me to tell you not to worry. It will be over soon, and he ... oh, uh, said a bunch of mushy stuff to tell you he loves you. I'm not delivering that verbatim, okay?"

Ruby laughed. She could see where Dan would be embarrassed to tell her the exact words from Mark. She thanked him, and he promised to call again soon.

Ruby was so relieved she could not contain herself. She practically danced throughout the remainder of the evening. Chloe was confused by her mother's change of mood. After getting the news from Dan, Ruby did not think there could possibly be anything that could upset her.

She was mistaken.

Early the next morning, Jordan showed up in a black disposition, wondering—nay, demanding—where she'd been and why the assignment was not finished.

"It is! And it's my best work yet! I mailed it yesterday. Are you getting out from under the fire damage at your office?" Ruby deliberately changed the subject because she did not wish to discuss or change her work to Jordan's paradigm, which had already been submitted anyway. He left without raising her ire. Even flack from him would not have destroyed her relief over Mark being okay with his court challenges. It would simply be a matter of white-knuckling it to the conclusion.

After he'd gone, Ruby and Chloe went out to a matinee and dinner at the Olive Garden. They had yet to populate their butterfly garden, but first they needed the proper flowers to attract them. They spent some time in BAM researching books and resources. Next, they strolled through Jolly Lane gardens and had fun choosing a colorful array of flowers. Their work was definitely cut out for them for the next few weeks, but Ruby was grateful for a project. She managed so much better when she had goals to take her mind off the obvious. She smiled indulgingly at her happy daughter and allowed different scenarios of possible explanations to march across her mind as to when it would be appropriate to tell Chloe how much in love she was.

Out of the blue, Chloe shyly asked Ruby, "Mom, is it too soon for me to think about who I want to marry?"

"Whom," corrected Ruby. Then she checked underneath her body to see if her legs had buckled. They were still supporting her weight—barely! "Why, how, what ..." She could not articulate a coherent sentence for a second. "Uh, no, not too soon to think about it. But definitely too soon to do it! I mean ... oh, I don't know what I mean! Of course you should think about it all day long, every day of your life, about as many boys as you wish. Because ..."

"Because, why?" Chloe wanted to know. She rather enjoyed dragging adult information out of her mother before she was supposedly old enough to hear it.

"Because it takes a lot of thinking, planning, and deciding. You want to make the right decision." Ruby's mind whirled madly at her own paradoxical thoughts, behavior, and desires.

"You and Dad didn't make the right decision?" pressed Chloe.

Ruby was quick to say, "Yeah, no, but it was the right decision at the time. Life just changes, and people change. Feelings do too. Besides, we got you out of our ten years of marriage!" They were reduced to mother-daughter giggling glee.

Chloe threw her arms around her mother, a little girl again. "I don't ever want you to change, Mom!"

"I'll never change where you're concerned, Chloe. That's a promise!"

Chapter

25

LOLLIE AND RORY had spent days gathering and canning their neglected harvest, but Lollie needed a change of pace. She suggested they go stay for a couple of days in Nebraska City, relaxing. Rory agreed; they required only a couple of hours' preparation and then hit the road. They had just enough time to arrive before dark—less than an hour and a half drive from Omaha. Neither of them ever regretted serendipitous ideas from each other. Nebraska City, home of The National Arbor Day Foundation, was continuous work and activity—which other people would be doing rather than them!

While Mark was showering, getting ready for court, and slamming down coffee after coffee, he wondered whether Zane would still be representing him and what kind of shape he'd be in. He also envisioned several brief (albeit demoralizing) scenarios of actually facing prosecution, and possibly conviction, alone.

It wasn't long before he found out. He found Zane sitting in his usual chair at their usual table, starched, immaculate, and professional. Under his breath, Zane whispered hoarsely, "I've contacted the Group. They have as many models available as we need to testify to all sorts of nonessential, non-information, and nonsense that will confound any charges. Your girl, whoever she is, won't have to become involved or even be identified. You can thank me later." His ego and arrogance was back.

Mark thought this may not be the best time to throttle him, but his hands were itchin'! Dan dropped a note in his blazer pocket and unobtrusively moved toward the back of the courtroom. Proceedings had barely begun when the judge asked where the young woman with the long, wavy hair was.

"Well, Your Honor, you will understand how frequently and drastically these days women change the color of their hair. I'm afraid pursuing this angle is not going to lend any conclusive evidence to our case. We respectfully request that you reconsider and dismiss this part of the evidence."

"Objection! Prosecution thinks identifying this accomplice is central to the case."

"The young woman will appear and be questioned," the judge said as the gavel crashed.

"Very well, Your Honor. We need travel time."

"Counsel, are you deliberately trying to obfuscate this process? How much time does your long-haired lady require?"

"Two days."

"Counsel, you've got until tomorrow."

Zane sat down. Mark felt totally compromised and glared at him, wondering if there was any gray matter between those ears.

"Meanwhile, prosecution may proceed with cell phone records," the judge continued.

The jury was invited back into the courtroom.

Mark imagined his life flashing before his eyes, and he wondered if it was humanly possible to die from boredom. At the break, he must communicate to Dan to get him out of town, where they could think, plan, and get this fiasco expedited and solved. He reached into his pocket and squinted to read the message on the note in the dark of his pocket. It said, "After court today ... National Arbor Day." So his buddies had come through again! They were heading out to one of their favorite hangouts to hash out a plan. He tried to remain nonchalant until this scourge of an afternoon was over. To keep busy and focused, he wrote down verbatim everything verbalized, accused, and intimated in court. He scrawled until his hand cramped. The ruse worked. Both prosecution and defense thought he was paying attention.

He was tripping out, subconsciously adoring Ruby ... with a little lust thrown in. He made a list of her attributes, talents, and personality. He realized he could write a book. He loved that woman more than a man probably should love a woman. *Whenever you're not looking, there she is ...*

In light of the multiple surveillance failures, security had been drastically expanded around Mark to avoid any more embarrassing escapes or the possibility of entirely losing their subject. Mark sat through the next three hours, wondering how to slip through their fingers once more. Greg and Jim were purposely absent so they would never be seen as a connection to him. All he knew was that whatever he did, the plan had to be glitch-proof.

Upon leaving the courthouse, Dan breezed past him and told him to jump up into the back of the Wal-Mart semitruck parked across the street, hop out the front door of the truck (which was out of view of the courthouse), and get into the taxi-cab. The cab would take him one mile to a designated corner, where he would transfer to Jim's navy Hummer—his company car minus the company name.

It worked. How it worked, Mark didn't know and didn't care, but he sighed in relief that it had. The four were heading 150 miles out of town, out of view and out of earshot. He would easily be back in court by tomorrow—reassured with a viable, foolproof strategy to wrap up this chasm that was keeping him from his one and only true love. His friends were awesome! After almost two hours on the road, Mark began to relax and seriously think about the task ahead. Several plans were mentioned, and all were scratched. Still, he couldn't guess what Zane had up his sleeve.

Lollie and Rory had freshened up, and after strolling around the National Arbor Foundation campus, they landed in the Timber Restaurant for a superb dinner together. They loved watching people, tourists, and retired folks as they gaped and marveled at the beauty of the log beams from native trees used to support the all-natural lodge. They were seated and soon ordered their meals; then they talked quietly about Ruby and Chloe, when they would visit next, possible plans for the Fall holidays, and a million other looming family ideas.

Lollie, facing the opposite direction from Rory, was privy to the group of handsome, successful-looking, young men entering the restaurant, looking unattached. How she longed for Ruby to find a really nice guy. She wished she could pick out one of those men and take him home to her daughter, though she knew that was crazy. Without being too obvious, she tried to assess them from across the room; they seemed very intent about some issue. People passing by between her and them helped disguise her curiosity. She could not help but wish for a life partner for Ruby, someone with whom to share. Of course, there would be problems, adjustments, and differences, especially with a 'tween involved. Lollie continued to size them up (and down) until it was time for her and Rory to mosey to their room.

Rory suddenly suggested, "Wanna go up in the tree house ... with *me*?" He tried his best to look the part of a pervert and reduced Lollie to giggles. Her laugh had said yes for her. They began the walk toward the beautiful, out-of-doors structure that offered tranquility, harmony, and rumination. Soon Lollie and Rory were lost in each other's minds and plans; they barely noticed that the same young men from the restaurant had gathered below and were engaged in a intent conversation. They had heard just enough that it would be awkward to try to exit, so they nervously remained still.

One of the men said, "Dan, never would I expect Julie to pose as Ruby. Just as I'd never ask your newfound love, Angela, to appear."

Dan answered, laughing. "She's spunky. Already offered to pretend she is the woman in the picture. She's even got the long, auburn hair. Besides, she said it sounds incredibly exciting; not much happens in her little Montana municipality!"

Lollie sucked in her breath. Ruby? Montana? Were they talking about *her* Ruby? Were they talking about the mysterious woman in the photo of the arson suspect that had been plastered all over the papers and media for weeks? No, it could not be! Then she looked to Rory for a denial and saw that he was almost as stricken as she was.

Below, the men moved on to the parking lot, where all four piled into a dark-colored Hummer and peeled out. Rory noticed the Kansas license plate. Rory and Lollie looked at each other in shock, and then they headed to their room. Neither of them was going to get a good night's sleep. It was far too late at night to call their daughter or bother their darling granddaughter. This jumble of information meant that their Ruby was interested in—no, was dating an arsonist? *The* arsonist?

The next morning, Ruby and Chloe flew out of bed to arrange butterfly plants inside the small chain-link garden space that would protect the butterflies from birds, cats, and nomadic, nocturnal insect-eaters. Even without the butterflies, the flowers had responded to the fertile soil and water given to them, and they bloomed in profuse color. However, an industrious honeybee had already found nectar, and the vital pollinators would eventually carry on with their important business. Ruby was adoringly proud of Chloe's help and interest in their nature project.

"Shall we taste some of your grandfather's maple syrup on our pancakes this morning?" enticed Ruby.

"Yeah, sounds good!" Chloe kept staring at the butterfly garden in appreciation of nature and the circle of life. Ruby didn't want to turn away either, until Chloe was satisfied. Mother and daughter enjoyed their moment and then went into the kitchen, smiling.

The telephone rang. Chloe grabbed it, answered, laid it down for Ruby, and said, "Mom, do you have a new customer? I've heard his voice before ..."

Ruby picked up. It was Dan checking in. Ruby was disturbed by Chloe's comment. *Did I just get busted?*

"Sorry, I heard her too," sympathized Dan. "Was just trying to stay in touch. Shall I call later?"

"Yeah, maybe it's best," Ruby anxiously murmured. "How is he?"

"I think it's coming to an end. Don't worry. I think the Group's going to fill in with ... Uh, guess I'll drop it. Try not to worry. Later."

By the time Ruby said, "Later," Dan had disconnected. *Why is it when people ask you not to worry, that's exactly what you do? Life is so messy sometimes!*

Chloe was still chattering about Ruby's new client from upstairs; Ruby tried to ignore her, pretending not to hear— but she scrounged her mind for another busy activity or project for them to engage in for the rest of the day. Biking? Hiking? Kayaking?

In spite of the bomb dropped underneath their hideout last evening, and talking and worrying half the night, Rory and Lollie had fairly leaped out of bed to a hurried breakfast at the lodge of cinnamon-applesauce oatmeal. Afterward, they waited for the sun to rise in the western time zone, and then they reluctantly made the call.

Ruby's phone on the wall jangled for the second time in ten minutes. *Is Dan calling back already? I thought he said later! Now what's happened?*

"Good morning, girls," chirped Lollie.

"Good morning, Mother," Ruby chirped back, "What are you two wild sixties hippies up to today?"

"Do you have a few minutes, dear? And is Chloe within earshot?"

Ruby was immediately alarmed. "No, she's upstairs ... Talk!"

"We were at Nebraska City last evening for dinner, and we climbed up into the tree house and overheard something quite strange." Lollie went on to explain how both she and Rory thought those young men, ostensibly from Kansas, were talking about *her*, their Ruby! Could it possibly be such a coincidence? Could it be a mistake? "We were absolutely certain they were talking about the arson trial going on in Kansas City. Honey, it is plastered all over the media!"

Seriously? Ruby thought. *This can't be possible!* This was not her parents—they didn't overreact to anything!

"Well, what did they look like? Did you see their faces? Did they see you guys up in the tree house? Did you hear any names?"

"We heard *your* name, Ruby—just your first name. There was stuff about arson. Then we heard Julie ... isn't she the Montana cousin? They sped off in a Hummer." Lollie was panting with the news and desperately hoping for a denial. "Then there's that waitress at the Redrock who—way back—said it looked like you in that newspaper photo ..."

Did all these bizarre events add up to a connection to her Ruby's new love? She was holding her breath for Ruby to say it couldn't possibly have been the man with whom she was in love ...

Ruby interrupted. "Mom, I think it's possible you may have inadvertently met him ..."

"Met who?" chirped Chloe.

Ruby jumped from Chloe's comment behind her, and her own voice choked. She coughed. "Whom," she corrected when her voice worked again.

"Okay, whom. Met whom, Mom?" she persisted, now petulant.

Ruby felt like her hand had been caught in the cookie jar. "Mother, tell Dad hi for me; we were just going on a hike. Here's your favorite grandchild ..."

"We were?" questioned Chloe. "That's Grammie?"

"Yes. Would you like to say good morning to them?" Ruby grasped the opportunity to change the subject and exit.

"Hi, Grammie! What was Mom talking about? Who was Mom talking about?"

"So, you're going on a hike ... to Harney Peak? Around Sylvan Lake? To Bear Butte?" Lollie tried to continue the charade.

"I guess. I dunno, maybe. I just wanted to know who Mom was talking about," finished Chloe.

"I'm sure she'll explain everything. Gramps and I were just heading home from Nebraska City, honey. Sure wish you'd been with us. We climbed the tree house!" Lollie was hoping Chloe would drop it. "Tell your mother bye for us, and perhaps we'll get out to visit before school starts, okay?"

"Yeah, school ..." Chloe said good-bye and immediately went to pester her mother. "Mom, is there something you want to tell me?"

Ruby laughed. "Yes, indeed. Get your backpack and fill your water bottle. I'm grabbing us some sandwiches and cookies, and we're leaving for Bear Butte in two minutes! Hurry!" Chloe scrambled away.

Nine o'clock in court. Everybody was putting on a good show of normality. A long-haired blonde beauty sat alongside Zane. Mark had no idea who she was.

The gavel slammed.

Prosecution could not wait to start shooting questions at the hapless woman now called to the witness stand. Apparently, this was Zane's best effort at filling in with this person to pose as someone she was not. Did she know what was expected of her? Could she pull it off? From where did Zane pick her up? The nearest call girl agency? Maybe she was one of his consorts!

"State your name, occupation, and how you know the defendant."

She said her name was Crystal, she was an administrative assistant, and she'd had one date with Mark Smythe. Mark did not recall ever having a date with this blonde—especially not a bleached blonde.

Prosecution asked if she remembered a camera flash upon leaving Mark Smythe's residence on or around the middle of June.

"No, not really."

"Were you in Mr. Smythe's car with your head facing over your left shoulder?"

"I'm pretty sure."

"What kind of car does Mr. Smythe drive?"

"A black one."

"Do you know the model of his car?"

"No. Um, maybe a BMW?" So she *had* been coached!

Prosecution held up the enlarged picture of the obnoxious getaway. "Can you ascertain if this is the back of your head and your hair?"

"No, but I think so." Mark liked her answers. He was boggled at the thought of possibly having to produce her name.

The judge was looking disgusted at this useless chain of events. Zane was hiding a grin behind his palm.

"Wind up this line of questioning, Counsel."

"Yes, Your Honor. Do you recognize the defendant, and would you be so kind as to point to the person with whom you had this one memorable date?" Prosecution's questions dripped with acrimony.

"Yes, that's him! That's Mark Smythe," she said, pointing to Mark.

He thought, *Oh, well. If she gets me off and doesn't implicate Ruby.* "No further questions."

"I should hope not," hissed the judge. "Defense?"

"Yes, sir. I have quite a few questions for Miss Crystal."

Crystal smiled at Zane and then at Mark.

"Crystal, relax and just tell the truth, okay?" Zane hoped to massage the jury with that word, *truth*. The woman nodded, looking very nervous.

"You testified that you had one date with Mr. Smythe, correct?" She nodded. "Where did you go on your date?"

She said, "We went to his favorite restaurant, a Chinese place."

"Do you know the name of the place?"

"Shogun."

"That's a Japanese place."

"Oh, sorry."

"You testified that you do not remember a camera flash leaving his residence. Correct?"

She nodded, but the judge ordered her to speak. "Correct."

"Crystal, are you or have you ever been any part of an environmental activist group, or do you know anyone who is?"

"No, I do not travel in those circles of activists, arsonists, environmentalists, or law-breakers." Again, coached!

"Do you ever color your hair?"

"All the time. I probably change the color of my hair every other week."

"One more question, dear. Why were you looking over your left shoulder in that photo?"

"I was setting my purse on the back seat."

"No more questions, Your Honor."

The judge was stunned. "That's it?"

"That's it."

He looked dumbfounded at prosecution and then called both attorneys to approach the bench. "This is beyond foolhardy! What was the point of bringing that brainless type into my courtroom?"

"Because you ordered it, Your Honor," Zane calmly reminded him.

"Anyone could see she was lying, Your Honor!" sputtered the prosecution.

Zane took a step back to let them duke it out, and to avoid getting spittle on his new suit.

"Anyone with any brains could see absolutely nothing, Counselor! These theatrics will discontinue, or I will hold you in contempt!"

Zane thought, *You asked for it, buddy—and you got it!*

Defense and prosecution glared at each other on the way back to their respective tables. Mark thought he vaguely remembered the young woman; but as a redhead, not a blonde. He'd certainly dated enough and had never gotten serious. He swung around to Dan's empty seat. Judge called a recess, and Mark followed Zane back to a private room.

When they closed the door, Zane whispered, "That woman was my wife. Turned out the Group could not come up with a substitute overnight."

"Yeah, I was pretty sure I'd never dated her."

Zane sighed out an apology for some of his egotistical, off-the-wall tactics. "I think the whole damned thing is coming to an end. They've got nothing or, at least nothing they can prove." Mark knew Zane was psychologically finished with his case. They strode back to the courtroom together, not speaking, awaiting the final showdown with the prosecution.

Prosecution had a vault of evidence, DNA, boot prints, hair samples, eyewitness accounts, tire tracks, phone records, and the very peculiar accelerant concoction that hadn't been analyzed to evidentiary perfection. However, they had nothing that matched anything or anybody, and certainly nothing that matched the defendant.

The judge could not admit defeat so easily. He was so certain of there being a big, crass blowout of media, fame, admiration, and everything short of a statue being erected in his honor. His gut told him a crime had indeed been committed by this defendant. Unfortunately, prosecution proved to be incompetent, and he may have to make a ruling.

Thinking ahead, the judge's common sense, finally operational, told him prosecution would never be able to fumble together a cohesive crime story, let alone a charge of arson. Therefore he could slap on a substantial fine because he could not abide Mark's condescending triumph; perhaps, he'd tack on a jail sentence of one year so Mark would never have a clean record. The defendant would be rewarded for time served from house arrest, and with good behavior, he'd receive leniency for a first offense, *(though the judge doubted with all of his soul that this was this defendant's first offense).*

His lawyers would contest all of the Judge's rulings; he would probably not legally have to serve a single day. He might suffer a bit with probation—just a slur on his character and future; but he would make him wait as long as he was lawfully allowed for the sentencing, setting it for one month away. However, the jury still had to report—as a formality—and he sent them into session immediately. The judge didn't think the jury could possibly come back with a verdict yet this afternoon, so he dismissed court for the rest of the day. The jury was ready in less than one hour.

Ruby and Chloe had arrived at Bear Butte State Park with backpacks, snacks, and energy to spare. Nothing was more exhilarating than tackling a small mountain, appreciating nature and its gifts, and spending time together. They slowly and methodically picked their way up the winding path, reverencing the prayer ties placed there by the Cheyenne and the Lakota. In spite of the scenic perfection, Ruby's mind kept backtracking to Mark as they climbed, took photos, munched on granola, and quenched their thirst. When they reached the pinnacle, terra firma lay below in spectacular wonder, in unspeakable, breathtaking magnificence. *This is truly a sacred place,* thought Ruby, and she watched her child *ooh*ing and *aah*ing over the colorful rocks, bird nests, and striations on scattered driftwood. She then reckoned that she was compelled to change professions in order to curtail the monstrous, wasteful advertising; she now found it to be in disagreement with her values and what she wanted for Chloe.

They sat side by side, trying to normalize their heart rates, with the spectrum of the world lying as far distantly as the eye could see. The sky was azure blue from horizon to horizon, clear and distinct with no clouds—flawless. This was western Dakota! There was a holiness about the place. A slight breeze rustled the pines below and grasses in an landscape of divine perfection.

"Wow!"

"Yeah, wow!" Ruby agreed. They stared for a long time at the plethora of beauty around them and leaned against each other with a sense of accomplishment, bonding them tighter than ever. They felt strong, satisfied, and exercised.

"We did it!"

"Yep, we did it. Together!"

"Mom, how far away can we see?"

"I'm sure it's at least one hundred miles before the curvature of the earth dips …" Ruby trailed off and thought, *How much more of a perfect setting could we be in?* She decided to share her exciting secret with her daughter. Ambiance hung poised.

"I've got to tell you something, sweet girl …"

Because it was late Friday afternoon, Mark had thought he'd be free to go. It was looking promising that he would get his life back, no matter the dollar amount—he didn't care! With a clear conscience, he could pursue Ruby, now and forever the love of his life. Money didn't matter anymore anyway; he'd give it all up for Ruby.

"Don't disappear, Mark," cautioned Zane as they were leaving the courthouse, which was already thinning out for the weekend. "We've still got to contend with the jury, and actually, I'm not sure that this ballistic judge won't have another shocker up his sleeve. A whole month to wait for sentencing! So don't do anything crazy, okay?" Zane offered to drop him off at home. Mark said he'd get a cab; he didn't want to put him out. Actually, Mark never wanted Zane to see where he lived. If he could slap together a Hail Mary ruse such as having his wife pose as a witness, who knew what he was capable of?

This was definitely an issue to be discussed with the Group … along with his resignation. No more arson, and no more environmentalism. No more hopping one step ahead of the law. He was trying not to let it show that he was elated to be free for the weekend. He had plans; Dan was already busy pulling them together.

Zane called him about fifty minutes later. The jury had reached their verdict.

"Too bad, Counselor. Not coming back!"

Chapter

26

"YOU'RE UNDER HOUSE arrest! You'll come back, or I'll have you dragged back to court!" Zane blasted into the phone.

"Listen, it's 3:30 p.m. on a Friday afternoon. Court is usually dismissed at 4:00. Nobody is going to get back to court in time to hear the jury! In fact, the judge is the one who dismissed court! He's just going to have to deal with it! You're going to have to deal with it!" Mark disconnected without a by-your-leave. But after clicking off, Mark thought, *Who would have thought they'd reach their verdict in less than an hour—the last hour of the last day of the final week?* Anyway, reaching a quick verdict was usually not a good sign.

Peaceful clouds drifted across the young women on the mountain.

Chloe turned to her Mother, listening.

"Remember you telling me that you thought you were in love with Marcus?" ventured Ruby. Chloe nodded. "Remember you asking me if it was too soon for you to think about marriage?" Chloe face was stone still. "Well, I haven't been in love for a very long time, sweetie, but I think I'm in love now. I'm sure I'm in love, Chloe." She hesitated before continuing. "We met sort of accidentally. We've talked on the phone, and I've spent a couple of weekends with him—but mostly just talked on the phone." Ruby waited for Chloe's reaction.

Chloe's calm was disconcerting. Finally, she said, "What's he like? Who is he?"

"Very nice, intelligent, gentlemanly."

"What's his name?"

"Mark."

"Mark? Like my Marcus in Denver? Do you remember me telling you ...?"

"Yes, of course, I do! And how is that Mr. Marcus these days?"

"I don't know. I kind of forgot about him, I guess, with all our traveling and activities and fun. I'll probably see him again next summer."

"Hmm. You don't e-mail or text or anything?"

Chloe shrugged and made a noise sounding like a very muffled *"I don't know."* Ruby respectfully waited for Chloe to process. Then Chloe blurted, "When am I going to meet him?"

"I don't know, honey. It's complicated. Maybe soon."

"How soon?"

Ruby shook her head. "Don't know. Wish I did ..."

"Well, thanks, Mom, for not treating me like a baby. And thanks for telling me your secret. Was that the guy who called yesterday, who I thought was a new client? I won't tell anyone!"

"No, but that was his friend Dan. He's Mark's best friend. It has been so long since I've dated, or even met anyone I thought about dating. It's been you and me for so long. I think I was as surprised as you are! I never would have kept it a secret, except I wanted to make sure that it was right for both of us." Ruby was running out of justifications; anything more, and she'd probably be chattering senselessly.

"Well, Dad went on with his life, so there's no reason you shouldn't." Chloe stated the obvious so pragmatically that it was hard to believe it had come from one so young.

Ruby hugged her and murmured, "I'm glad you're so understanding, sweetie. Are you ready to hike back down?"

"Can't we stay just a little bit longer? I like it up here."

Several other groups of people came and went. Mother and daughter sat glued to each other, watching the surreal activity of nature and hikers interacting. Chloe got up to explore some more and peer over the edge. Soon Ruby stood by her side and asked if she was ready to go.

"Sure." They loaded their backpacks onto their shoulders, picked up the area of trash, and moved in the direction of the path.

Ruby's cell phone rang. She reached into her fanny pack thinking it would most likely be Dan with news. "Hello?"

"Mrs. Smythe?"

"Mark!"

"No, it's Mr. Smythe!"

Chloe stopped in her tracks and turned around, shocked. She whispered, "Is it him?" She could see from the look of pure pleasure on her mother's face that it was.

"Darlin', it sure sounds good to hear your voice. Wish I was there, wherever you are!"

Ruby nodded to Chloe and then uttered almost inaudibly, "Oh, yeah. Me too!"

"What are my favorite girls doing on this unfaultable day?" Mark made a conscious effort to include Chloe. With the end of the trial in the crosshairs, he recognized it was imminent they would meet. He thought it extremely important to lay groundwork for success in that department.

"Actually, we're up on Bear Butte, hiking. And what are you ...?"

"With only thirty seconds left to cajole, Mrs. Smythe, you will consider marrying my pitiful, love-sick, humble self, won't you?"

Still being cautious where Chloe was concerned, Ruby laughed at his feeble attempt at humility and said, "You know the answer to that!"

"Yes, I do; but I still enjoy squeezing it out of you!"

His comment delighted Ruby, and she almost lost her footing on the path over his suggestive remarks. Ruby was so concerned that the phone connection might break up, she temporarily braked while Chloe continued the descent.

"Uh, on a more serious note, Ruby … Have you ever told your daughter about us?"

"This very afternoon. Don't worry, okay? I think she's going to be fine with the situation."

"Whew! Good! Uh, I mean, it's just that I don't have much experience with kids and no kids of my own …" Mark had been obsessing over meeting Ruby's daughter.

After a few more hushed, sweet nothings, Ruby and Mark hung up their phones. Ruby sped up to catch Chloe, who was significantly ahead. When she caught up and Chloe again asked the sticky question regarding what Mark had to say, Ruby nodded and stepped carefully into the unknowns of telling Chloe more about him.

"So how did you two meet? Oh! Please tell me you didn't meet him online. Did you?" she tried to scold. Then she switched right back to the Chloe who was completely naive of her mother's clandestine activities while she'd been busy with friends, or her dad, or at school.

"No, sweetie… Bet you won't believe this, but we actually met across the street from where we live!"

Chloe screwed up her face, "What? Across the street? There's nothing on the other side of our street! How did that happen?"

Ruby said, "At the Redrock. You remember those sirens that blew through town several months ago?" Then she realized she was opening the can of worms regarding Mark's arson. She stopped, ruffled Chloe's hair, and retorted, "Maybe I will try to answer your questions one at a time. But right now, let's get down this mountain in one piece and head to the Olive Garden, okay?"

That was not going to do for Chloe, now that she'd steered her mother onto this path of adult conversation. "We're pigs! We can't go to the Olive Garden. They probably won't even let us in!"

"True, let's grab a pizza from the Lintz Bros. instead, and go home to a relaxing bubble bath.!"

"Great idea!"

They threw their gear into the back of the truck and headed south. Near Hermosa, they picked up their pizza and munched most of the way home. Between hot, spicy bites, Chloe still attempted to return to the subject of her mother's newfound love. By the time they reached Tepid, light had faded, and a blue dusk was settling over the curving highway. Ruby suggested flipping a coin to see who got the shower first. Chloe won.

"Great! So I have to do the unpacking?" Ruby jokingly complained.

"I'll help you," promised her sweet daughter. Feeling so mature after their girl talk all day, Chloe offered to be more responsible. She headed straight for the bathroom; soon Ruby could hear water running and imagined bubbles gleefully swimming down the stairs. She dragged gear into the house, scattered it at the back door, and stumbled between backpacks, rolling water bottles, and hiking boots. They had dropped their smelly clothes there too. Ruby had jumped into some comfortable black exercise clothes and began sorting their laundry from dirtier to dirtiest.

She had just stuffed in a starved-animal-sized bite of pizza when the doorbell rang.

Chapter

27

SURPRISED, RUBY STEPPED to the door. Dan was standing there, grinning like a hound who had just swallowed a bird. Moving up behind Dan was none other than Mark with a roguish expression which was almost uncontainable.

"Mark!" was all Ruby could utter. "When did you ...? Why didn't you ...? What are you ...?"

Mark's mouth, arms, and body found hers for no other reason than to shut her up—tastefully. They engaged in a long-denied, anticipated moment of passion as Dan respectfully breezed past them into the house—and straight into Chloe, who was scantily clad and quickly whipped her towel more tightly around herself.

"Who are you?" Chloe shrieked.

Dan sprang across the room and respectfully turned his back to Chloe. Over his shoulder, he replied, "Hi. I'm a friend of your ..." Dan tried to calm the alarm on both of their accounts.

Chloe went marching to find her mother and demand to know why there was a strange man in their house. She blasted through the doorway to find yet another strange man kneeling behind a huge bouquet of red roses with several happy face balloons floating in front of her. Chloe looked incredulously at them, and she asked her mother for an immediate explanation.

"Mom, there is a ..." she had been spouting on the way to the door.

Her mother looked entirely too calm. In fact, she was actually smiling! Chloe looked back toward the apparition with the roses in front of her. She could not see his face but instead saw a very tanned, muscular leg with one strong hand resting on a knee while holding the bouquet with the other hand. Then a voice tentatively came from around the floral bush.

"Hi... and so you must be Miss Chloe, beautiful daughter of Ruby Jewel, I would very much like your approval to be your mother's very special, good friend."

Chloe slowly pushed aside the fragrant roses to see who was behind the flora. She innocently looked into the handsome face of Mark Smythe, who was wearing a goofy smile and looking like a pitiful, hopeful puppy dog.

Zane was ticked off that the jury had come back so soon. Nobody was expecting them to come back in less than an hour, and never in a million years did he think it could happen before Monday morning! That probably meant only one thing: despite all their efforts and work and appealing, Mark would be found guilty! Zane immediately notified the defense team and Mark, and he got absolutely no one on the phone.

"I instructed him to stay nearby!" lamented Zane, who could still not reach any of the other attorneys assigned to Mark's case. He'd retraced his steps to Mark's condo and paid the manager to open his room; it was cleaned out lock, stock, and barrel. Zane swore for ten minutes.

He showed up at the courthouse at 3:45 p.m. on this bizarre Friday afternoon, and he could perceive the judge was beside himself with mirth. Not even the prosecutors showed up. Therefore, the verdict was forced to be postponed until Monday anyway, sending the judge into an explosive tirade. *There would be consequences!* Zane was stressed to the max; he did not relish losing! When questioned about where his client was, Zane blatantly lied to the court and said Mark had been involved in a previous commitment, but he would be walking in the door any moment. He took a gamble that he could extrapolate the truth with only five minutes to spare, until the courthouse was legally closed. Luckily, his wild gamble figured right.

Mark and Chloe remained locked in an interminable stare as both parties realized the magnitude of this inevitable meeting. Ruby observed silently, holding her breath.

Mark instinctively knew this situation could not be rushed, coached, or engineered in any way. He remained silent and precariously patient.

Chloe looked from Ruby to Mark and back to her mother as they waited for her reaction. She took a deep breath and nodded, because she could not trust herself to speak. Chloe turned to go back into the living room; Ruby laid her hand on her daughter's shoulder to follow. Mark still stood where he was. Chloe turned and motioned for him to come; she took two steps toward him and filled her arms with roses. Soon she was looking for a vase and pouring in water.

Mark and Dan settled on the couch, Ruby grabbed her sun tea jar, quickly filled glasses with ice, and handed them all around. Chloe set the roses on the coffee table and continued arranging and burying her face in them. She'd never received roses in her life.

Mark took that precise moment to hand a card to Chloe; she timidly accepted it and hopped up the stairs to her room.

"Well, you two certainly have a way of blowing all normality out the window," began Ruby, almost chiding them. However, she was so deliriously happy to see Mark that she didn't know whether she should laugh or cry. She kept patting her hand on her heart and gave not a care about her post-hike appearance. Apparently, neither did Mark.

Dan, not wishing to be any part of this engagement, said nothing. He was not about to exit and jeopardize Mark's near freedom or future by allowing these two lovers their own penchant for emotional thinking or planning. Their next brain-addled idea may be to consider running off together! Mark definitely could not stay here, and Ruby could not go with them back to Kansas City. He observed them longing for each other; it was no different than his own longing for someone in Montana. Common sense told him not to trust his own decision making in this love-demented condition—so he obviously could not trust these two. He would stay and make sure Mark got back to his verdict. But just in case, if the jury ruled against him *(God forbid)*, it may be the last time he would see Ruby for a long time. Not that a team of wild horses could keep her away from jail, *(with her own newly developed penchant for breaking the law).*

Ruby moved over onto the couch with Mark to be near him and feel his body heat against her, and so they could touch. He raised his arm, and she nestled against his left side and swore not to move for the next ten hours. Dan, also on the couch on the right of Mark, was now glad he could avert his eyes toward the street and away from the undisputed attraction they had for each other.

Mark whispered in Ruby's ear that they only had until midnight on Sunday. Court would resume on Monday for the verdict, and hopefully it would be his last day in court... ever! They could view everything happening over at the Redrock, but they were in low lights and did not think the patrons of the cafe could view them. They talked, filled in the blanks, questioned and answered, and caught up on everything else newsworthy. The precious few hours drained out of the hourglass, grain by grain. Even so, Ruby took a fleeting moment to dash into the shower for less than five. She returned to Mark's side, her hair wet, fragrant, and wound into a wavy mane.

Chloe had been upstairs for quite a while. Ruby was on the

verge of tearing herself away from Mark's ribcage to go check on her when she shyly appeared.

Mark noticed immediately that Chloe was wearing the delicate jade four-leaf clover necklace with a pearl in the center. He did not mention it and waited for the daughter to show her mother. Chloe smiled and murmured, "Thank you for the card." The front of the card was a lovely mother pushing her darling daughter on a swing; they had beautiful, loving expressions that revealed how much they cared for each other, even in doing a simple activity. It was very much how Ruby and Chloe lived. The verse was simple and sentimental, and it would make a hardened criminal weep. Mark had neatly written,

My Dear Sweet Little Chloe,

This truly must be a shocking surprise for you, but, I hope it will be fun getting to know each other. I am in love with your mother to the point of insanity, so I can only surmise that her precious daughter must be very much like her— lovable, intelligent, caring, cute, and beautiful beyond words—and will also be easy to get to know and love. My commitment to your mother will be the same for you: that I will love her (and you) for better or worse until the day I die. There was something about her. I knew from the moment I set eyes on her while she was working away in her studio months ago. I hope and pray it will be the same with you. I will do my best to love and respect you, and I hope when you're ready, you can share a little bit of the love you have for your mother with me.

There are several promises in my heart that I feel I should mention so we have a better chance of starting off on the right foot.

(a) I will never tell you what to do; that is always between you and your sweet mother. If I request anything from you, I will ask politely, and you always have permission to say no. I will always agree with her where you're concerned, so please never ask me to disagree with her.

(b) I will not be your peer, but I hope to be your friend; I will not try to take the place of your father, because all any kid needs is one father. I know you love him, and I will not criticize him or be disparaging toward him, or toward you.

(c) If you ever want me to get out of your life, I will go; because if you don't want me here, then I probably won't want to be here either. Then at some future time—maybe when you go off to college—I will try again to see your mother. But I will never let go of her unless she wants me to, and I don't care if I have to wait for the rest of my life. My hope is for she and I to be together always.

(d) The last promise is one that I wish to ask you in person. Whenever you're ready and want to hear it, just let me know. Don't worry about it; there is no hurry and no pressure. Ask me whenever you're ready. I'm a very patient man.

All my love to both of you,
Mark

Conversation had drifted to choices of movies they'd watch until it was time to crash. While it was dark, Ruby suggested moving her car to the street so Dan's car could be hidden behind the studio building, thus remaining out of sight in the morning. Chloe chose *Princess Bride,* which Dan and Mark had never seen. They enjoyed watching Ruby and Chloe laughingly quote nearly every line of the script rather than actually seeing the movie for themselves. The good times rolled until midnight and past.

At about 2:00 a.m., Mark and Dan slipped out to a nearby motel. Ruby did not want them to leave, but they would not compromise Ruby and her child so tantalizingly close to the end of the court business. Ruby and Chloe would drive out to meet the men on Saturday, where they could tour and continue the frolicking fun.

Ruby observed Chloe very closely. Chloe was shyly warming up to both Mark and Dan. Ruby was relieved. When she got a chance, she was going to maim both Mark and Dan for not letting her know they were coming. She found out later that by the time they impetuously made the decision to bomb in on her, it was way too late to let her know because both of them had thought the other had called. Even while Mark was calling Ruby while hiking up on Bear Butte, they were flying at five thousand feet.

That was also why it was so imperative to find out whether Ruby had talked to Chloe about him: because he would have cancelled out if Ruby had not yet spoken to her daughter about him and prepared her for the inevitable situation.

Chapter

28

THE NEXT DAY, the group headed to Scott's Bluff, where they could hike unobserved, talk freely, enjoy each other's company, and allow the lovely child her own pace in learning just about anything she wanted to know about Mark or Dan. The only exception was court. If at all possible, they would omit his arson activities. No parent would be thrilled with wrong messages from negative examples of adult behavior. Mark was proud of his commitment to environmentalism, but he was not proud of breaking the law. As far as Ruby was concerned, Chloe would never find out about her little foray onto the dark side. Ruby was actually appalled at her own parents setting property on fire during *their* college days.

The weather was glorious as usual. They began the day tentatively trying to do everything just right. They ended the day laughing, teasing, and talking like old school chums, or as if Mark and Dan had both been long-lost favorite uncles. They returned to Ruby's apartment toward dark, to be less noticed.

The group defaulted to a quiet Sunday morning of pancakes and maple syrup (Rory's label) for breakfast before the men set out for their flight to Kansas City. With the trial so close to being finished, even Ruby and Mark could say good-bye without their hearts being yanked from their chests.

Monday morning in the courtroom was heart-arresting and breath-suspending tense. Zane would have liked to yell at Mark, but he couldn't under the circumstances... since prosecution also had not shown up last Friday for the last fifteen minutes of the roller-coaster week. Still, the judge was not going to let a good tongue-lashing slip by him. Before the jury was led into the courtroom, he had a few choice words for prosecution, and then he laid into Mark, threatening him that he ought to slam him with the maximum penalty of twenty-five years in jail and a fine bigger than all combined damages, which figured to be in the millions. Mark did not care; he knew the judge did not have sufficient cause to do such a thing. It was only a threat and he knew his Group would appeal and win, based on the lack of evidence.

His mind was on Ruby, his freedom, making a good impression on Chloe, and getting on with their lives. Like Dan, he was beginning to gravitate toward thoughts and plans in Montana. What a gem of a place, one of the best-kept secrets of the universe. No wonder the Indian tribes fought so hard for it. The West was sacred—*Wakan Tanka* territory, highly revered by the Lakota, Cheyenne, Shoshone, and so many others.

As the jury filed in, Mark returned to the present, but not before he mentally revisited Chloe approaching him about what he'd wanted to ask her.

She was a very smart, mature-beyond-her-years, sweet child. Mark felt a stab of regret at never having had a child of his own. But he'd never cared enough about getting married, so why complicate life with children? He'd never gotten around to it and had never found the right woman. But there was that quote again: "Whenever you're not looking for someone, there she is ..."

Curiosity had finally gotten the best of Chloe. She waited until they had hiked up to the top of Scott's Bluff to shyly mention to Mark that she wanted to know what he was going to ask her. He smiled, looked pleased, and enjoyed her sweetness and honesty. Chloe really had no experience with older men other than her father, so she needed to figure out when Mark was teasing, when he was serious, and many other nuances and confusing actions that adults seemed to possess. Chloe responded to the kindness in Mark's eyes; if she'd had any experience with older men, she would know his eyes were dancing with mischief. She was happy that her mother liked Mark so much, and she could tell they were completely in love.

In only two days' time, Chloe had learned that Mark was one man full of surprises. She also learned that Mark was a man of his word. Mark first started with whatever it 'was', had to be a secret. He explained it would be the only secret they would ever share, and he asked if she could keep a secret under pressure, even from her mother. Chloe assured him she could. It was incredibly exciting to be in on an adult plan. Of course she could be trusted; she would not tell her mother! That was a hard decision, because she and Ruby never kept secrets from each other. Except for one little issue: hadn't her mother kept Mark a secret all summer? Therefore Chloe didn't think it would be bad if she had one tiny secret with Mark.

Mark whispered an invitation for Chloe to go with him to pick out an engagement ring for her mother. Chloe sucked in her breath and nearly choked. She had not expected to be included. The promise had been made and sealed with their budding trust, so there was no going back, and she wholeheartedly agreed. She could not believe it—Mark had asked her to pick out her mother's ring!

She'd ventured, "You mean *diamonds?*"

He'd answered, "Yes, diamonds!"

Chloe had never been in an expensive jewelry store, let alone a store that sold just diamonds! Her innocent little heart was all aflutter. Chloe queried, "What about the, uh cost ...?"

"No problem. That's my part to worry about!"

Then Chloe flippantly said, "Well, Mom does not like sweater snaggers!"

Mark laughed until he thought he would bust a vein. What an expression! Only two women living together like this mother and daughter could come up with a unique phrase for an unworkable, undesirable, frivolous piece of ostentatious jewelry. Mark thought of all the men who had laboriously purchased flawless, expensive diamonds for hopeful, anticipatory, engaged women in the world whose singular thoughts while accepting the baubles and proposals were, "Sweater snaggers."

Chapter

29

MARK SMILED AS he remembered Chloe's childlike innocence, total surprise, and willingness to participate in subterfuge for her mom's sake. But he nearly fell off his chair thinking about sweater snaggers. The judge was asking him what he thought was so funny, and whether or not he realized the unfathomable extent of the precarious position he was in.

Mark looked at Zane, trying to silently ask him to answer for him. Zane gestured for him to speak to the judge. Mark thought, *Thanks, buddy!*

"Uh, yes, sir. Uh, no, sir. What was the question, sir?"

The judge merely said, "I thought so. For being in the heap of trouble you're in, Mr. Smythe, your attitude has certainly not convinced this court that you're not a future danger to society or have, in the least sense, been remorseful or rehabilitated!" His recant sounded pretty much like he'd already been sentenced.

He motioned for the jury to deliver their verdict.

Ruby thought Chloe was acting strangely and tried to cajole her into talking. Chloe was smart enough to know that if she got started, her mother could probably weasel information that might give a clue that would spoil her surprise. She clamped her mouth tighter than if she'd been at the dentist. For some reason she couldn't even articulate, she wanted to prove to Mark that she could be trusted, especially because he said that would be their only secret he would ever share with her without her mother's knowledge.

Ruby was walking on air, so she really couldn't complain about Chloe being happy. She gave her teasing a rest but never gave up on trying to squeeze Chloe's inner thoughts out of her. They did many things together, mostly bike riding. They had precious little time to go on any long rides with school so close to starting. Friends who had been gone over the summer were calling and making plans with Chloe. Life was busy, busy, busy.

Ruby was trying to concentrate on projects, anticipating the end of the trial, and pontificating about her *(and Mark's)* future. She knew they would be together soon. She could not see herself continuing in advertising. She spent long hours on the phone with her Mom. Lollie tried not to pry, but she was very unsettled at Ruby's involvement with such a questionable, maybe dangerous, relationship. At this point, Lollie and Rory did not know for sure whether the man in whom Ruby was interested was indeed the one on trial in Kansas City. They were almost afraid to broach the subject; all they got from Ruby was assurances that everything was going to be okay, she was not in any trouble, and Chloe was okay.

Ruby filled in her parents on their surprise visit from Mark and Dan—meeting Chloe, having fun, and circumventing the prying eyes of the small town. As they talked, Ruby was pretty sure her parents had indeed seen the group of friends who always had each other's backs. However, they still probably did not know which one was the man in whom Ruby was interested.

Ruby finished lamely by saying it would be a matter of time before they met. Lollie retorted, "Sounds like an Elvis song."

The jury foreman stood when asked if they'd reached a verdict. "Yes, Your Honor, we have."

"Please ..."

"We find the defendant, Mark Smythe, not guilty of the charge of arson."

"What?" derided the judge. The entire court fell deathly silent upon the recrimination of the judge. "How could you possibly ...? You were in session less than one hour, and you found him not guilty?"

The judge was busy shuffling papers, moving desk objects, obviously flustered, everyone could hear his feet tapping. His body language spoke loudly and clearly that the jury had gone amuck. Soon he was standing, red-faced, wielding the gavel like he wanted to throw it at somebody. He directed them to go back into session.

"Court resumes at 1:00 today, and everybody had better show up!"

Mark was flabbergasted. Zane was insane with fury. The Prosecution was smug. The court room emptied in a shuffling, bustling, nonverbal two minutes.

The car was waiting—always in a dissimilar location at an obscure time, always a different car, and always a riddle for surveillance to anticipate or follow. It seemed they were still confused about where Mark was getting his support from.

"Can you believe it?" Mark was elated. Not guilty! Dan was deliriously happy. It meant he could fly to Montana soon to see Angela. They found a nearby cafe, and no one seemed to be following now that the verdict was coming down. But in Mark's business, it never hurt to be cautious. They popped the cork on some celebratory wine. It felt so good, calming, and victorious.

"Wow!" was all Mark could repeat over and over.

Dan relaxed. "Who would have thought ... Just like that!"

"There's no way they will come back with anything different, do you think?"

"No, they got it right the first time. Still, when the jury is out for such a short time, it's usually *not* good news."

They had three whole hours for lunch, talking and planning.

Mark said, "Let's get going on a trip to Omaha. My next goal is to meet Ruby's parents." He went on to mention that they might have been observed in Nebraska City.

"What? How? Are you kidding me?" Dan was incredulous.

"I know," admitted Mark. "What are the chances?"

"Okay, I'll get the machine talked into it ..." Dan trailed off. He was referring to the plane.

Ruby was peeling tomatoes from her garden and getting ready to can a few pints. Chloe was washing jars and lids. The cell phone rang. They had retained the cell phones just in case.

"Hi, darlin'," rumbled the suave, sexy voice of Mark.

Ruby's knees went to jelly. "Hi!"

"Are you busy?"

"Uh ..."

"Too busy to hear the verdict?" *Busy* was the code word for a Chloe sighting.

"Yes! But ... No! But, wait!" She told Chloe she was going out to pick more tomatoes. "Okay, talk!"

"Well, the first verdict was not guilty. But the judge apparently did not like the verdict and sent them back to discuss some more. How do you figure that?"

Ruby breathed a sigh of relief, held her heart, and said, "Oh, thank goodness!"

"Gotta get back to court. Hey, do you think you and Chloe could meet us in Omaha tomorrow night? That is, if you're ready yet for me to meet your parents ..."

She gave a slight hesitation, so he continued.

"That is, darlin', only if you're ready. I guess they kind of know quite a bit about me already, and maybe we've already inadvertently met?"

"I am trying to figure that out." Ruby was not questioning Mark; she was questioning the direction of her life, her so-far successful career, her goals, and her all-consuming desire to be with Mark. Her love for him *was* all-consuming ... but was it also addle-brained and impractical? Too flighty? How was life going to converge? She was independent and had been single for a long time. She had to consider Chloe and their future. She had many life-altering decisions to make. Simply being in the position of having to make decisions—that was what was so discombobulating. The biggest speed bump in her and Chloe's life so far was what color of bike helmet to wear.

As usual, Ruby was questioning *herself*. It was not that she wouldn't throw it all away for him. It was simply that she and Mark had not had sufficient time to really discuss the nitty-gritty, the challenges, the specifics of their future.

"Well, about Omaha ... My parents are coming up for a visit before Chloe starts school, perhaps this week," she began. "In fact, school starts in only two weeks."

"Great." Mark slowed down his thinking and began planning and rearranging. "Then Dan will fly me to Tepid Springs as soon as this thing's over. Perhaps today, perhaps tomorrow?"

"Yeah, sure." Ruby's mind accelerated down the tarmac... first to the excitement of romance... then, more practically, to lists of chores, stress sweat, and a future involving much that she hadn't had to deal with for a decade and a half—marriage?

She said more positively, "Yeah, that will absolutely work. It will be fine... great. And of course, I can't wait to see you— permanently," Ruby tried her best to come off in an attitude of *keep calm and carry on,* but her nerves were working overtime ... and failing.

My parents? Mark? Getting everything done? All of us smooshed into one locale, one little corner of the world, together? For how long? She was embarrassed to admit it, but she always worried over what her parents would think of her getting involved with a debatable person—even for love. By now, she was certain they had put two and two together.

"Don't worry, darlin'. We'll stay out of your way until we're invited, okay?"

Ruby sighed in relief, as quietly as she could. *Wow! Close call!* She was thankful that Mark was such a perfect gentleman; it only served to make her love him more. The easy part in getting off the phone was declaring their forever love for each other. Mark headed back to court for the finale. Ruby headed into the house for a marathon of cleaning and preparing for company. Chloe was poking her head out the door and waiting petulantly for instructions ... and explanations. She was such a sweet helper to her mother, when Ruby needed her most. Obviously, Ruby was unaware of Chloe's motivation and excitement for Mark's return.

They dove into the task of spring cleaning. Yes, Ruby did her spring cleaning more toward late summer and fall, so their living quarters would be fresh all winter when they were cozied in for snowy, icy, western plains weather. The carpets got rolled up and cleaned underneath, mattresses were flipped, all blankets and sheets were washed and hung outside to dry, and a few cupboards were cleaned and rearranged. They gathered clothes, kitchenware, and shoes for the Salvation Army. The windows were washed inside and outside, and nearly every horizontal surface was dusted, wiped, and refreshed—even the cobwebs behind the pictures on the wall. At the end, they were two tired, lovely, but well-exercised young women. They headed to the Plunge for a natural-spring soak.

Everyone filed into court as quiet and reprimanded as they had departed. The judge had castigated the jury for wasting everybody's time and thousands of dollars by delivering a not-guilty verdict. He sat confidently flaring his nostrils while he reigned over his diminutive, if temporary, kingdom. He wasted no time in calling for the verdict again. Wielding power was fast becoming an addiction for this inept purveyor of justice.

"Not guilty!" came the second pronouncement of innocence. But not so fast—the jury had stipulations.

The harried judge, stone-faced, asked each individual juror, "What say you?"

They individually replied, "Not guilty," once again, as if anyone besides the judge needed further clarification. He resigned, defeated to the fact that the jury was in charge after all—as it should be. He gave his court over to the bailiff. The jury foreman went on to explain that they would not send someone to jail for twenty-five years with such a glaring lack of evidence, and that the only evidence the prosecution had presented was circumstantial at best. In their hearts, the jury reported that they felt Mr. Smythe had probably committed something unlawful where arson was concerned—but nobody had died or been injured as a result. Still, arsonists could not be allowed to run roughshod over the country doing their devil-may-care damage, and certainly not in the name of environmentalism.

They unanimously suggested community service for one to two years, and perhaps teaming up with police departments to coach them on how he'd accomplished his strikes against corporate America without leaving evidence. In that way, he could serve his time and prevent future damage to property and/or human life, as well as curtail the millions of dollars' worth of wasted money from arson across the nation. It was happening everywhere, up and down the highways, and logistically Mr. Smythe certainly could not have committed all of them because he couldn't be in two, three, or half a dozen places at once! The jury also figured that they were probably just scratching the surface on discovering the whodunits, and it must be an extremely organized group. One person should not be made an example while dozens of others go free. Whoever and whatever was behind this epidemic needed to be ferreted out, and that was the problem, the goal, from the jury's perspective.

"Case closed," whined the judge as he smacked the gavel for the last time on this matter. He stepped down with black robes flowing behind him.

Zane grabbed Mark's hand, shook it like a dead fish, and said, "Congrats, buddy. See you around." He quickly slipped out the side door. Prosecution ignored Mark, keeping busy shuffling their papers and ceremoniously snapping shut their computers and briefcases. Mark gestured to the jury his appreciative thanks and went out the front to throng through the media. Dan exited toward the back door of the courthouse heading to the plane. Mark sent a quick text to Ruby.

Rory and Lollie threw in a couple of overnight bags and started toward Tepid Springs by noon. They took their time, enjoying the beautiful sunshine and the lighter humidity the farther they traveled west. They involved themselves in the typical, mundane spouse chitchat. Motorcycles rumbled around them. They were glad to be free of their estate responsibilities for a few days; upkeep on a farm like theirs was very tedious. As they cruised through small towns along Highway 20, they noticed billboards that knew how to insult one's intelligence. One said, "Get America back to what we deserve!" *(A bit braggish, they thought.)* Another touted, "The L. Bow Room restaurant." *(Cute—nice play on words.)* Still another bragged about how advertising was the only way to run a successful business. Then there was the usual 'Freedom isn't free' *(perhaps from a Vietnam veteran)* and the typical abortion atrocities. Rory and Lollie were reluctant to verbalize the obvious: that some signs were too extreme to display, and there were entirely too many of them. Billboards were wasteful, and maybe such an onslaught to the senses deserved to be destroyed.

The signs thinned out, the subject material mercifully changed, and they tossed around the idea of taking their girls to the Alpine Inn in Hill City, one of their favorite spots. Lollie hoped they weren't too tired to go anywhere, because she could predict how maniacally Ruby could act in her zeal to get everything done in one day. Nearly every "lick and promise" began with emptying three years' of a closet, cupboard, or nook and cranny. Her habit was to get it done before school started so there would be no distractions during school days with jobs piling up.

Rory checked the time; they had less than a hundred miles before arriving at Ruby's house. More motorcycles, on their way to Sturgis, vibrated around them; small planes droned overhead. They had rested in Valentine and downed a couple of Cokes. Now they were nearing the Nebraska and South Dakota state line. No fewer than a hundred cyclists had stopped to take pictures and remove helmets.

"Maybe we should move out here, where it is so blessedly sunny with blue skies all the time. Every time we come out here, it's gorgeous! Not overcast or humid."

Rory laughed. "Definitely, And what would we say to our son and family?"

"Yeah, true," agreed Lollie, "Guess we could visit them during the week of Sturgis!" They were still kibitzing and laughing about that prospect when they reached Tepid.

Mother and daughter felt refreshed and massaged after their hot-tubbing and swim. They got back to their apartment, dressed in comfies, and collapsed on the couch to anticipate their company. Ruby was obsessing over the meeting. Chloe wanted pizza, Ruby wanted a kegger, and they settled for the last of the leftover lasagna. They had accomplished quite a bit working as a team all afternoon. Ruby still wondered what burr got under Chloe's saddle to convince her to work like a little Merry Maid! They were both exhausted, leaned against each other, and slipped easily into catnaps. Before long, someone was rattling at the door. Ruby's heart sped up to borderline palpitations and near hyperventilation.

"Mom, Dad!" yelled Ruby. "I'm so glad you came!" Interrupting erupted from every direction as if all was normal. Ruby was exasperated. *Is the word* normal *even in the dictionary? Because it sure didn't exist in real life!* She absolutely did not feel like anything was normal. In fact, she felt like she, or something or someone, was about to implode!

They got settled down into the evening and sleep, and nothing much happened until next day. Ruby spent half the night wondering whether Mark had made it into town. Why hadn't he called? Was he going to drop by? Was she going to have to face an awkward, abrupt meeting, with a tongue-tied, embarrassing introduction? How was she going to handle it? Over and over the nagging thoughts of how, when, should, could, and would invaded her head. She could not figure out a reasonable, workable, natural plan.

Ultimately, the next day came.

The coffee was burbling, and yogurt, fruit, and granola were set on the table. Everybody was up, yawning and sleepy. The day was pristine, giving no reason in the world to be crabby. Ruby could not yet seem to get her frown upside down. Chloe was bouncing and ready to boogie; she ushered Rory to the butterfly pavilion, insisting on it being called a pavilion. While they were yonder, Lollie put her arm around Ruby's shoulders and asked if everything was all right.

Ruby smiled and said, "Yeah, pretty much." Lollie dropped the subject and her arm, dissatisfied.

Lollie said, "Let's do something different today. Not shopping or eating out."

"Yeah? What, then?" Ruby was glad to move off the uncomfortable moment and go forward. "We've never toured the Landstrom's Black Hills Gold Factory, in Rapid, have we?"

Lollie said, "No, we haven't. I've been wanting to do that ever since you moved to the Hills."

"Hey, great idea. Okay, it's a deal!" Then Ruby decided to hop over to the cafe and get a white mocha, listen for the local gossip, and take a relief break from her stress. She was glad they'd formulated a forward-moving plan. *Just get me my mocha!* screamed her addiction.

Lollie stood, wondering and watching her trot across from the studio window. What pride she had in her daughter! Ruby was such a good mother and a responsible parent who provided well for her daughter. She was a creative, practical thinker who was independent. Perhaps she was an underachieving career gal. Lollie so wished for Ruby to find a significant other, a companion, friend, and mate. But was Ruby flirting with danger?

As she gaped across the street at nothing in particular except the wishful thoughts in her own head, two athletic, handsome men sauntered into the cafe. At the same time, an elderly woman was stepping out onto the sidewalk. They moved aside to let her pass, took her hand to steady her, and held the door. It was apparent that both men chatted the little darling up a bit as she continued on her way with a smile. Lollie thought, *How respectable, chivalrous, and gentlemanly. You don't witness that much anymore. That is exactly what I want for Ruby!* The young men somehow seemed familiar ... She was briefly distracted as she heard Rory and Chloe banging in the back door; they must have exhausted the thrills of the butterfly cage—or *pavilion*.

Ruby thought she detected an audible hush after entering the cafe. She chose to ignore it and ordered her white mocha. Marcia, at least, was overly glad to see her. Ruby placed her order, and the verbal buzz resumed.

Marcia said, "Well, that trial is done with down in Kansas City, finally."

"Yeah." Ruby was trying to brush it off as insignificant to her. "Great."

"Great? The guy got off scot-free! How is that great?"

"Oh, I hadn't heard." But, of course, she had heard. Mark had texted her immediately when he was found innocent—the *second* time he was found innocent—and warned her (very desirously) that his first stop was Tepid.

"It's all over the Internet!"

Suddenly, a strong, familiar hand went up against her back—so much like the fantasy she frequently revisited of that first time, months ago, when Mark had touched her and laid down money for her white mocha. A growling, deep whisper into her hair said, "Whenever you're not looking, darlin'." Ruby's knees nearly dissolved, and shivers crawled all over her body. His other hand came across in front of her, paid the price of her coffee, plus the standard generous tip for the waitress, whose eyes were ready to pop straight out of her face and dangle like those springy fake glasses.

Ruby was deliriously happy to see and feel Mark. He was free! She let the worry, the stress, and the thoughts of impossibility dissolve, gone forever. There was no turning back. In a delicious moment of reckless abandon, she turned toward him, surprising herself and all cafe onlookers. In a deliberate disregard of modesty, propriety, and decorum, she threw herself into his arms, accompanied by a long, sensuous lip lock while the graveyard-quiet shock of the patrons of the entire place hung in the air.

Mark was happy and was most willing, if not convivial, to fly in the face of convention. He enthusiastically accommodated and returned the embrace with ornery, unabashed passion. He rationalized that they'd held back for too long already. Two beautiful people so obviously in love in their long-denied embrace—it was almost like the ending of a perfect chick flick giving nearly everyone present the rare experience of a heart flutter or two.

Across the street, Lollie was lollygagging at the window. "Rory!" He had already gone off with Chloe again. "Come look! Our Ruby is brazenly kissing a man over there in that café, right in public, in front of God and everybody! Oh, what is going on? Oh, my goodness gracious! Oh, Rory!"

Chapter

30

BEFORE LOLLIE WAS finished with her mortifying sentence, the reunited couple were holding hands and sprinting between tourists, traffic, and Harleys, across the street toward her. Lollie turned to the door, and Rory and Chloe magically appeared by her side. Ruby and Mark blasted behind them into the apartment, with Ruby exclaiming, "Mom, Dad, I want you to meet someone!"

Soon the dreaded event that Ruby had feared, rehearsed, and emoted over for weeks was accomplished in a swish of a wand. Done, out in the open. All fine and good. In fact, everything was better than good! It was not that her parents hadn't expected it, and Lollie had known that Ruby was interested in someone. The more they'd connected the dots here and there, they were simply concerned that he might be an arsonist.

Dan strolled in behind the two lovers. For a fleeting moment, Lollie hoped and speculated that perhaps Ruby could see something in this handsome man rather than this *arsonist* whose mug shots had been plastered all over every TV screen in America. But, no, it was clearly apparent with whom Ruby was crazy in love.

The group revved down somewhat and lounged around the living room couch for a few hours to decompress. Questions needed asking, and answers needed explanations. Everybody was hungry, anxious, and hesitant, but excitement blew through like the famous, unrelenting South Dakota winds.

The trial was over, the verdict was final. Mark was a free man, and two strikingly beautiful people had found each other and minced no words or actions telling the world about it.

Dan had discreetly offered to take Chloe around town so she could give him the official Tepid tour. She showed him her school, her gymnastics class, and their church. They saw the Mammoth Site, the historic Veteran's Home, the Plunge, and just as many other landmarks. Dan enjoyed avoiding the ghastly scenario where he could escape what Mark had to go through: *the inevitable meeting of the parents*. He knew it was coming for him too! Chloe enjoyed being the center of attention and the expert tour guide.

Ruby was supremely thankful for Dan offering to take her so all the court drama could be processed and laid to rest. It didn't take much interaction to find out that Mark was an upstanding citizen; he was responsible and a good match for their precious Ruby. Rory and Lollie could clearly see that Mark's good character far outweighed their concerns.

By the time Dan and Chloe returned, there was a plan to visit the Landstrom's Gold Factory. Dan wanted to look at necklaces for someone special and asked Ruby to help him out; Lollie and Rory were looking for matching fortieth anniversary rings. Mark and Chloe would have the opportunity to authentically pull off their little secret. Ruby was basically clueless and absolutely suspected nothing since it had been her own suggestion to tour the gold factory. She would look for a special little ring for Chloe to celebrate their summer of mother-daughter bonding. Ruby had also easily succumbed to the usual parent trap of "All my friends have a Black Hills gold ring except for me" complaint that Chloe implemented to weasel some jewelry out of Ruby.

Everyone was in favor of the Alpine Inn for dinner.

They rode in separate cars in order to mix up the configuration of passengers. Hopefully, Chloe would not suspect it was all to prevent her from learning anything about unlawful activity. Ruby knew the knowledge would come out eventually, but they needed to mete out smaller doses of this revelation for Chloe at a more mature age. Mark had mentioned Montana, and she soon realized there was not going to be any slowing down of life any time soon. She also graduated to the fact *(as the country song goes)* that she was ready to see Lubbock, Texas, in her rearview mirror—and probably trash her advertising career along with it.

In the factory, they moved from group to group to see gold creations beautiful enough to drool over. Dan seemed to be dragging his feet on choosing a necklace for Angela. Ruby learned much about Angela while helping Dan. Angela loved horses and riding. She was a physical science teacher at their local middle school and high school. And she quilted! Ruby raised one eyebrow and disdainfully repeated, "Quilting?" She thought, *How dull.* The last garment she'd attempted to sew was a pitiful pleated skirt in seventh grade home economics. Mrs. Olson was such a crank, and Ruby briefly wondered whether she'd died of old age yet.

Dan continued looking at rings with Ruby. Ruby said, "Well, if she works with horses, she probably doesn't need a sweater snagger ..."

Ruby kept gazing over to see how Mark and Chloe were faring. They sure seemed to be laughing a lot. From across the display cases, Mark and Chloe heard the term—sweater snagger—exactly what they were avoiding for Ruby, and laughed even more. Dan was not as familiar with the term and looked confused. Chloe was having the time of her life being an important part of this adult group and looking at very expensive diamonds. With huge eyes, she gasped at price tags.

Rory and Lollie were oblivious to the young people and involved in their goal to update their vows.

After a couple of hours of watching the history of gold mining and looking for jewelry, the group moseyed to the cars to head for the hills.

The Alpine was busy, backed up with reservations, so they hung out in Hill City while they waited. They toured art galleries and then western stores, where Mark and Dan both donned cowboy hats and boots. They sampled the chocolate factories and a few free spoonfuls of homemade ice cream. They spent an hour in Everything Prehistoric, the fossil and rock shop where, apparently, the town's Tyrannosaurus rex skeleton was pretty much stolen out from underneath the city.

One could shop all night in this touristy little town. Soon their number was called, and they were seated in the inn, where more decades of history told the story of the German folks who'd operated a restaurant and hotel here in the 1800s.

The evening was naturally air-conditioned, indoors and outdoors, and the ambience was perfect. Everyone was having a great time. Around this particular table, the people were animatedly sharing stories, conversation, and food. Their group was an enviable interaction of good people having good times in a very good place.

Chloe blurted something of concern, and the adults all dropped their forks. "Mom, I think when I grow up, I want to work for Greenpeace ..." While they were recovering from that bold, decisive statement, she added, "Or maybe be a paleontologist!"

After all the stress and living on the edge that Ruby had been through, would her sweet daughter end up in a compromising and controversial situation similar to Mark's? *No way!* Then, at the sudden twist to paleontologist, the adults relaxed and surmised her reference to Greenpeace was a coincidence rather than a reference to a subject akin to a bombshell about a certain unlawful activity. Whew!

"Oh!" went all the way around the table. Smiles of relief ensued.

Then Mark took the opportunity to slip out of his chair, drop to one knee, and propose to Ruby with all of his heart. He made his declaration of eternal love for her in front of everyone at the table. Chloe sat at her elbow and whispered, "Just say yes, Mom!"

Everybody seated on the fringes of this happy table clapped until Ruby had turned the color of her namesake. Ruby was dazzled by the ring, an emerald cut diamond, brilliant and lovely and nestled flat into the gold. It was certainly not a sweater snagger. Mark slipped it on her finger, kissing the top of it and her hand, where it would stay for the rest of their lives. She could see that the ring was way beyond expensive.

"Mark, you have court fines to pay," she protested.

"That is not for you to worry about, Mrs. Smythe," he declared. Rory and Lollie raised eyebrows at the 'Mrs.' title. He was most definitely a fast mover.

Chloe said, "Yes, it *was* expensive, Mom. But I am sworn to secrecy!"

Ruby sucked in her breath. "You know?" Chloe nodded and smiled a conspiratorial smile while beaming at Mark. She'd just proved she could keep a secret, however out in the open it was now. Mark knew then how fortuitous it was to include Chloe in the conspiracy.

When the gawking and marveling was finished, Mark got down on his other knee on the other side of Ruby, proposed to Chloe, and promised that he would treat her like his very own daughter. He accompanied this with a refined, angelic, Black Hills gold ring that was dainty and specially fashioned for a young girl, complete with a sapphire to complement her sparkling eyes. Chloe was agog with happiness and surprise.

Again, the tables around them clapped in congratulations. First she was speechless, then shade by shade she turned all sorts of pinks and red. She was struck with a horrible case of the 'tween giggles, as junior high girls were prone to do, and she could not find a way to stop. Every time someone looked at her, she burst into laughter again.

The night continued. Their table was a plethora of uproarious gaiety and distraction within the whole room. Even the restaurant owners took time to applaud and encourage the merriment going on. What neither Ruby nor Chloe knew at first was how Mark was playing both ends against the middle. In order for Chloe to shop for Ruby's ring, Ruby had to stay with Dan, shopping for Chloe's ring and Angela's necklace.

Did all of that make any kind of sense? Of course not! It was just what one did when one loved people and wanted to create loving surprises and happiness for them. Mark, donning a smug grin for the little trick he'd accomplished, was elated when Ruby determinedly promised to wipe that grin off his face once and for all when she got him alone. And, oh, how he would relish that wiping!

Dan, the friend and gentleman, absorbed this incredible feeling of family, love, and caring. He knew Angela would fit right in; he and she would be as much a part of this family as they would Angela's side of the tree. Dan was almost as happy for his friends as he was for himself; this was the first event of a guaranteed series of memorable traditions in the making.

Mark and Ruby jumped into the rented car. Dan chauffeured Chloe and her grandparents back to Ruby's apartment, and then he hoofed the short distance to their motel across town. Dan hit the pillows, gleeful and satisfied over the necklace Ruby helped to pick out for Angela. He anxiously anticipated their reunion in a few short days. He crashed into the business of his own dreams, assured he would not see Mark until morning.

However, Lollie and Rory did not know. Neither did Chloe. When they awoke, it was to breakfast on their own—no Mom, no daughter, no Ruby. Within the morning, Mark and Ruby reappeared in Tepid to lunch with the family. Rudimentary plans needed to be sketched out about a wedding in the very near future. Chloe wanted to orchestrate the entire event, and Mark and Ruby laughed uncontrollably.

Chloe said, "After all, if I'm going to be a fashion designer and wedding consultant ..."

Mark and Ruby heaved huge sighs of relief that she wanted to participate. They gave a second huge sigh that the Greenpeace idea had been shelved. They were more than pleased to indulge her.

Lollie and Rory beamed with happiness over the past two days' grandiloquent events. How else could they act or be, except ecstatic for their daughter? They were content that Ruby's life was heading down a beautiful, primrose path.

Of necessity, the friends and family temporarily scattered in various directions: Lollie and Rory to the east, Mark and Dan to the west, and Ruby and Chloe staying right where they were in order to manage their eminent Tepid exit. Now, there was an impossible growing list of preparations to formulate and execute.

Epilogue

LOLLIE AND RORY rolled out of town, waving good-bye until loved ones were no more than two inches tall. It was perhaps the last time for a long time they'd be in Tepid Springs. The journey home was anticipatory and promised them much needed hours and peace to settle down. Wow! After this overload of information, it would be a hundred miles before the happenings of the last three days soaked in. *Would Ruby, Mark, and Chloe move to Montana? Would they move before school started? Oh, well. Just another pristine place to vacation, right? What type of work would they find in Montana?* Mark mentioned returning to computer programming or actuarial science. Ruby briefly gave some thought to teaching or dendrochronology. Rory and Lollie guessed this was not their problem anymore, and they smiled at each other. Perhaps it was a new phase of their lives too, and they were utterly happy.

Dan and Mark flew straight to Angela's back door, as Mark had promised he would do, after everything Dan had done for him. Dan had waited long and worked hard to maintain Mark's cover and *(thankfully)* innocence. He'd denied himself personal goals and activities in order to stand by his friend whenever and wherever he needed him. Now it was over.

Hopefully, now the places he would fly Mark to would be more on the legal side. Dan was free to visit his new girlfriend, Angela. He was as crazy about her as Mark was about Ruby. Mark loved Angela too, and he agreed with Dan that they would always be a part of each other's lives and families. Mark revered Montana, and he thought of Julie and her family. They would drop by Julie's and fill her in on his narrow escapades, as well as his and Ruby's engagement. There was so much to talk about, so much to do. He was so much in love with Ruby and with life! Mark and Dan vowed to pester Jim and Greg until they succumbed. *All for one, and one for all.*

Life was so promising and incredible. Ruby was nearly delirious with relief that it was over. Every minute spent getting ready to leave was an unforgettable ritual—saying good-bye to one life. Every minute spent embracing a new life and love, was an anticipatory ritual—saying hello and 'wide-open-arming' the future. Chloe was just as anxious and excited for a change in their lives. Leaving her friends was no problem, with Facebook and texting at a finger's touch.

A month later, Mark, Ruby, and Chloe were traveling west in a luxurious RV, *a small token from the Group for Mark's court inconveniences.* Mark could not prevent himself from occulogyrating over the 'gift' and mustered an insincere, ironic thanks. He was determined to ditch it ASAP. *Really? Forever drive around in a gas-guzzling tank of a pampered chef-mobile and glorified outhouse?* Ruby laughed till her throat hurt over Mark's description of the nonsensical highway barge. The affluence! The audacity! The ostentatiousness! That was most certainly not their style, especially after burning dozens of signs that were deemed ugly, greedy, wasteful, and wrong. She couldn't wait to hop into her economical little truck. Mark simply asked himself again if the whole world was going mad, or if it was just him.

They had only traveled a couple of hundred miles west on Interstate 90 when—disgustedly—along came the worst of the worst signs either of them had ever encountered. It bragged about having "heavy showers" for their motel guests. Enough water to waste without reservation, preservation, or conservation? No attempt for concern about the planet, for others, for the Seventh Generation?

"What?" they exclaimed simultaneously. Were people such as these even remotely aware of the fragility of Earth's number one resource, of every human being's need for water? With a shortage of water, droughts, and fire danger, and with western states, pipelines, entities, and corporations fighting over water rights, such people were really going to advertise that they possessed ample water to waste? It was a pretentious claim—asinine and superficial, a total disregard for everything natural. Unfortunately, it was too blatantly ignorant to let go. Filthy, filthy greed!

Mark looked at Ruby, and Ruby looked at Mark. They were reading each other's minds these days, thinking exactly the same thing: *One final burn.* It had to be, as a concluding strike, a final memorial to a transcended past, creed, and philosophy. They both knew they would never again risk burning another sign, no matter how offensive. But of all the signs that had to go, this one was tops. This burn would be the ultimate conclusion of a sealing, clinching, celebration of a complete end to activism for both of them! Nobody in his right mind would jeopardize the love Mark and Ruby had found. This was definitive!

Graciously and miraculously, Chloe lay sound asleep in the back of the RV in her personally chosen bunk.

There was no human activity for at least forty miles in either direction. Mark rationalized, *How could these advertisers ever hope their sign could be safe out here in the middle of nowhere? How could they hope that with such a careless, insipid message, it would not be considered detritus by cogitative people who cared about natural resources, the future of their world, and—most important—the generations to come?*

Mark idled the RV on the pavement, both for a quicker getaway and also to avoid leaving any traceable tire tracks in the gravel on the shoulder of the highway. He slipped outside to the rear of the motor home, not even wanting Ruby to ever learn *(or be responsible for)* his method of destruction. He drilled a small hole very low at the base of both wooden posts, inserted Jim's fool-proof chemical concoction, and lit the fuse. The fuse would smolder and consume the entire base for several hours before actually igniting, destroying the evidence along with the fire. They would be long gone before the sign would fully catch fire and be gobbled up in a quick, raging inferno. Heck, it might flare up and be consumed, and the fire would be nothing but ashes by the time an observer might happen along this lonely stretch. He obscured his shoe prints *and made a note to slosh through many puddles, street water, and mud as soon as possible to wash away forensic dirt from the treads that could be matched to the crime scene.* He climbed back up into the behemoth and cleaned his hands with Clorox wipes. The smiling, conspiratorial lovers headed west.

Printed in the United States
By Bookmasters